DEDICATION

To my wonderful husband and mom. Thank you for always believing in me. And to my marvelous Street Team! It is so much fun getting to chat with you all on a daily basis. I'm so lucky to have such a fun group of people surrounding me! Per your suggestion, I've included the playlist. Great idea, Heidi!

.

BOOKS BY KARICE BOLTON

THE WITCH AVENUE SERIES
LONELY SOULS
ALTERED SOULS
RELEASED SOULS
SHATTERED SOULS

THE WATCHERS TRILOGY
AWAKENING
LEGIONS
CATACLYSM
TAKEN NOVELLA (A WATCHERS
PREQUEL)

BEYOND LOVE SERIES
BEYOND CONTROL
BEYOND DOUBT
BEYOND REASON - COMING SOON

AFTERWORLD SERIES
RECRUITZ
ALIBIZ-COMING SOON

THE CAMP

ACKNOWLEDGMENTS

I want to say a simple thank you to Amazon, Barnes & Noble, and all of the other avenues available for the indie publishing world. It allows the art of storytelling to continue to flourish in unexpected ways!

Thank you also to:

Cover artist: Phatpuppy
Typography: BB Designs
Female model: Anya Kod
Male model: Steve Alario
Makeup/Hair artist: Nadya Rutman
Photography: Teresa Yeh

CHAPTER ONE

The elevator chimed, barely bringing me out of my morning fog, and I took one graceful step forward, tripping right into the carriage. My mishap scared the yawn right out of me, but I was met with a deep, gravelly chuckle, and my heart instantly skipped a beat. I wasn't expecting an audience so early in the morning.

"Good morning," a vaguely familiar voice greeted me.

Oh no! How could this be?

"Having a little difficulty staying upright?" he teased and that was all it took. I knew who was on the other side of the voice before I even looked.

I raised my head and locked eyes with him—the one man in the universe who was off-limits, my best friend's brother. He was also the one man who'd managed to sneak into my dreams last night and take charge.

Heaven could be so cruel in the love department.

The intense charisma he projected from just one smile was enough to melt me, or anyone, in place. His features were magnificently chiseled, and his eyes held a playful curiosity as he raised a dark brow waiting for a response of some sort.

I felt a blush creep up my spine landing on my cheeks as my mind wandered to a few of the images that my memory left behind from the night before. His hands skirting along my belly, his mouth following—just to name a few. I usually loved my active imagination but not so much at the moment.

To top it off he looked out-of-this-world delicious, even this early in the morning. And that should be illegal. His dark hair was mussed just right and his black suit stretched along his chest, matching my dreams from the night before. He flashed another smile and his brown eyes immediately warmed as he took me in. Tiny little creases around his eyes formed as his smile grew larger at my apparent inability to stop gawking, or reminiscing. Either way, I got the feeling that he knew he had the upper hand, and I had to change that.

I turned around quickly and pushed the lobby button. The silver doors slid shut, and the elevator felt like it was the size of a narrow, toothpick holder as I debated what to do or say. My inclination was to hold onto the railing, but that would be a dead giveaway that he was taking my breath away. The elevator began gliding down swiftly when I became one with my words again.

"What are you doing here?" I blurted, refusing to turn to face him.

"It's nice to see you too," he laughed.

I felt his gaze run along my body, and with every fiber of my being, I wanted to be the good friend that Gabby deserved. I wanted to be repulsed from his adoration.

But I wasn't.

In fact, I loved the feeling this encounter stirred inside of me. It didn't help that the images my mind conjured the night before were on fast-forward as I squeezed my eyes shut.

"Brandy, wasn't it?" he asked, slicing my strength in half. His voice was so masculine, and beyond a doubt, the sexiest voice I'd ever heard.

Get a grip, Brandy!

I nodded, allowing my mind to take control.

"Jerry, was it?" I asked, knowing damn well his name was Aaron. And I remembered calling it out a time or two last night in my deep sleep.

His laughter boomed inside the elevator's tight quarters, and I was unable to hide my smile. I felt the magnificent energy run between us, and my body tingled at the thought. Of him. Of me. Of him and me. But were these feelings only brewing because I knew I couldn't have him, and he was nothing more than a safe and casual flirt?

The elevator hit a bump right before it landed at the lobby, and I was thrown off-kilter as I took a step toward the doors.

I let out a sigh just as his fingertips gripped my arms from behind, taking me completely off guard. My belly muscles contracted as I felt his soft touch signal something deep inside me that I wanted nothing to do with.

"Glad I was so memorable," his voice rumbled. "It was Aaron."

"What do you think you're doing?" I asked, spinning to face him.

"It looked like you were about to go over again," he said, smiling innocently, his eyes piercing. "Just wanted to protect my sister's best friend from tumbling."

Neither of us could deny the energy that was running between us, but I was going to do my best. My friendship with Gabby was far more important than anything this could ever amount to. That I was sure of. He was trouble. I could tell by the gleam in his eye, his mussed up hair, and that look. I would only amount to a prize he could stack with the other females he'd acquired. I could sense that much about him. If there was one thing I got out of college, it was how to sniff out a player. And he was a player—among other things.

His phone rang, and his one hand let go of me as he grabbed his phone out of his pocket. He silenced it quickly, before he slid it back in his pocket and locked eyes on mine once more.

I shrugged his remaining fingers from my other arm, turned around, and proceeded off the elevator in a quick strut but not before he caught up to me.

"Where were we?" he asked, knowingly.

The magnetism he exuded was impossible to miss as he moved ever so smoothly through the lobby. I noticed all the necks turn to watch him glide after me, and I got the distinct feeling I was in over my head. I still wasn't sure of what terrible things Gabby's long lost brother had done, but if she said they existed, then I believed her.

"I was headed for a latte, and I have no idea what you were up to. As of now I'm beginning to feel like you're stalking me," I said, pushing my way through the revolving glass doors.

The sidewalk was bustling with workers headed to the many skyscrapers that were stationed in this corner of the city. I passed by a gardener and said a friendly hi as he was watering the building's large planters. I hoped that Aaron would get the message: the gardener was more interesting than you, buddy!

"Do you think that's how I operate to get a woman in bed?" he asked, his lips tugging into a smile. "I tend to like my women agreeable and excited, not frightened and on the run."

The shock of his statement did nothing but delight me, which told me my only line of defense was to pretend he didn't exist. Besides, he couldn't exist, not in my world.

I ignored him, trying to stifle a laugh and decided not to go to the coffee shop across the street. My plan was to shake him.

I had to shake him.

"Still going to get coffee?" he asked, his low

voice vibrating my common sense right out of me.

"Yes. That was the plan," I said, attempting to act dismissive. But that's all it was—an act.

"Is there a problem with the Starbucks across the street?"

"I don't like it." I pursed my lips together and kept walking. And that was a complete lie. It happened to be my favorite near the office. They knew my name and drink before I even got to the counter.

"You don't like Starbucks or you don't like that particular Starbucks?"

"That particular one," I replied, walking quicker.

"And why's that?"

I stopped dead in my tracks and turned to face him.

So much for my plan.

"Are you always used to getting what you want?" I narrowed my eyes at him.

"Mostly." The corner of his mouth turned up slightly, and I wanted to deck him and jump him simultaneously.

"Then what is it you want?" I asked, his eyes intense as amusement filled them.

"How about I buy you a cup of coffee and we can discuss."

"I can buy my own, and I was planning on it being a solitary act."

"You know you're curious," he whispered, taking a step closer. "I can see it in your eyes."

I wondered what else he could see in my

eyes...the fact that he was the main character in all my fantasies the night before, or how about the guilt that was pulsing through me since I allowed him in my dreams in the first place? Either one was a viable option, but I hoped I wasn't that transparent.

Against everything I stood for—and the friendship I cherished above everything in my life—I nodded in agreement.

"I'll give you five minutes and that's it," I muttered, unable to look him in the eye.

"Great. I think I can relay my proposition to you in that amount of time," he grumbled, as I spun around to the crosswalk.

Proposition?

Trying to shake the gnawing feeling of desperation tinged with excitement, I darted across the road and landed at the Starbucks that was completely out of the way, and he was right behind me.

The line wove through the coffee shop, allowing me to peer at all the mugs and trinkets as I stood waiting for what seemed like hours. I needed to do anything but look at him. Keeping myself busy tracing the lines of the mugs with the space needle etched onto the ceramic, I was surprised that he wasn't speaking—relieved—but surprised.

And then I jinxed it by sneaking a look out of the corner of my eye.

"So I'm sure you've heard all sorts of things from my sister," Aaron began, completely throwing me off guard.

"Actually, I haven't heard a thing about you. Ever. And the ride home with her last night provided just as many insights," I said quietly, before stepping up to the counter to place my latte order.

Digging for my debit card, I felt Aaron's body come deathly close to mine as he recited his drink order to the waiting cashier. He was no more than an inch or two behind me, and with one accidental wiggle, I'd find my body pressed up against his. He swiftly handed over a twenty-dollar bill to handle both of our drinks, and I let out a disgruntled grunt. He placed his one hand on my shoulder as he waited for his change, and my body wanted to sink into his. Even though it was an innocent gesture, it felt far more escalated and like he was staking claim, or at least that was what I hoped. My heartbeat quickened as I felt the space between us shrink. This was absurd. The feelings that were crashing around inside of me from merely being in close proximity to him were crazy. It felt like all my nerves were on end, tingling with the slightest movement, the slightest touch.

He was good.

Too good.

Too experienced.

Anger began to quickly replace the amusement that had momentarily settled in my mind as I got my wits about me. Who did he think he was?

I didn't want to make a scene in front of everybody at Starbucks. But, again, who did he think he was? He took his change and dumped it all into the tip jar before taking a step back from me. Was that supposed to impress me?

A big tipper. Whoopie!

Letting out the breath that I didn't even know I was holding in, I scowled at him and marched to the end of the bar.

"You're welcome," he said, grinning as he came up behind me.

"Thank you," I muttered, staring at the barista as she placed the lid on my cup.

"Have a good day," the perky barista said. But somehow her gaze didn't include me while she stared at Aaron, smiling.

"We will," Aaron replied. I could almost hear the wink in his voice as he grabbed his drink off the counter.

The nerve!

I walked away from the bar toward an empty table for two. The morning paper was scattered across it, which I shoved to the side. I had to get my head on straight. He was off-limits. He flirted with anything that had a pulse. He was a creep. He was a player. And most importantly, he was my best friend's long lost brother.

But he was gorgeous, and there was something so intriguing about him.

"Beneath that scowl, I know there's more," Aaron said, pulling out the chair from the table.

"You are bad news," I said, confident in my best friend's assessment. After all, he was her brother. She would know.

He arched a brow and crossed his arms,

stretching the suit jacket's material to its maximum. I could only imagine the definition under that material. No, let me rephrase. I already had imagined the definition under the fabric, and it was not for the faint of heart.

"I won't disagree with that," he said, clearly amused.

Annoyed, I took a sip of my latte and let my gaze fall to the brown tile floor and then to my phone. It was a quarter to eight. I didn't have to be to my lovely cubicle for fifteen minutes.

"So what was it you wanted to discuss with me? A proposition of some sort?" I scoffed, feeling his eyes on mine.

There was silence. He was waiting for something.

I looked up and his gaze fastened to mine. That's what he was waiting for.

"I thought Gabby would have told you about me," he began.

"All I know is that I didn't even know you existed until last night." And I wished it had stayed that way. God, his lips were full and...

"I don't know what I was expecting," Aaron said, his tone softening, the playfulness leaving. "I've done some things I'm not proud of."

"Yeah?" I asked, not amused. "Care to elaborate?"

"Listen, I want the chance to talk to my sister, apologize to her, explain things to her. A lot happened and..." his voice trailed off, catching me off guard. The confidence completely evaporated from him, and his ego dissolved into nothingness. He ran his fingers through his dark hair as he thought about what next to say. His mouth puckered as he blew out air and looked toward the ceiling. He looked so vulnerable, nothing like the man chasing me down the sidewalk.

"I think you're the key to getting to speak with my sister," he replied flatly.

Shaking my head, I broke my gaze from his. "Not going to happen. If she wants to talk to you, she will. I'm not going to force anything. I don't know what happened between you two, but I want no part of it. She's my best friend and as far as I'm concerned you don't exist until she says you do."

"Brutal," he muttered, scooting forward in his seat.

"Whatever bad blood is between you two... is between you two. Buying me a cup of coffee isn't going to make me forget where my loyalty resides. She's like a sister to me and what we've been through binds us together forever. Having a good looking, not-so-sweet-talking brother pop up out of the blue isn't going to shake that. You may be able to weasel your way with others but not with me. You want to talk to her? Grow a pair and talk to her."

And with that, I grabbed my cup and purse and walked out of the Starbucks. But something inside me told me it wasn't going to be the last of him, no matter how hard I tried to make it so.

CHAPTER TWO

Twelve hours earlier...

"Are you going to be okay?" I asked, noticing Gabby walking a bit like Frankenstein. "Your shoulders look like they're up to your ears."

Gabby nodded, and I felt her discomfort from here. Poor girl. I had no idea what was happening, but the almost perfect life I thought Gabby lived seemed to be shattering with every step closer to this stranger. I wanted to be angry that my best friend didn't tell me she had a brother, but I was just baffled. Yet, here I was about to meet him. I continued following her through the scattered tables until we slowed some. Her hesitancy worried me.

I looked around the ballroom and still felt a little out of my comfort zone. Okay, that was a lie. I felt *completely* out of my comfort zone. It didn't matter what kind of dress I pulled over my head, this crowd—these people—were entirely out of my league. And not like in the "oh-woe-is-me" mentality, but more in the "I want nothing to do with this type of phoniness" business.

The ballroom was dressed majestically for the auction with flowers cascading from the ceiling, and gigantic flower arrangements tucked wherever there was an empty space. From the moment I had stepped into the Chateau, I felt like I was exploring a secret garden. And all this so that Gabby's parents could raise money for someone or some family that landed on their radar. It was a different world for sure, and not one I felt completely comfortable navigating in. I mean the money spent decorating the place could've been given to the family, right? I obviously didn't get it.

"Gabby," a male voice called, startling me out of my piddley contemplations. We had bigger fish to fry, and I was here to stand strong and support my best friend. With what? I had no idea.

My head snapped up to follow the low, gravelly voice, praying that he didn't look as sexy as he sounded. I couldn't see who called Gabby's name, but she froze in place. It was obviously her brother. I had never seen Gabby like this—ever. And we had been through a lot. It was like all of her confidence had been zapped right out of her.

But how did I not know that she had a brother? Why would someone hide that? We were best friends all through college and now we're roommates. We never hid anything from each other. Or at least I thought we never hid anything from each other. However, now was not the time to get caught up in details. Gabby needed me and with every passing second that became more and more apparent. She glanced at me and her eyes held a deep sadness, one that ripped at my heart. It looked like someone had kicked her in the gut. It killed me to see her like this. Who was this stranger?

I watched the crowd disburse in front of us, leaving a shadow of someone in front of Gabby. I couldn't see him from my vantage point, but Gabby grabbed my hand and began walking toward him, dragging me with her. I saw Gabby look at the exit sign a couple times and wondered if she was going to bolt. That would be awkward, but I'd do it. For her. She had a habit of running whereas I liked a good fight. It was the best way to hammer things out.

Navigating between some chairs, I almost tumbled into Gabby when she abruptly stopped. I wasn't sure I wanted to look at the stranger—at Gabby's brother.

"Hello, Aaron," Gabby said, coolly. "Surprised to see you here."

This wasn't good. Whenever Gabby used that tone, all bets were off. I raised my gaze from the floor to the man standing in front of us and almost gasped aloud.

Shit! I was looking at the most attractive man in the world. The energy coming from him was intense, his expression bold, eyes alert but sensitive. Why was he Gabby's brother? Why?

He was dressed in a fitted tuxedo that hugged his broad shoulders. The definition—more like hardness—of his contours hovered under his shirt, stretching the material. My eyes traveled down to his waist, and it was impossible to ignore the way his tux fit him in all areas. And I mean all areas. Aaron's hair was dark, cut short, but it had a messiness that meant one thing. And that one thing would have to be ignored. It was my own theory, but it had been a hundred-percent proven time and time again.

I glanced around the room and wondered where his girlfriend was or whoever it was that he encountered so early in the evening to give his hair that quality. Bringing my attention back to him, I watched his mouth part slightly, and my eyes slid up his strong jawline, darkened by a day or two of missed shaves. I had to avoid his eyes. I knew I had to avoid his eyes. As he stood in front of us, the cockiness I sensed earlier was being swapped with concern for his sister.

"I'm guessing dad didn't tell you I was coming?" her brother replied. I saw the muscles in his neck strain as he spoke and my stomach knotted. His voice was so deep and masculine.

"Dad?" Gabby asked, releasing my hand. "Interesting. You ran out on us, and I never heard from you, but you can call him dad?"

Oh no. This was going to get ugly and fast.

"A lot of things happened. Many that I'm not proud of, but—" he began.

I shifted my gaze to sneak another look at Aaron and felt like a complete traitor. My reasons for wanting to look at him had nothing to do with Gabby's assault.

"Save it," Gabby said, flashing her palm in front of him. "This is my best friend, Brandy. Imagine her surprise tonight finding out I even had a brother."

Please don't look at me. Please don't look at me. You're an enemy. An enemy!

"Aaron," he said, giving me a slight nod as he extended his hand toward me. My eyes flashed to his. The warmth in his brown eyes almost melted me all over. Almost. After all, this was Gabby's brother and I wouldn't go there. However, the longer he held my gaze, the more I wanted to forget whatever this mess was that Gabby was dealing with. I mean this guy couldn't be all bad, could he?

What was going on in the universe tonight? First, we rear-ended someone on the way here who was God's gift to women, and then this? It was like heaven was dangling all the men we couldn't have right in front of us!

Aaron's gaze intensified as he waited for my response, and I felt my mouth become completely dry and heat rush through me. This was not good. I was sure Gabby was seeing right through me.

Shame on me!

I needed to redeem myself somehow.

"I know. I heard," I replied. My voice sounded strong and confident—maybe even reserved. Possibly snarky? Was it too much?

I felt the firmness of his handshake. His strong

fingers wrapped around my hand and my mind imagined those fingers crawling up my spine. I caught a flicker of amusement in Aaron's eyes and my stomach clenched.

Damn him!

My breath caught as his gaze held on to mine, and I let out a noise like a strangled cat to hide it. His mouth curled slightly, and I noticed how deliciously soft his lips looked. He nodded, and a smirk was hidden behind the seriousness of what was set before him to deal with.

I just prayed Gabby didn't notice.

And I prayed that he would quit looking at me. His gaze twisted me up inside and that wasn't good.

"I didn't want to ignore you all night, although that was my natural inclination, but I think it's time I go find a seat," Gabby muttered.

Thankfully, his gaze broke from mine.

"Gabby, I hope you'll give me a chance to explain things. Maybe over coffee?" Aaron asked, his voice softening.

Gabby was already turning around when she muttered her response, and I was quick to join her.

"You going to be okay?" I asked as we made our way to the table.

"I will be. I don't understand why he's back. Shit. I don't even know where he's been, or why he left in the first place." Gabby sighed, and I felt her hurt and wasn't even sure over what.

"I'm here for whenever you want to talk about it," I whispered, feeling an odd sensation scatter down my spine. I quickly looked over my shoulder and caught Aaron's gaze falling down my body. I narrowed my eyes at him and pushed down the feelings of pure delight that pulsed through me.

I. Am. A. Horrible. Friend.

CHAPTER THREE

I glanced under the stalls in the ladies' restroom, and after finding absolutely no anonymous feet, I let out a sigh. I looked at my phone and slid it on the counter. I had five minutes before work started. I had to pull it together. After being accosted by Aaron this morning, I was left with so many unanswered questions. Like, why was he in this building? I promised myself after last night that I would forget him as quickly as I met him. Then I dreamed about him all night. But being the good friend that I was, at least I was riddled with guilt all morning. I even convinced myself that he was truly undesirable. All was going according to plan. It really was.

Unfortunately, running into him this morning did nothing but reignite the images I tried so hard to put out of my mind. I had to have lunch with Gabby today. I needed answers, and I prayed those answers would confirm what a creep he was.

"Okay," I whispered to myself, glancing in the mirror. "Aaron is bad...bad...bad."

But even as I recited the chant to myself, I caught a glimpse of a smile surface on my lips just by uttering his name. I grabbed some more mascara out of my purse and dabbed it on my lashes, hoping that would make me look less guilty, maybe brighten my eyes up. My brown eyes, usually held a brightness on their own, but after last night and this morning, they were definitely absent of any such spark.

There was something so absorbing about the idea of him. The way he smiled at me earlier was electrifying.

Enough!

Tossing my Starbucks cup in the trash, I grabbed my phone and trundled off to my desk, shaming myself the entire way.

After a morning of scheduling travel and turning in expense reports for the team, I was hoping that the nagging guilt would dissolve but it didn't. And now I was completely exhausted from pretending to be disinterested in Aaron. My cell phone rang and not recognizing the number, I sent it to voicemail.

Peeking over the cubicle wall, I watched Gabby on the phone and knew now was my chance.

I grabbed my phone and quickly texted our third musketeer, Lily Novak. Maybe she knew about Aaron.

Did you know Gabby had a brother?

I tossed my cell on my lap and grabbed a folder to file when the cell buzzed with Lily's message.

She's an only child

I shook my head and let out a deep sigh. So Lily was fooled too. How could our best friend not mention this? And why?

Nope. Apparently not. I met her brother last night and ran into him this morning. And let me just say WOW but not... Shame on me. I will burn. I will burn for this I tell you!! Not to mention he did something horrendous which was why he wasn't around. What is wrong with me?

I had to admit that it made me feel better that Lily didn't know that Gabby had a brother either. All three of us were best friends—had been since college—and this whole secret—keeping thing was really worrisome and made me wonder what else was out there that she hid. My phone buzzed once more, and I glanced down to see what every best friend would tell another in this situation, which was why I loved Lily.

You will not burn. But I would try to find out what's up. That might solve your problem. Unlike me, you have good judgment-lol. xxx

I chuckled and wrote back,

You, my friend, don't know all the thoughts that crossed my mind. But yes, time to find out what mystery man did to our bestie. Will keep you posted. xxx

Setting the phone down, I noticed a voicemail from the earlier call and pressed the speaker button. Listening intently, I heard nothing but silence for a few seconds followed by shallow breathing. My pulse quickened slightly, but I knew this had to be a mistake. Probably just someone with the wrong number and a bad case of asthma.

As I sat listening to Gabby recount everything that happened or, more to the point, didn't happen with her brother, Aaron, I couldn't help but wonder if his vanishing was that big of a deal. I knew I'd be heartbroken if either of my two brothers left without a hint of where they were going, but there was something inside of me pushing me to find out Aaron's side of the story. I couldn't pretend to know the depths of despair that Gabby felt after her mother died, especially when her brother took off right after. And from the sounds of it, Aaron was more than just a brother while Gabby was growing up. He was the one and only dependable male figure she learned to rely on because her father was always busy working. Unfortunately, all that did was make me want to learn more about Aaron, not penalize him. Maybe if I reached out to him and found out what he'd been up to or where he'd been for ten years, I could help Gabby repair the relationship with her brother.

I became lost in my world, daydreaming about Aaron and wondering if the pull I'd felt was imaginary or not. There was only one way to find out, and I wasn't sure I was strong enough to see him again without wishing for so much more.

Gabby started laughing once she realized I'd zoned out, and I turned scarlet red and began giggling. I felt like I was in grade school, hiding my first crush from my brothers so they wouldn't tease me endlessly.

"Sorry!" I babbled as she polished off the two éclairs, and I finished my sandwich.

But then my mind drifted back to the mysterious stranger with the beautiful brown eyes, and I knew I was seriously in trouble and needed to message Lily immediately. Besides, I knew the stress of Gabby's brother reappearing was getting to her, and I might need some backup if it got worse. With everything Gabby had gone through, I'd imagine it made her fearful of reconnecting or even connecting in the first place. It explained a lot as to why it felt like there was a wall there at times. She had to learn to deal with life on her own, and not even all the money in the world could have prepared her for what she had to face with her own health issues.

I glanced down quickly so that Gabby couldn't

catch the tears that were surfacing as I thought about her heart transplant and everything she went through to become strong again, both physically and mentally. I shouldn't be worrying about anything but making Gabby's life better and less complicated, mixed with a little fun of course. And I think that was going to start the moment the sexy bike builder dropped off her new bike. Each time I transferred his call to her, I detected something more behind his words than just scheduling a time to drop off her new bike. It was going to be my mission to make sure that Gabby didn't blow him off as quickly as she usually did. Forget Aaron. I needed to put Gabby first, like she always had done for me.

CHAPTER FOUR

"Well, Gabby's got a little surprise coming her way," I confessed to Lily as she hopped out of the booth to give me a hug.

Lily drove up from Portland and met me at one of our favorite pubs since we were both in a bit of a self-imposed crisis mode. A pitcher of ale was delivered to our table, and I knew tonight would be a good confessional night for us both. The lighting was low and the place was just beginning to fill up with the after work crowd. The dark paneling provided a homey vibe, but the funky lighting and zany artwork completely twisted the décor into an artsy atmosphere.

"Smart thinking," I said, laughing as Lily gave me one last squeeze. "A pitcher is definitely the way to go tonight. And you look fab, by the way."

A text came over my phone, and I glanced down at the number—another unknown number with a bunch of garble. This was really getting annoying.

"What's up?" Lily asked.

"Are you getting weird texts? I think my number somehow got on a robo call list or something." I showed her my screen and she shook her head.

"Huh-uh. I haven't been getting anything like that."

I deleted the text and pushed my phone away, glancing at Lily.

Lily's auburn hair was piled on top of her head, and she looked calmer than normal. Although, I could still detect a slight note of frantic hidden behind that façade. But that was her nature, which was why a job at a PR firm was great for her. All of her crazy energy would produce something great in the end, and nothing would slip by her. I, on the other hand, preferred a bit more of an organized life. It had gotten me this far, and I wanted stability to carry me forward as successfully as it had done in the past. I had wanted to go to law school ever since I was a little girl. Planned for it, dreamed about it, and now I was finally about to enter the program. I had been studying hard all summer just to prepare for my first semester, and finally my plan would start to take shape.

"I can't tell you how much I've missed you guys," Lily said, shaking her head. "I feel like even this small distance is driving me to make absolutely insane choices."

I stared at Lily for a split second before I burst

out laughing.

"What?" she whined, shoving a curl behind her ear.

"Yeah, I'm sure it's the four hour drive that's screwing with your judgment." I rolled my eyes and poured myself a glass of ale.

There was a reason she commanded so much male attention. She was downright gorgeous. Lily's hair was a unique shade, but I think what made the red stand out even more were her green eyes. Dressed in a pair of baggy boyfriend jeans and a loose red tee that exposed her cleavage, she was covered up more than most but still oozed sexiness. She never seemed to notice exactly how much attention she received from the opposite sex, which somehow always got her into trouble with the women around her.

I, however, added a little more zest to my dressing hoping for the same result. I actually wasn't sure how that was going to work once I started law school in the fall. They all dressed so conservative and boring. Just because I wanted to go into law, didn't mean I wanted to dress like an old lady. I enjoyed the few assets I was blessed with and wanted to show them off, at least a tad. Tonight I was in a pair of black leggings and an oversized gray top with a v-neck that went as low as one could get away with, but I had a lace camisole under it. Really, all three of us were different, but we complimented each other so well.

"Hey, not nice. But what were you saying about Gabby? Why can't she get her butt down here to see me?"

"She is waiting for her new bike to be delivered that *daddy* bought her," I said grinning. "And it's being delivered by the insanely hot bike builder, who I think has the hots for her. Anyway, she was expecting him to arrive in an hour, but he left a message on our machine and arrived early."

"Rich people's problems...And?" Lily's brow arched.

I started laughing again, and I knew she was kidding, considering her family rivaled Gabby's in wealth. I was like the odd man out in this group. But I loved Lily's humor.

"I let Jason in and told him to make himself at home while Gabby chilled on the patio in the tub. When I last left her she was relaxing in the hot tub in a beautiful lavender bikini that would make even the happiest man in the world weep."

A basket of tortilla chips arrived, and I plopped a chip in my mouth, crunching loudly to avoid the mix of guilt and evil delight.

"Are you serious? Are you sure he's okay to just let—"

"Yeah. I would bet my life on it. She's being too wishy-washy and needed this kick in the ass. Besides, her dad installed a camera system along with the security system, which I told Jason all about."

"You told him he's being recorded?"

"Yup...even though he's not. We screwed up the channels somehow, but still the law has been laid. That will keep him on his toes."

"I'm certainly glad you're our friend and not our enemy." Lily crinkled her nose and grabbed a chip. "Now spill the beans on Gabby's brother."

I sat back in the booth and tried to shake the images that flooded my mind the moment Aaron was brought up. From the second I'd met Aaron he'd invaded every private moment and thought I'd had. My dreams, fantasies, musings... there he was. And no matter how hard I tried to focus on anyone else, it was like he'd appear, wriggling his finger and grinning like he knew he could get whatever he wanted. The big reveal from Gabby's past didn't help either, especially since it didn't seem quite so big to an outsider like me.

"Not to discount Gabby's feelings, and God, I can't imagine..." I shifted uncomfortably and noticed a group of guys come into the pub. Lily followed my gaze.

"Now we're talking. But continue your thought first, men later."

"Well, it's just what she went through sounds riddled with loneliness, and I can't even begin to imagine the rejection she felt *because* of her brother, Aaron. It explains a lot about how she is now, but I also can't help but wonder what else there is to the story. His side, you know? And what he did to her was bad—horrible—, but I do wonder what made him abandon his baby sister. I know there's more there that might paint a different picture."

"And you're feeling guilty because if he looked like a toad you might not be so willing to hear his side," Lily said.

"Sometimes your bluntness is really over the top..."

I tossed a chip at Lily and took another sip of the ale as I wondered what bothered me the most. The fact that I was contemplating going behind my best friend's back to talk to her brother, or that I hoped whatever we found out about his side of the story would somehow make up for his past mistakes.

"Well?" She sat back in the booth and her eyes flashed to the group of men.

"I'd like to think I'm a better person than that."

"Wouldn't we all?" Lily grabbed a napkin and wiped her mouth before throwing another glance to the group of guys who came in and stood next to the bar. "So how about you just answer my original question and tell me about her brother."

The pub's lighting dimmed slightly as the music went up a notch to welcome the dinner hour, and I scooted forward on the bench.

"He happens to be the most attractive man in the world as long as he keeps his mouth shut."

"I feel like that's been a statement said about me at times." Lily frowned. "I like him already."

"Seriously, as soon as you see him you'll completely understand my quandary. All he has to do is walk into a room and people just feel his presence."

"You're sure about that?"

"I am! I saw it in the lobby and at Starbucks. The way he carries himself...he's so sure of himself. And God, his body…"

"Go on."

"He obviously works out. He's got dark hair and there's this thing between us. Or at least I think it's between us. I hope it's not one-sided. You know what? I'm just gonna leave it at that because the more I talk about him, the worse I feel. I'm done. He's just a distant relative of Gabby's that obviously has problems, and I'm never going to think about him again. See? I feel better already."

"Okay. So other than the fact that you were arguing with yourself for a good part of a minute there, it sounds like you've got a solid understanding of why you should avoid him. Now, I'm going to play devil's advocate."

"Of course you are," I grumbled, watching our server make her way to our table.

"Sorry for the delay. A big group kind of swarmed me over there," our server said, pointing at the group of guys.

"Yeah. They look to be a little out of control," I teased, noticing just how loud and obnoxious they were getting.

"Would you like to order any starters?" she asked, glancing over her shoulder back at the guys.

"I think we'll just order our mains. I'll take the Beecher's grilled ham and cheese with a side salad," I said, handing my menu over to her.

"Did you want the salad in place of the fries or in addition," she asked. As my eyes landed on the group of men by the bar, my gaze quickly fell to one in particular. Could it be? No. That was ridiculous. There were a lot of well-built men in Seattle, kind of.

"Umm. In addition. Thanks," I muttered, feeling my heart rate rise as I continued to watch the guy. I only saw the back of him, but the way he was telling stories it looked like the other guys were just his puppets or... God. There was something about him. No way. Now I was getting obsessive. It was not Aaron.

"And I'll take the turkey burger with fries, but I'd like the sweet potato ones. And let's get two duck farts," Lily said.

I snapped my neck back to focus on Lily as our server left and started laughing. "Are you serious?"

"Hell yeah, I'm serious. And what was with that whole zoning out thing while ordering? Did you spot a target?" she asked.

Leave it to Lily.

"No. Just thought I saw someone I knew."

"Okay, so back to the important stuff. Let's think about this Aaron person. As of now, the only negative is that he's Gabby's brother."

"No. That's not the only negative. He left her, abandoned her without a word for over a decade. I mean come on. You know what she's been through."

"Let's try this again...He was eighteen and he left and never called or communicated with home. I don't think that's a crime, and it certainly, at least in my book, doesn't make him a bad person. And if he didn't know about her health, I mean he can't be blamed after the fact for that. None of that started until she was in high school, right?"

I nodded.

"So he was obviously long gone by then. Maybe there was some serious behind-the-scenes stuff that made it impossible for him to be in her life."

"Okay. My turn. So let's say you're right. Does that mean he's going to run anytime something gets tough? That's not anything I'd want long term anyway, so why waste my time? You know, I even dragged poor Gabby out to a club just to get her brother out of my head! How pathetic is that?"

I watched Lily as she took a sip of her beer and placed it back down. She didn't say anything for a couple of seconds but just sat quietly. This wasn't Lily.

"You know what just dawned on me?" she asked.

"What?"

"Here I am trying to persuade you to do something you obviously don't want to do. And who am I to do that? I have the worst track record when it comes to men." Lily's lips pulled into a smile.

"None of us have really excelled in that area," I laughed. "Otherwise I wouldn't be daydreaming about a completely unattainable man."

Our food was delivered, and I heard the voices raise another click as the drinks continued to circulate among the crowd.

"This will be the last thing I say on the matter." Lily raised her hand in oath. "But I have never seen you light up the way you did when you mentioned his name. You get this look in your eyes, almost a dreamy stare..."

I rolled my eyes and shook my head as I thought about Lily's words. Going forward I'd need to try my hardest to look detached and uninterested whenever Gabby brought up her brother.

"The truth of it is, I'm all dopey over a guy I can't have, and all he probably wants is a way to get to his sister." I shrugged. "So I swear I'm officially over it."

"Uh-huh." She watched the crowd near the bar grow, and my eyes went back to the stranger at the bar right when he turned around. The butterflies in my stomach were quickly squashed when I realized it wasn't Aaron. I let out a sigh loud enough for Lily to catch as she munched on her fries.

"Sounds like leaving him in the dust is working out for you. Enough of that, though. Now let's get on to me. I think I might have found someone."

"And is he available? Like actually available?"

She pulled her brows together and scowled at me. "He works at the PR firm and is definitely available. He's actually asked me out twice, but I declined both times."

This did not sound like the Lily I knew. She usually jumped at the chance to go out.

"Really? I didn't know that no was even in

your repertoire," I teased.

"Hey now. I may have made my share of bad choices, but I'm trying not to do that any longer. I'm taking my time. Plus both nights that he asked, I had events I needed to attend. One for a lip gloss launch and another for a brewery."

"A day in the life..."

We continued eating and chatting, catching up on everything since she moved to Portland. The pub was one step past lively, and it was getting hard to hear Lily so we both decided to call it a night here and find a place where we could chat. When the server brought our check, I quickly paid and we began wandering through the crowd.

"Wanna hit the bar down the street? The dancing's only in the front, and there are usually places in the back to sit."

"Totally," I said, weaving my way through the final horde of people before landing at the exit.

Lily heaved the large wooden door open, right when I heard my name called from behind. And this time there was no mistaking who it was.

CHAPTER FIVE

"Lily," I hissed, but she couldn't hear me. Instead, she pranced out to the street leaving me stranded in the doorway. "Lily," I tried again.

She turned around, only to reveal a huge grin as she looked behind me, obviously spying the source of the voice.

Drats! It really was him.

"Excuse me, miss. Do you mind closing the door? You're letting the AC out," the bartender called over the crowd.

Gladly!

I gave him a quick nod and ran through the door. My fingertips released the wood, letting the hinges close it silently.

"Let's get out of here."

But it was too late. The door pushed open, and Lily's huge grin turned to one of complete adoration as the male calling my name came into her view.

"Hey, Brandy," Aaron said, his voice calm.

My body completely betrayed me as I turned to face him, but not before I realized he had someone with him. The excitement in my belly was quickly replaced with disappointment and jealousy. The tall blonde next to him was definitely the exact opposite of what I had to offer. Every hair was in place, and her tan couldn't get any more golden if she rubbed it in hourly. My skin was olive, not orange. Her features were harsh. No. That was mean. They were dramatic and certainly hinted of not wanting to get on her bad side.

He tilted his head slightly, and his eyes grew curious as he waited for my reaction. He slid his right hand into his jean pocket and just waited. Was this a test? Did he want to see what I thought about him being with someone? Or did he only want to size up how to approach me about his sister?

"What's up, Aaron?"

Aaron hooked his thumbs through his belt loops and watched me closely while my agitation level grew. I was sure a hint of a smile was threatening to take over his lips as he toyed with me.

Lily stood next to me, and I could tell she was giving the once-over to the blond. I wasn't sure if that made the situation better or worse.

"Didn't I make myself clear the other day?" I pressed. My brows pulled together as my arms folded in front of me.

"The other day?" blondie asked, looking up at Aaron.

Ignoring her, he took a step forward. "I was hoping you'd reconsidered."

"Nope. Still feel the same way. Listen, my friend and I haven't seen each other in a while so we're gonna take off."

Aaron followed my gaze to the slobbering and very possessive female by his side as I took a step back. The blonde nodded in victory and grabbed his hand, staking her claim. He paid as much attention to her as he would a scarf wrapped around his neck and shook her hand from his. Normally, I would have been delighted, but in this instance, I actually felt sorry for her. Rather than the blonde say something to him, she turned around and walked back into the pub.

He took a step closer, and his voice dropped, sending electricity through me. "Would you at least give me your contact information?"

Lily patted my shoulder and walked down the sidewalk, which was exactly what I didn't want her to do. Privacy wasn't something I needed to have around this guy.

"You know where I work, which is the same place your sister works. That should be enough. Besides, wouldn't your parents just give you the information for your sister?"

He cocked his head and grinned. His brown eyes piercing as he caught my wrist in his hand, allowing me to feel his restrained strength as my feeble attempt to flee failed. A flurry of excitement ran through me, but I shook my head in protest.

"I wasn't asking for her information. I was asking for yours."

He released my wrist, his eyes raking over my body as I crossed my arms.

"And get in between you and the blonde? I don't think so."

Aaron smiled and smirked. "I get it."

"Get what?"

This wasn't what I was in the mood for. This guy had some nerve. Gabby and he couldn't be more different. Watching how he treated his date was bad enough, but asking for my information while she scurried off? No thanks.

"You're worried."

"Worried? Please. I just have more respect for myself than apparently the poor souls you choose to lead on."

I watched as a couple went into the pub, and Aaron's fingers touched my chin softly bringing my attention back to him. Unfortunately, his touch produced a flutter in my stomach, and my cheeks warmed instantly.

"I only met her tonight," he mumbled.

"Is that supposed to make me feel better? Because it doesn't. Besides it's of no concern to me. I could honestly care less."

His eyes narrowed on mine, and I watched as he twisted his lips, contemplating what to say next.

"Listen, I wish nothing but the best between you and Gabby, but that's all I've got for you." As I stood staring at him, I realized the duck fart and half a pitcher had completely caught up with me. I wanted to find a tree to lean up against or maybe...

"So you *are* worried about that," his voice low. There was a tenderness behind it that caught me off guard.

"Yeah. And you should be too, especially if you're trying to repair anything with her." I snapped out of the fog.

There was silence between us. The warm summer air began to feel unbearable, or maybe it was his gaze that produced the heat through my body. I had nothing else to say to this guy, and I just hoped he wouldn't make it any more difficult than it already was to shove him out of my mind.

And then he did.

"That night at Chateau Marx I spotted you across the room and my world stopped. I'm not that kind of man, but you took my breath away, and I damned near spilled my wine all over when you glanced in my direction." He took a deep breath in and continued. "And then you stepped to the side as you grabbed something off a tray and my sister came into view...I was in shock. I knew she was going to be there that night, but I still wasn't ready for it. And seeing that you two were together... That just seems to be my luck." He stopped himself.

Realizing my balance was completely off-kilter, I shifted my weight slowly from one foot to the other as I debated what to say. The woozy me was willing to soften the seriousness of the situation, but thankfully a wave of clarity appeared.

"Well, I guess it's just an unfortunate set of circumstances for us all," I whispered, my pulse roaring in my ears. "Besides, something tells me you were able to keep yourself amused that night without my help."

His eyes became incredibly intense, and I felt my body succumbing to his potent gaze. Even as my body betrayed me, I prayed that my mind would not. If there was one thing I possessed ample amounts of, it was self-discipline. But that was generally not when I'd had a few drinks.

I saw Lily leaning against the brick building, texting and chuckling to herself, and I wondered if there was more to her work-romance than she let on. Nothing would surprise me with her. I brought my attention back to Aaron, which was a mistake.

"I guess it is a very unfortunate set of circumstances," he agreed. "But you're not someone I'm willing to give up on. I think you'll come around."

I frowned as his words settled over me. The one thing I was sure of was that the longer I stood in front of him, the stronger the attraction became. He scratched his chin as his eyes danced with playfulness once again, and I imagined his fingers gliding along my flesh.

Damn my imagination!

Attempting to gather my thoughts and my balance, I took a step away from him.

"Would you at least take my number on the off chance my sister wants to get ahold of me?"

"I thought you said this wasn't about your sister."

"Man. You're good," he said, bemused.

I didn't have any clue about how to respond. I didn't want to betray Gabby and that wasn't my intention, but being in his presence sent something thrumming through me that dislodged all common sense. It was as if my subconscious was begging for him to take control, and he somehow picked up on it and used it to his advantage.

His phone buzzed and he grabbed it out of his pocket.

"What's up, Jason. Make it fast," Aaron replied into the receiver.

A few moments of silence was followed by Aaron quickly running his hands through his hair.

"What do you mean she took off? Where'd she go?" Aaron asked.

And then it dawned on me that it must be Jason, the bike builder Jason, and they're talking about Gabby.

"What's going on?" I interrupted, staring at Aaron.

"Why was she angry?" he continued, and a few more moments of quiet. "You're sure she went back?"

Aaron hung up and looked at me, his expression filled with exasperation. "Does Gabby have a habit of taking off?"

"It has happened once or twice. Seems to run in the family. Now tell me what's going on. Was that *the* Jason?" I asked.

"Yeah. It was *the* Jason, and for some reason, Gabby got upset with something he said and took the bike out for a joyride."

"Oh, my God. Did she say where she was going?"

"Well, Jason thinks it was more show than go because she circled around the block a few times and landed back in the parking garage."

I couldn't help but laugh. That was definitely Gabby.

"I hate those things," I muttered.

"That's not what I wanted to hear," he said quietly.

"Listen, I'll give you my number, but it is only for emergency use concerning Gabby."

The moment I spoke the words I regretted them and rather than tell him my number, he reached for my hand that was tightly squeezing my phone. Teasing the phone gently out of my fingers, he slid it on and dialed his cell.

Victory flashed in his eyes as his grin widened. "See how easy that was. Now you have mine and I have yours."

"Does it ever get old always getting what you want?" I asked, feeling the anger stir again.

"Not yet," he murmured. "Nice seeing you again, Brandy."

And that was it.

I watched as he turned away and walked back into the pub. The lingering sensations pulsing through my body left me on edge, and I had no idea how I was going to get through the weekend without having him visit my dreams once again.

My insides twisted into knots as I thought about him meeting back up with the blonde or anyone else for that matter. I sulked over to Lily and smiled.

"I better take off. It sounds like Gabby's getting a little unruly with her new motorcycle. At least that's what Jason called Aaron about. Do you know what makes me so mad?"

"Do tell..."

"He managed to weasel my number from me."

"The nerve."

"Come on. You know what I mean. He's just assuming that I'll fall down at his feet."

"I think that's a fair assumption," Lily laughed.

I rolled my eyes. "Not even. I know he went right back into the pub and picked up where he left off with the blonde. He obviously has no shortage of women in his world. He won't miss not having me, and I certainly won't miss the trouble. He's far too arrogant and sure of himself. And for that alone I'll stay far away. I don't need another player."

"You know what I find absolutely intriguing?"

"What?" I asked.

"For someone who left home before even graduating from high school and being hidden for ten years, he certainly has fine taste in luxury items."

"What do you mean?"

"He was wearing a Sky Dweller."

"A what?" I asked.

"The watch he was wearing was a Rolex, a Sky

Dweller Rolex. His suit is Hugo Boss and his shoes looked to be as well. He's got money."

"How can you tell all that just by looking at him?"

"That's my job. I have to know who, what, when, and why just by looking. Image is everything in PR."

I was quiet for a few minutes as we walked down the sidewalk.

"So like how much money?"

"Those watches go for $40,000, at least."

My mouth dropped open and I stopped walking. "What the hell has he been doing for the last ten years that would provide that kind of income?"

She turned to face me, smiling. "See? Intriguing. I don't know, but I might snoop around when I get back to the office next week."

"Well, regardless, it only adds to my theory about him. I'm just another figurine to add to his collectibles."

"I wouldn't be so sure," she whispered, catching me off guard. There was something behind her gaze. A sadness or regret possibly? "In his mind, you're already his. You might as well not fight it."

"What the hell are you talking about?"

"The possession in his eyes when he looks at you..."

"Yeah?"

"I've only seen that type of look once before and that's what it meant then, and I'm certain that's what it means now. You belong to him."

"I don't belong to anyone. And when?" I asked.

"It was another lifetime ago," she muttered, dismissing my curiosity. "But God, I miss living close to you guys. Try not to have all the fun in the world. I'd like to think of you as lonely and as screwed up as me."

We stopped in front of the hotel she was staying at and she glanced at her phone. "Perfect timing. Mike was going to meet me for a nightcap."

"Who?"

"You remember Mike. He graduated a year before us? He's working in the city."

I raised a brow. What happened to the guy from the office she was interested in?

"I don't know who you're talking about," I said, laughing. "Well, tomorrow you'll make it to my brothers' birthday party, right?"

"It's not like that, silly. He's bringing his wife, who's pregnant. And of course I'll be there. Can't wait to see the twins. It's hard to believe they're turning twenty-seven."

"Tell me about it."

She gave me a big hug and turned into her hotel. I looked back behind me to where the pub was and fought the urge to go see exactly how Aaron would be spending his night. I didn't care! I was *not* going to turn into that person. No way.

I needed to get home to Gabby and make sure her butt was anchored to a chair and not a bike seat and find out what made her so mad. And hopefully by tomorrow, Aaron would be a distant memory as I celebrated my twin brothers' birthdays.

If only it were so easy.

CHAPTER SIX

I pulled into my parents' driveway, lifted the parking brake and didn't bother rolling up the window. The street was already lined with cars, and the red, black, and silver balloons tied to the mailbox swayed in the gentle breeze. The excitement of the barbeque was already running through the air. I heard the low bass of music coming from the backyard, bringing a smile to my lips. I was truly lucky to have such a wonderful family.

I loved the house I grew up in. It was mid-century modern and had an updated *Brady Bunch* quality. My parents took a lot of pride in their home and our family, for that matter. Over the years, the outdated brick had been exchanged for flagstone, and shake accents were added under the eaves. My father owned a construction business, and whenever times were slow, he worked on our home. Thinking of my father brought such a warm feeling to my heart. I never really got that fuzzy feeling when I saw Gabby and her father together. It made me feel bad for her, and that was even before any of this stuff with her brother popped up. I understood that her father threw himself into his business and that certainly made for a cushy life for his family, but I wouldn't trade what I had for the world.

My family certainly wasn't wealthy, especially now that I knew what that really entailed, but we never went without. Or maybe I just didn't know what I was missing in the first place. Both of my parents were hardworking and loved what they did. My mom was an attorney, practicing in a non-profit that she founded. She worked with clients who couldn't afford legal representation. Her foundation grew tremendously, and I'd be remiss if I didn't acknowledge just how quickly it grew once Gabby's father contributed and highlighted it in his portfolio of non-profits to watch.

As I sat in the driver's seat, I thought back to how wonderful it was growing up with my brothers, and how devastated I would have been if either of them had left me without saying goodbye or telling me where they were going. For that reason alone, Aaron needed to become a thing of the past—just a momentary lapse of daydreaming judgment.

The front door opened and my brother, Mason, popped his head out. "Hey, how long are you going to sit in the car, sis?"

He was dressed in a loose pair of shorts and a black polo. His dark blonde hair was shaggy and his blue eyes vibrant. He worked with my father in the construction business, and as a result, his olive skin was even deeper than usual.

I swung the car door open and jumped out, leaving their birthday packages in the car.

"Hey," I squealed.

Mason jogged to the driveway and gave me a big hug. "It's so good to see you."

"Where does the time go?"

"Hey now! Don't hog my little sister," my other brother, Ayden, yelled from the doorway. He was the oldest between the two and took full advantage of those couple of minutes. Looking identical to Mason—a fact that Ayden would argue—was where their similarities ended. While Mason was conservative, Ayden was a free spirit. And not one of those lazy, I run-with-the-wind couch surfer types, but rather, he always trusted his gut and ran on instinct, while executing his plans flawlessly. He saw an opening in the energy drink market, and leaped on it. Now he was the leading manufacturer of organic energy drinks. Not bad for a twenty-seven year old. My father used to tease him about ending up a thirty-eight year old couch surfer if he didn't start applying himself. And, boy, did that pep talk work.

Ayden shoved Mason away from me and inserted himself into a grand bear hug.

"It's been too long, knucklehead," Ayden

teased.

I started laughing as he let go of me. "Well, maybe if you didn't call me knucklehead you'd see me more."

"I can't believe the last time we were all together was at your graduation in June," Mason said, smiling. "You must be really busy at your new job. Or maybe you have a new guy?"

"Yes to the first and definitely no to the second. Thanks for your concern." I glared at Mason who couldn't help but smile.

"That's good news because Cole has been anxiously gulping his beer—"

"Whoa. Not so fast," I interrupted.

Cole was one of the guys my brothers ran around with in college. I never understood what my brothers had in common with him and got even more annoyed when he seemed to show an interest in me. I think my father should have given Cole the pep talk instead of my brother.

Mason and Ayden both wiggled their brows up and down, and all I could think to do was punch them both in the shoulder.

"Don't even think about it. You know how I feel about him."

"He's matured," Ayden replied, dropping the act and Mason nodded in agreement.

"I don't even think when he's ninety, I'll be able to handle him."

"Our little sister, the heartbreaker," Mason said, wrapping his arms around my shoulders, leading me into the house.

"Your presents are in the trunk, but if you try

anything, I'll take them right back."

As soon as I got inside, I smelled the delicious aromas coming from the kitchen. I was able to sniff out my mom's world famous meatballs, chicken wings, and something very garlicky. The entry hall carried on the tradition of helium balloons, and the staircase was wrapped in silver garlands with my brothers' names spelled out in giant, cardboard letters. I started chuckling as I thought about the event I had just attended, put on by Gabby's parents, and how horrified Gabby's stepmom would be if our family volunteered to do the decorating. But, hey, it would have saved a ton of money.

"What's so funny?" Ayden asked, coming from behind carrying both packages.

"Just remembering why I loved home so much."

My mom came out of the kitchen, dressed in jeans and an oversized teal tunic, and held out her arms. "My baby."

"Everything smells so delicious."

My mom gave me a quick hug and kiss and trundled off to the kitchen with my brothers and me trailing behind her.

"Dad's outside trying to get the barbeque to light. He's put so much lighter fluid on the coals, I'm afraid the neighborhood's going to go up in smoke."

For some reason, my dad wouldn't switch to a gas barbeque. We had tried convincing him that it would be easier, but he vowed he'd never do it. My brothers used to wet the coals just to mess with him. I glanced at both of them wondering if they were up to their old tricks again and judging by the sparkle in their eyes, I'd say yes.

"Poor dad." I grabbed a cup and filled it with raspberry lemonade with a kick.

"Did your brothers tell you who was excited to see you?" my mom asked, stirring the meatballs and giving me a sideways glance.

"Not you too?"

"He's cute and he's doing very well for himself."

"He could own or run the entire city of Seattle, and I still wouldn't be interested. You know I'm not into that stuff. Besides, I'm not interested in dating. I need to concentrate on law school."

"Is my girl in here?" Lily's voice rang through the entryway. "I think I overheard something about law school and dating?"

Lily rounded the bend, beaming and gave both my brothers a quick hug. She had a pair of jean shorts on and a hoodie. She had straightened her hair for the occasion, and it looked really cute. She handed each of my brothers a silver gift bag.

"Is she babbling about Gabby's long lost brother?" Lily rolled her eyes as I froze in place.

"Hadn't mentioned it. Thanks for that." I dropped my gaze to the floor.

My mom smiled and shook her head. "Long lost brother, huh? How does that work?"

"I guess he took off right after Gabby's mom passed away. He was eighteen and just kind of disappeared until a week ago. Or so the story goes," I said.

"That's odd," my mom replied, piling the meatballs into the warmer.

"Well, I happened to run into him last night and he is gorgeous," Lily continued. "And wherever he's been for the last ten years has certainly been productive."

I furrowed my brows at Lily to make her stop, but she was having none of it.

"And how did you find this out since last night?" Ayden teased. "Do you do this to all potential victims?"

"First, I spotted what he was wearing wrapped around his wrist. Second, I asked one of my coworkers at the firm where I work. They would love to sink their teeth into his business. And third, I'm not interested. He's got his sights set on our dear Brandy."

I let out a groan and shook my head.

"Right. I'm sure you would turn him down." Mason raised a brow at Lily and grinned. He knew her well.

"What? I did this strictly for business. I always have to be on the lookout for new clients." Lily and my mom laughed.

"Well, Gabby has a bike now and she's riding that thing everywhere," I said, switching the subject.

"She finally got one?" Ayden asked.

"Her dad surprised her with one. And she happens to be dating the guy who built it."

"Is that why she didn't show up?" he teased.

I nodded. "I wish she wouldn't ride it. It's so unsafe and with everything she's been through, I would have thought she'd be more careful."

"It's probably because of everything she's been through that she wants to live a little," Lily chided in. "A new heart might do that to a person."

I smiled and knew it would be a losing battle. Just because I was afraid of those machines didn't mean the world had to be. It didn't help that I woke up last night from a nightmare where the bike was the main attraction either. And it wasn't the first time.

"Well, I'm proud of her for not only riding but allowing herself to dabble in the love department. We could all learn a thing or two," Lily said.

And with that, I grabbed the pot full of meatballs and began my escape plan with my brothers right on my heels.

Walking through the family room and out the open sliding glass door, I beelined toward the picnic table that had all of the food spread out on it. I quickly grabbed the extension cord and plugged in the pot. I glanced around the backyard, noticing the tiki torches stuck around the patio and lanterns dangling from the trees.

"So what's the story with this mystery man?" Mason said, his overprotective ways emerging.

"There is no story. He's Gabby's brother. Therefore, he's off limits." I spotted Cole sitting with a beer at one of the tables taking selfies and rolled my eyes. Mason and Ayden turned to follow my gaze and their laughter rang throughout the yard, but it still didn't interrupt

Cole. He was obviously on a pursuit to find the perfect self-portrait to post to our poor unsuspecting world. He was the only man I knew who would make friends take pictures down if he didn't think he looked perfect.

"Need I say more?" I laughed. "Do you really think I want to date a guy who is so concerned with getting a flawless shot to share with Facebook? I mean look at him. He's actually positioning the beer bottle perfectly next to his grinning chops."

"Do I hear my baby girl?" my father turned around, lighter fluid in hand.

"Daddy, you really ought to think about switching to a gas barbeque."

"Enough of that out of you and give me a hug."

He wore his Barbeque Master apron with pride, and I couldn't help but love him for trying. Unfortunately, Cole spotted me heading for my dad and quickly stood up.

I gave my dad a quick hug so he could get back to the task at hand and backed up with my brothers.

"So we may have to be on the watch," Ayden told my father.

"For what?"

"Brandy's still blushing from a mere mention of some guy, which tells me it might not just be some guy."

Turning quickly, I could feel my cheeks blazing as I socked him one in the arm. Suddenly feeling like I was back in high school, all I could blurt out was to shut up.

"Is that so?" my father asked, as he tended to the unlit coals.

"Dad, have you ever wondered why you have such bad luck with your coals?" I took a step away from my brothers, but unfortunately, it landed me closer to Cole.

Ayden and Mason quickly exchanged glances. Mason's mouth opened, but he shut it quickly when my brow shot up daring him.

"That's part of the challenge," my dad answered.

"You might want—"

"To let us buy you one of those stainless steel barbeques that even has a burner," Ayden interrupted me.

"So who is it that Brandy's interested in?" Cole asked, taking a sip of his beer.

I saw Lily come outside with my mom and another group of my brothers' friends. I hoped she'd see the desperation in my face and come save me.

"Yeah. What's his name?" Mason grabbed a beer from the cooler just as Lily settled into our expanding circle.

"Who?" Lily asked.

"Gabby's brother." Mason knocked the cap off of the bottle and took a chug.

"Aaron," she replied, completely oblivious.

"Aaron who?" Cole asked, his hazel eyes flicking to Lily's.

"I'd imagine his last name is Sullivan," Lily replied, grinning.

"Aaron Sullivan? The Aaron Sullivan?" Cole

started laughing viciously and my insides began to ignite with fury.

"What about him?" I asked, narrowing my gaze on him.

My mom was moving a bunch of the balloons to the far side of the yard so they wouldn't keep interfering with the food table, but she stopped to glance at me. My voice must not have been as calm as I'd hoped.

"Only that he's the king of players. I don't think I've ever seen him with the same date twice."

I could feel the blood pumping mightily through my veins.

"And when exactly is it that you're bumping into him? I wouldn't guess you two to be running in the same circles." My brows shot up.

"Ouch," Cole said, grinning. "Believe it or not my MIS degree is paying off. And yes, we do frequent the same functions quite often."

"It doesn't matter to me. He's a single guy and can date whoever and however many he wants." I walked over to the cooler and grabbed a hard cider, twisting the top off.

Cole came up behind me and lowered his voice. "Look, I get that you're not into me, but this Sullivan guy is bad news. I just don't want to see you getting hurt."

I turned to face Cole and couldn't help but soften. "For that I thank you."

"Truce?" he asked.

"Truce. But enough with the selfies, Cole."

CHAPTER SEVEN

I had spent the last couple weeks on autopilot and was relieved to go that long of a stretch without having any accidental run-ins with Aaron. I was back at my desk and buried in Monday morning madness, looking forward to getting some chapters read later in the afternoon on formatting legal pleadings when I heard a laugh from Gabby's office. It had to be Jason on the other end of her phone. A nagging feeling of envy began to rear its ugly head, and I squashed it quickly. What I needed to do was concentrate on getting all the calendars updated and airline reservations made for the team. Once I got all that out of the way I could sneak in some reading and shake these ridiculously unfounded feelings. I wanted to start law school with a bang, and the only way I saw that as a possibility was to begin reading the textbooks ahead of time.

Gabby was softening on her brother, and I was positive Jason had something to do with that. Whether Gabby recognized that or not, I didn't know, but at least she was willing to consider the possibilities. It was nice to see a genuine smile on Gabby's lips since Jason came into her life. And her laugh was definitely signaling a turn in the relationship. I'd almost bet money that pieces of the wall around her very guarded heart were actually beginning to crumble.

My email bleeped, and I looked up from the files I'd been sorting through. My heart started pounding when the letters came into focus.

How could this be?

To: Brandy Rhodes
From: Aaron Sullivan
Subject: Cole

Ms. Rhodes:
It was a pleasure bumping into you a couple weeks ago. I'm surprised our paths haven't crossed since. I want to express my astonishment at what a small world it is. Beyond the obvious connection we seem to share, it seems the universe has a mind of its own.

I was playing golf with Cole on Sunday, and he mentioned running into you at a function. Can you believe that? It sounds as if you two certainly have a history. Is it...

My cheeks ignited. What history? There was no history with Cole. What in the world did Cole tell Aaron? The preview screen cut the remainder of Aaron's message from view. But that was completely fine since I was in a frozen state of shock. How did Aaron get my email? Sitting motionless at my desk, I slowly rose from my chair, popping my head over the cubicle walls, and scanned the top of everyone's workspaces on the off chance Aaron was on the floor, spying on me. He didn't seem to have any scruples when it came to tracking me down. I looked around the room and saw no sign of sexy-as-hell-stalker-man and sat down quickly.

Okay, I had definitely turned crazy on this one.

I stared back at the screen not wanting to open the message fully. I refused to engage with him, and something told me that a control freak like him would have tagged it to see if his message was read. I knew I would have. But it was killing me to find out how he got my email address. Who would have given it to him? I positioned my cursor over his name very carefully and right clicked the properties. My mouth dropped open as I saw the same parent company where I worked in his email stamp. The bastard worked here, and I bet Gabby had no idea.

Damn him! Damn me for not figuring it out sooner.

Even though the curiosity was pounding through my veins to take a look at his email, I highlighted his message and clicked the trashcan.

There!

That made me feel a whole lot better. I wanted

to tell Gabby, but that wouldn't be a brilliant idea because she'd wonder how I'd found that piece of information out.

I turned around to see the receptionist bringing me a bouquet of flowers, and my stomach dipped to my toes. No way!

"These are very pretty," she cooed, placing them on my desk. "Great date last night?"

My heart was beating so fast. How could he do this when his sister was bound to see them?

"No date at all," I said, searching for the little card and only finding one with my name on it and no sender.

"Well, they're gorgeous," she said, before turning around.

I shoved the arrangement to the corner of my desk and tried not to focus on them, but the thought of the weird texts and phone calls that I'd recently received made me a little uneasy. But I was sure these came from Aaron. The timing was too impeccable and I was just being a worrier, reading too many thrillers late at night.

I heard a male's voice calling for me down the way and almost panicked mistaking the tone for Aaron's. This pins and needles thing was really getting tiresome. Decker came into view, and my insides did a conflicting tumble as disappointment and relief duked it out.

"Hey, Brandy. You doing okay?" he teased, leaning over the cubicle.

Decker transferred to our division around the same time as I arrived, and I enjoyed his sense of humor. His dark hair, chiseled features, and hazel eyes weren't bad to look at either.

"Yeah. Why?" I glanced back at my email to see if any new messages arrived and it looked all clear.

"You kind of look like you saw a ghost."

"Just got a random email that was meant for spam."

Decker started laughing, and I couldn't help but notice how strong his forearms looked in the rolled-up shirt he wore. "Some of those can be pretty spicy. Just don't click on them...whatever you do."

"I'll try to remember that." I grinned.

Why couldn't I be into Decker? He's available, friendly, and hot...in a newly-minted college graduate kind of way. Aaron, however, exuded an entirely different persona. He was full of confidence, and he wasn't that much older than Decker. Somehow, Aaron's mannerisms conveyed an entirely enticing way of thinking and being. I also had to admit to myself the deception was a little intriguing, which added mystery in a way that wasn't explainable...

And shame on me!

I had done great all last week.

"I was just checking to see if you'd like to do lunch? A new pizza place opened up that offers lunch specials by the slice." Decker smiled, and I noticed the flicker of more behind his eyes.

"Totally. What time you wanna head out?"

"11:30 work?"

"Perfect." I gave him a quick wave and watched him wander back to where his cubicle was hidden.

Exactly what I needed. I turned my attention back to the file I was organizing that contained everyone's itineraries as Gabby came out of her office beaming. I couldn't help but smile. There was no way I was envious of her, only confused about my own choices.

"Nice conversation about cheese?" I teased.

She leaned over my cubicle, a dreamy expression plastered on her face as she rested her elbows on the plastic wall.

"There is something so familiar about Jason. Like we can talk for hours and it never gets old."

"Sounds like how it's supposed to be," I reminded her.

"I know I'm still in the honeymoon stage, but I hope that it never ends."

"Something tells me it never will."

"Wanna do lunch today?" Gabby asked.

"I would but Decker just asked. You want to come with us?"

She smiled and nodded knowingly. "No. I don't want to be the third wheel."

"It's not like that," I whispered. "It's totally professional."

She shrugged, still grinning. "Listen, who knows when and where love will..."

"Enough." I shook my head. "Not happening with Decker."

"Well, when that attraction does happen, don't ignore it, my friend. We've only got one shot at this life." She patted her chest where her borrowed heart resided, and I had to push down the lump that formed in my throat. She really did have a different view of things than most.

"Promise." I rose my hand in a pledge and smiled. "One more thing."

"Yeah?"

"Do you promise me you'll be extra careful on your bike?"

"I'm always careful."

"I know, but I just want you to be extra cautious."

"For you, anything," she vowed, winking. "Okay, off to grab a coffee. Need anything?"

"Nope. I'm set."

I glanced at the clock and only had about an hour to run through everything I wanted to get done before lunch. I made my rounds, dropping off mail and picking up a few small business requests along the way.

Decker was waiting near my cubicle when I returned. He was leaning against the wall, and I had to admit that he really did know how to dress well. He finished an email on his phone and glanced up when I'd grabbed my purse.

"My treat," he said, ushering me toward the elevators.

"No way. You did that last time. I owe you."

We stepped into the elevator and the cart glided down to the lobby. Once the doors opened, I stepped into the large space that bustled with people as the noon hour became closer.

"I think I'll owe you one after this lunch."

I turned to face him and raised a brow. "What

does that mean? Did this place get really bad reviews or something?"

"No. I just. You'll see."

I stopped mid-stride and turned to face Decker.

"What are you not telling me that you obviously want to tell me?"

His eyes fell to the marble floor and then moved up to a large ficus tree near the security guards.

Decker still didn't speak, so I lightly punched him in the arm. Maybe this was a date. "I'll let you buy. Now let's get going before the place fills up. Lead the way."

I followed him down the hill and over two blocks before seeing a large outdoor eating area that was nestled in between two towering skyscrapers. It was filled with people drinking coffee and eating all sorts of food. I spied frozen yogurt, sandwiches, burritos, and burgers scattered on people's trays. How did I not know about this spot? It was lunch hour heaven.

"Is that the place we're headed?" I asked.

"It is. There are over ten restaurants and cafes lined up in that little atrium area so if the pizza place doesn't look so hot we can always grab something else."

Decker looked a little uneasy, and I realized this might be a lot more than I realized. I totally needed to give him a break.

As we wove through the patio tables and lines of hungry people, we made it to the corner pizzeria, Bella Pies.

"This the place?" I asked, standing next to him.

"It is." He reached into his pocket and dug around. "I don't have my wallet." He slapped his head. "I left it on the desk."

"No sweat. I'll pick up the tab."

"I can't let you do that. Just buy your own slice and I'll be right back." He wouldn't look me in the eye and took off before I even had a chance to relay how ridiculous that was.

"Next," the cashier called.

Realizing I was that person, I ordered a slice of garlic chicken and spinach pizza and paid. I stepped to the side of the counter and wondered what in the world had gotten into Decker. When my order was called, I grabbed the tray with the slice of pizza and cheese bread and found a place to sit. I felt awkward as couples and groups were taking up tables all around, and I hoped Decker would hurry up and reappear. Plus, I didn't want my pizza to get cold.

Snagging a sliver of spinach off the top, I slurped it up and delighted at the lack of manners I displayed when no one was looking. I had never actually been to this area of the city before and noticed the amount of techies that congregated rather than the suits, and then a rumbling laugh interrupted my people watching.

"Is this seat taken?" An all too familiar voice from behind wrapped around my body. The spike of excitement I felt was out of this world.

I turned around to see Aaron standing with a tray that held two slices of pizza and garlic bread. His smile was absolutely adorable and revealed a line of perfectly straight teeth. He was one of the suits, dressed impeccably in some designer I'd never guess, but Lily would be all over. The wind ruffled up the corner of his suit jacket as I sat staring, speechless. His brow arched up and his smile turned into a smirk.

"Well?"

"Sorry. I mean yes. It's taken. I'm here with a coworker."

"Decker?"

"How did you know who I was here with?" I responded, trying to keep my voice neutral.

He slid his tray onto the table, unbuttoned his jacket, and sat across from me with such quickness that I was stunned. His brows pulled together as he removed the napkins from under the plate, still not responding. The rays of sunlight that managed to sneak in between the buildings danced off his eyes, warming them up as he looked up at me.

"You're going to have to find another place to sit. Decker went back to grab his wallet and..." As the words left my lips, I rolled my eyes. Man, I was gullible. I glanced around the patio and back at Aaron.

"Decker worked on one of the teams in my division." He took a sip of water. "Before he transferred to yours. Good kid."

"Kid?" I rolled my eyes. "I'm sure he'd love to hear himself be referred to that way."

"He's got a lot to learn. His maturity level is—"

"About as great as Cole's," I interrupted.

Aaron's gaze caught mine and his mouth

parted only to shut quickly.

"You look completely out of place." I grabbed my fork.

"Doesn't bother me if it doesn't bother you."

I shrugged and took a bite of the pizza. It was delicious. Not as delicious as looking at him, but it would have to do as I stared at my plate, determined not to be swayed.

"You have my number. Why didn't you just call me?" I asked.

"Would you have answered?"

I couldn't help but smile at the obvious and felt my belly tighten as his eyes darkened with intent.

"Thanks for the flowers," I said, grinning. "But that wasn't very tactful considering..."

"I didn't send you any flowers," he said, bewildered.

"Oh. I just thought it was you," I said, completely mortified.

"The old send-flowers-to-yourself trick," Aaron laughed. "I think the person you're taunting is supposed to be in the office to see it or it doesn't quite have the same impact."

"Very funny." But the uneasiness began to creep up each vertebra as I thought about who might have sent the flowers.

"So why did you delete my email without opening it? That's a bit rude, don't you think?" His eyes pinned me against an imaginary wall, and it was all I could do not to slink away. "I won't go away that easily. And I don't think you want me to either." His gaze drilled into me as he watched my cheeks ignite.

"I saw the direction the email was heading and didn't want to waste my time. And don't be so certain."

"Direction the email was headed?" he questioned, ignoring my confession.

"Cole. There *is* no Cole. He's my brothers' friend and contrary to what he may have told you, I have never been nor would I ever be involved with him."

"I realize you have some internal code about not being with him because he's a friend of your brothers, and not entertaining the idea of us because I'm the brother of your best friend. But I think..."

"There is no code with Cole. I just don't like him. End of story." I dropped my slice of pizza and wiped my hands on the napkin.

"So you have no code when it comes to dating friends of your brothers, but you do have a code when it comes to me?" My eyes fell to his lips and my traitor of an imagination pictured his mouth tracing down my collarbone. I shook my head to squash the vision. His eyes were full of amusement when I looked back up, and I swore he knew what I was thinking. The tension between us was almost unbearable, and I caught myself shredding my napkin under the table.

"That's not what I meant. Of course, I wouldn't date my brothers' friends, but it also happens that I don't like Cole. He's lazy and he gives me the willies."

"The willies?" Aaron's laughter caught the

attention of some of the techies in line, and I couldn't help but smile. "So quite possibly, it sounds like I don't give you the willies, which is in turn why you enacted your code with me. You needed some forsaken reason to keep me away."

He was wearing me down. He knew it and I knew it. And I no longer cared as he watched me closely.

"There is no code. And I think we both know why I'm keeping you away."

"I don't think you should hide us from my sister," Aaron continued.

"There *is* no us." I fumbled with my napkin as my heart started pounding.

"Not yet. But there will be."

CHAPTER EIGHT

His frankness was disarming and so was his intent. There was no escaping from him this time, and I'd be lying to myself if I tried to run anyway. It no longer seemed as if we were in the middle of a lively city. It felt like it was only the two of us on the patio as his eyes bored into me, stilling everything around me but my hammering heart.

"All I'm asking for is one date. A proper date," he said, sliding his tray to the side. "And then make up your mind whether I'm worth investing any time into." The coy smile reappeared on his lips as he awaited my answer as if he knew I'd be unable to turn him down.

"What about the others?"

"Others?" he repeated. His brow quirked up slightly, as he sat back in the chair.

I nodded, watching the intensity of his

expression change behind his eyes.

"I'm asking for one date," he muttered, glancing at the lunch crowd. He looked uneasy and I wasn't sure if it was because I knew there were others or because I was pinning him down.

"And I'm asking whether that one date will just put me in the lineup?" I stared directly into his hardening gaze. "Because that's not what I'm looking for."

"What are you looking for?" his voice was low, and I watched the strain in his jaw as the muscles contracted.

"Something more if the fit is right, and I'm not sure you're capable. From what I've heard—"

"Heard?" His eyes stayed on mine. "From who?"

"That doesn't matter, but I've seen it for myself. The way you treated that poor woman."

His laughter was cold and distant. "At the bar?"

I nodded suddenly not feeling so sure of myself.

"I had just met her. I had no interest in her. Should I have led her on and made her feel like—" He removed his jacket and my eyes couldn't help but stumble over his chest. God, he looked sensational. "Like I make you feel?"

"Who said anything about me feeling any sort of way," I protested, shaking my head. "You, my friend, are sorely mistaken."

"Am I?"

I blushed immediately and clamped down on the garlic bread. This wasn't going how I planned.

"Now tell me, who did you hear what from?" he asked.

"Cole," I replied simply.

"You said yourself he wasn't a reliable source."

"And Google," I confessed, flushing immediately.

Yes, it was true. I had become one of those I had sworn I wouldn't and may have Googled him once or twice in the last few weeks. But I did find out some very interesting tidbits. For instance, it appeared he never made it to an event alone, including the one at the winery where I first met him, which added to my theory of only being added to a revolving lineup.

He was silent for a moment before his eyes flicked to mine.

"Have you seen any events where I was with someone since the night at the winery when I met you?"

Come to think of it, no.

I shook my head.

"Do you think that's a coincidence?" He leaned toward me and the shift between us was energizing.

"You expect me to believe you haven't been on a date with anyone since that night?" I arched a brow. The exhilaration that raced through my body at his proclamation almost tipped me over the edge. I wanted to believe it but found it almost impossible.

"It's the truth. I haven't been able to get you

out of my mind." He glanced at his watch. I was sure my lunch hour was up, but I didn't care. "And the brunette, Macy, who I'm sure you spied in the pictures with me that night, never happened. If that's what you're wondering."

God, yes! That was what I had been wondering; although I'd never admit it to him. The absolute pleasure that was pulsing through my veins was almost indescribable.

"Now will you give me one chance to prove myself?" he repeated.

I was silent.

"How about you just try responding to my emails or a phone call? You might find you like it."

I nodded slowly, smiling as I felt a rush of excitement. I knew I would like it and that was the problem.

"A friendship. That's all I can offer."

"That's a start." His eyes glimmered with victory. "I'll be in touch."

Wait. What?

"I've got a meeting I'm late for," he said, sensing my unease with the sudden brushoff.

My stomach knotted slightly as I worried that I truly was only a conquest. But I hoped not. I really hoped not. I watched him take off toward our building and wondered if I was making the mistake of a lifetime and jeopardizing a friendship in the meantime. I tossed the garlic bread and last bites of the pizza into the trash and made my way back to the office, worrying my way along the sidewalk, barely noticing that I was almost to my building.

As I rounded the bend, I saw Aaron and his sister talking in front of the entrance. Not wanting to be seen, I did a quick pivot and snuck back to where I came from. There was a side entrance to the garage that would suit me perfectly well. I gave a quick wave to the guard and beeped into the building, waiting for the elevator to deliver me to our floor.

The elevator opened up on the lobby and both Gabby and Aaron stepped inside.

Just my luck!

Completely puzzled as to who knew what or how much of anything, I just smiled and stepped deeper into the carriage to let them both fit in. Aaron gave me a quick nod and wink, which totally made my insides collide, but reality soon came knocking.

"Hard to believe Aaron works in our building," Gabby said, smiling, turning toward the closing doors.

Not hard to believe if you knew who he worked for I wanted to blurt.

Aaron took a step back and leaned against the rail.

"Sometimes things are meant to be," Aaron said, his eyes staying focused solely on me, sending a shot of pure electricity through me.

"That is true," Gabby said, completely oblivious.

The doors opened on our floor, and I quickly followed Gabby off the elevator. I felt his eyes still on me as I walked away, and he remained in the elevator. I needed a safe territory so I didn't stick my foot in my mouth.

"Did he say what he was doing in the building?" I asked.

"Guess the company he works for has headquarters on the twenty-sixth floor."

So he didn't mention that the company was owned by her father. Good to know.

"Are you guys doing better?" I asked.

"I think we'll get there. Part of me wants to gun him down with questions to find out why he left or where he went, but the other part of me doesn't really want the answers yet. I've made him such a monster for so many years, I'm hoping to make him human again before I find out anything that will disappoint me."

I nodded as I turned into my cubicle and Gabby took a seat at the opening. "That makes sense."

"Jason gave me a heads up about a dinner at my parents' house, and Aaron will be there. I was hoping you'd come for moral support. I talked to him about it quickly downstairs. I think it will be good. I hope it will be good."

Shit!

"Sure. You know I'll be there for you any way you need. Do you think you'll find out what's been going on?" I wiggled my mouse to wake up my computer, and my email popped up with a message from Aaron. I minimized it quickly and turned around to see Gabby staring at the floor. My heartbeat was racing and a rush of adrenaline flooded my system. I liked what this was doing to me, what Aaron was doing to me, and I really enjoyed the secrecy of it, which was peculiar.

"I do. But something tells me there's more to it than just my brother so I'm glad there will be other people there. Might diffuse my temper."

"You...a temper? I can't even imagine," I teased.

She rolled her eyes and leaned back in the chair.

"So who sent you flowers?" she asked, glancing at the arrangement. "It's like I'm distracted for a couple weeks, and your whole dating life blows up."

"I still have no dating life," I laughed. "But I don't know. They just showed up with no sender."

"That's weird."

Tell me about it.

"I'm guessing Shane?"

"I don't think he's gotten over you, and you're so nice to your exes that I don't think they ever quite get the message," she said, grinning.

"And the alternative is never speaking to them and changing my number?"

"Works for me," she laughed. "So I think Decker might be into you."

I spun around in my chair and laughed. "Really? What makes you think that?"

"I ran into him outside, and he seemed all flustered and completely unlike himself." She grinned and pointed at the flowers. "Maybe they're from him?"

He probably seemed flustered because your brother—his ex-boss—scared him to death.

"I doubt it. I think he just has a lot on his mind," I said. "I went around the office to see if there were any projects that I could help with, and everyone seemed set, so would you mind if I snuck in—"

Gabby held up her hand. "I told you not to ask. You know I don't care if you study when the workload falls."

"I just feel weird."

"You shouldn't. Just because you get your job done quicker than any other admin I've seen, doesn't mean you should get penalized and get more work dumped on you. Take advantage of it while you can. Now, I better get back to my office and see what fiery email my father sent about this week's lackluster results in the cheese department."

I couldn't help but giggle. I knew Gabby was doing all of this because it was what was expected of her to make her father happy, but she never really did care about the corporate world. I hoped that she'd find what would make her happy because spending twenty or thirty years trapped in a life that wasn't her own would wear anyone down. I knew I was lucky. My parents were supportive of anything any of us wanted to do. I just happened to be the oddball that enjoyed volunteering in my mom's not-for-profit legal center. I hoped to follow in her footsteps and make both my parents proud. But I had no doubt that being an attorney was what I wanted to do. Gabby used to have that passion and certainty when she was taking the culinary classes, and I hoped she'd find that again.

I clicked on my email and Aaron's message popped up. The thrill of hearing from him was now outweighing the doubt. I glanced at my flowers and then at the email.

To: Brandy Rhodes
From: Aaron Sullivan
Subject: Lunch

I hope it came to you who might have sent you the flowers. I only wish I beat whoever it was to the punch.

I'll be in touch and I do hope to see you at my parents' home tomorrow.

In Friendship,
Aaron Sullivan

My resolve was waning as the flurry of excitement took over. He was absolutely irresistible and he knew it. Now it was up to me to find out if there was anything more to him, to us, and I think I was finally up for the challenge.

At least as a friend…

Chapter NINE

To say I was confused was putting it mildly. I had finally wrapped my mind around going on a date with Aaron, and then the complexities of their family slammed into me like a semi-truck last night. I didn't want to make things more difficult for Gabby with everything she was dealing with, and I was pretty sure I was about to do so. Prior to the family dinner, I had an entire speech built up to present to Gabby about seeing her brother, but now it just seemed selfish and unimportant. Now was definitely not the time to whine about my secret crush.

I had gone to the dinner party at Gabby's parents last night, which was intense. Gabby found things out about her family that I knew she was still trying to absorb, and I felt absolutely helpless. But it also made me see Aaron in a different light. He was punished because of mistakes his mother had made, and rather than deal with everything, Gabby's father pushed Aaron away, essentially banishing him from the family. Finding out Gabby's dad wasn't Aaron's dad because their mother cheated on her husband was shocking and then to find out Aaron's father turned out to be the family's chauffeur was even more bizarre.

I could see why Aaron stayed away and made a life for himself elsewhere, and surprisingly Gabby understood that as well. I couldn't imagine what he had gone through just as I couldn't imagine what Gabby had gone through. It was times like these I was grateful for my overly nosey family.

Gabby was hurt by all of their actions, but I think what bothered her most were the secrets her entire family kept from her. After the family dinner, the anger and pain was evident when she spoke about her father. But that all changed this morning when she got a call that her dad was in the hospital.

It was early evening and I had just left the hospital a few hours ago. Gabby, Jason, and Aaron were all still with Gabby's father. There was a brief moment when Aaron and I were alone, and that's when it happened. I was completely caught off guard and agreed to meet him for dinner. Looking into his eyes, I knew I couldn't say no. He needed someone to talk to and Jason was obviously preoccupied with Gabby. I also couldn't tell Gabby. Now was definitely not the time. Besides, Aaron and I were clearly in the friend zone, and neither of us was in a state of mind for anything more.

And now here I was standing in front of my closet, throwing jeans, skirts, and dresses into a pile on the search for the perfect friend-zone outfit. The gnawing disappointment bubbled up again, and I hammered it back down as I reached for a cute floral sundress. One of the few non-clingy dresses I owned.

I changed out of my outfit and slipped the dress over my head, feeling the light fabric cascade over my skin. I stepped in front of the mirror to analyze my selection, holding my hair up and then letting it loose around my shoulders. The dress seemed harmless enough. It was cut above the knees, but it was loose and feminine.

Who was I kidding? I wanted to make him change his ways and follow me around like a puppy dog. Wishful thinking with his history, and I doubted his DNA was even built like that, but I could dream.

I noticed my boy shorts weren't the best choice for the dress as the outline in the mirror glared back at me. Laughing to myself as I rummaged through my drawer for my favorite thong, I wondered why it would really matter if we were going to stay in the friend zone and give him a bit of the granny panty to dream about. I went through my drawer and came up empty-handed, which was odd. I had zero laundry to do and they should be in there. I started searching through the drawer more thoroughly and realized that wasn't the only thing missing. I shut the drawer and opened the one underneath and there was nothing but my pajamas inside. Leaning over, I looked under my bed and in the closet. I sat on my bed, thinking, and was able to come up with at least three missing items. I walked over to my dresser and began looking through my pieces of jewelry and sure enough there was a sterling silver bracelet, a matching necklace and earrings all gone.

This was crazy. Maybe Gabby borrowed them and just didn't mention it. But she wouldn't borrow the lingerie. What would account for that? I got a sinking feeling as I thought about who all had access to our apartment. We did have cleaners come in bi-weekly, but there was no way that any of the crew would do that. It was a mother and daughter team, and the daughter was pushing fifty. I was positive that snatching lingerie wasn't either of their ideas of a good time but if not them than who? I laughed at the absurdity. I glanced at the clock and only had another ten minutes before Aaron was going to pick me up for our non-date. I could deal with this later. I was sure there would have to be some logical explanation, even if it was one I didn't want to face. Maybe Gabby was just messing with me since I've had the weird texts and messages.

My phone buzzed and I glanced down at the message.

Downstairs

Shoot! Aaron was already here, and I didn't have time to freshen up my makeup. I grabbed my purse and pulled out my mascara, dabbing it on quickly before I gave up and just headed out the front door, dismissing the case of the missing underwear.

As the elevator glided closer to the lobby, my pulse quickened. Exactly what a non-date shouldn't do to a person. I reached in my bag and grabbed a clear lip gloss, which I filled in my lips with. I could do this. It didn't have to be sexual with him. It didn't have to be romantic.

The elevator doors opened up revealing Aaron dressed in a pair of low-slung jeans and a silver button-down that hugged his visibly defined chest. The sleeves were rolled up, and I imagined my hands running along his muscular forearms. He had changed from what he was wearing at the hospital, and his hair looked slightly damp from a recent shower. He looked phenomenal, and worse, he was holding a beautiful arrangement of white roses.

"You didn't have to do this," I told him, taking the flowers as he quickly kissed each cheek.

"I thought I better start playing catch up to whoever sent you the others," he teased.

He took a step back, and his gaze traveled slowly along my body sending a trail of shivers in its wake.

"A friend doesn't have to worry about things like that, but I love them. Let me run upstairs and put these in water."

He smiled as his gaze met mine. "You look

beautiful."

His compliment melted me on the spot, but I didn't want to let it go to my head.

"Thanks. We do look pretty good for two friends just chatting over a casual meal. Wanna come up for a second?"

His smile deepened as I turned toward the elevator. "Absolutely."

The moment the doors closed, I felt the familiar electricity run between us and wondered if he felt it too.

"This is going to be harder than I thought," his voice low as he rocked back on his feet.

"Isn't it though?" I asked, afraid of the sensations pulsing through me.

"Yeah, it is." He took a step toward me, and I instinctively moved the roses to block him and started laughing.

The elevator doors opened, spilling us into the hallway.

"You know what I think?" I asked, unlocking the door. He came up behind me and I felt the familiar charge run through me.

"What's that?" he asked, his voice low as his hands slid along my hips.

"That you need to stay on this side of the door while I put these flowers in a vase."

He released his hands from my hips as laughter replaced the tension in the air. I quickly pushed through the front door and left him standing in the hallway.

CHAPTER TEN

I was completely at his mercy and had to get a grip. This crush was getting out of hand, and that's all it was. There was no future with him. He wasn't that type. My only hope was that when we sat through a dinner we'd bore each other out of our minds. But something told me that wasn't going to happen. I grabbed a vase out of the kitchen cabinet and filled it with water. I unwrapped the brown paper around the roses and snipped the ends off the stems and arranged them in the vase. Not wanting Gabby to run across them, I took the vase to my room and sat it on my nightstand. I took a step back and attempted to regain my composure, but knowing Aaron was waiting for me in the hallway was all it took to get my pulse going again. I needed to settle down. I needed just a few more minutes away from him.

"I got lonely out in the hall," Aaron said, jolting me right out of my wishful thinking as he lightly tapped on my door. I spun around to see him taking in my bedroom. He was grinning as he looked around, his eyes canvassing every section of the large space. My bedroom was quite roomy with a sitting area overlooking the city. The walls were taupe, the furniture white, and the decorative pillows turquoise. It was homey and far more sophisticated than any other bedroom I'd had up to this point. I could thank Gabby for that.

I followed his gaze to my bed, and pure delight shot through me as he glanced back at me, his eyes scorching.

"You don't take instruction very well," I huffed, turning him around and pushing him out of my room.

"Very true. Let's get going before they run out of tables."

I followed him back down the hall and kept to myself in the elevator, wondering if I was someone who actually enjoyed torturing myself. We stepped onto the sidewalk and the warm air touched my skin as we began our walk. Every time I felt his body move closer to mine, I stepped away, rerouting our direction slightly.

"Here we are," he said, ushering me toward a black door that was ornately carved. "They have patio seating on the side of the building. Thought it would be nice for a night like tonight. Being cooped up in the hospital all day was draining. I need some fresh air."

"I completely understand that."

He opened the door and I walked under his arm to a large seating area. All of the wood was dark teak and the long stretch of seating was covered in red velvet. The lighting was dim and the crowd of people in the bar was overflowing. I noticed quite a line of people waiting for a table in the restaurant as well.

"Mr. Sullivan," the hostess cooed. "It's so nice to see you again."

She glanced at me, her eyes sizing up his latest conquest, before turning her attention back to Aaron.

"Do you have a table for two on the patio, Tammy?" he asked.

"Of course," she replied, grabbing two menus. "Always for you."

I felt the distinct shift in the room as the large group of people who had been waiting for a table saw us get seated immediately. Feeling a little uncomfortable about it myself, I turned and grimaced an apology before quickly following Aaron and the hostess, weaving through the crowd of people.

Tammy showed us to our table, handing us our menus, and I caught a glimpse of folded money in Aaron's palm swiftly release into her palm.

"Thank you, Mr. Sullivan." She smiled and gave him a quick nod before turning around and leaving us alone.

"I see how it works now. I wonder if that would work at Applebees?" I smiled. "I'll have to try it."

Aaron started laughing and shook his head, but the moment his eyes connected with mine, I felt the tinge of excitement race through me. I needed to get my emotions back on track, keep the subjects neutral. Wait...That was neutral. God, I was in trouble around him.

"How's your dad doing?" I asked. "It's okay to still call him your dad, right?"

He laughed. "I do. He's the one who raised me. They think he'll get out tomorrow, and then he's got to take it easy for a few weeks."

"I'm so glad to hear it. Gabby felt so guilty."

"About what?"

"She thought she was too hard on your dad, and she's always paranoid about karma so..."

Aaron laughed. "Gabby was like that as a little girl too. If something went wrong in her life she would analyze everything that led up to it. I would've thought she'd grow out of it."

"It probably just got worse, especially after—" I stopped myself.

"The transplant," he finished, his voice catching slightly.

I nodded and glanced at the menu.

"I don't think I'll ever be able to forgive myself," he said, more to himself than me.

"We've all got our regrets," I said. "And I know she's just so happy to have you back in her life."

Our eyes met and I saw the relief flooding through his expression.

"Is she happy?" he asked.

"I think she's getting there. Jason has certainly

turned her on to a different set of possibilities. She'll kill me for telling you this, but she's really not all that into selling cheese."

His laughter was melodic as his eyes met mine. "Would you be?"

"Not really," I confessed. "But I'm thrilled to have the job. It will definitely cut down on my financial aid bill at the end."

"Have you thought about transferring to the legal department for—"

"There's no transferring within divisions for twelve months from the hire date," I stated robotically.

"There are always exceptions to the rules."

"Is that so?"

He nodded. "Think about it. You wouldn't be the first HR made an exception for."

"We'll see," I said, opening up the menu.

"The linguine with the mussels and oysters is phenomenal," Aaron suggested.

I shook my head. "No way. Not a seafood girl."

"And you live in Seattle?"

"I'm okay with some fish, just not things that look like they blend in with the rockeries."

"Have you ever even tried an oyster or a mussel?" he asked.

"No. I haven't had anything like that and plan on keeping it that way. It just looks like a rubbery mess of goo."

"You're how old and never had shellfish?" his brow arched.

"Food selection has nothing to do with maturity level."

"It very well may."

"It's not like I'm the only one in the world who isn't into seafood."

"How do you know if you haven't even tried it?" The smirk that appeared on his face was far too adorable for his own good, but it did nothing to convince me to try the slippery suckers.

I rolled my eyes.

"The smothered chicken sounds perfect."

"That's mature."

"What?"

"The eye-roll over shellfish."

"It wasn't over the shellfish. It was over how very persistent you are. You're quite controlling."

"And you're not? You're wrapped so tight, I'm worried one false move and you'll come undone."

"I just might." I stuck my tongue out quickly and rolled my eyes again.

And my heart nearly stopped when he did the same, revealing a tongue piercing. His smile grew as he waited for my response, and I saw a glint of silver reflect from his tongue once more. How had I not noticed before? A tongue piercing... a suit with a tongue piercing.

"Brandy, why are you blushing?" he teased.

I opened my mouth and then smacked my lips together, laughing.

He smiled, his eyes fastening on mine. "What's this I hear about you not liking motorcycles? Have you ever tried riding one?" he asked, changing the topic.

I shook my head quickly, trying to regain clarity. "I'd like to see my thirtieth birthday so I tend to avoid things that might make that impossible."

He whistled softly.

"What?" I asked.

"That must be a long list you've got going."

"It's not."

"I bet it is."

"It really isn't."

"So parachuting is out?" his eyes twinkled.

"Seriously? Come on. Who even acts like that's part of normal activity?"

He shrugged.

"Are you telling me you've jumped out of a plane?"

"Many times. And look, I've even lived to tell you about it."

"What did it feel like?"

"Incredible. The rush is something that's pretty hard to replicate."

"Is that why you did it? For the rush?"

"I did it because it was part of my job, but I loved it. The speed the body falls through the air..."

I shuddered just thinking about it.

"Too much?" he asked.

I laughed and nodded.

"So what's the craziest thing you've done?" he asked, leaning back in the chair.

Hmm. The craziest thing I've ever done? This was going to be a challenge.

"You got anything?" he asked, snapping my attention back to the question at hand.

"I've got one," I said.

"Spit it out."

"I went up in a hot air balloon for my eighteenth birthday." I sat back in my chair, completely satisfied with my answer.

"Not bad. Would you go again?"

He read right through me.

"Absolutely not."

"I think that's going to be my duty to you as your newest friend."

"What?"

"Make you live a little, face your fears..."

I groaned just as the server came to take our orders.

"And it's going to start with tonight's meal. We'd both like the Pasta allo Scoglio," Aaron said, handing our menus to the server.

After the server left, I looked at Aaron, who was completely amused with himself.

"I don't like being forced into doing things," I said, unfolding my napkin. "And I'm not afraid of shellfish so this shouldn't even count. I just don't like them." I wanted to be mad at him, but he looked so happy I couldn't be.

"I'm not forcing you. I'm only giving you a little push," he replied. "And you can't say you don't like them because you've never tried them."

"I don't have to try them to know I won't like them."

"If you could look at me and tell me without a shadow of a doubt that you hated shellfish, riding bikes, and rock climbing then I wouldn't push you into doing any of them. But by the sounds of it, you're making an uneducated guess, which doesn't sound very lawyer-like to me."

I scowled at him. "How'd you know I'm going into law school?"

"I've got my sources," he replied, his brow arched.

"Cole?" I asked.

"No. Not Cole. Not this time. So how'd you decide to go into law?" His question surprised me.

I glanced at the twinkle lights that outlined the patio and caught a glimpse of someone on the sidewalk staring in my direction. Our eyes met quickly before the shadow of a person darted into the night, leaving me with an uneasy feeling. I turned my attention back to Aaron who was waiting for my response.

"I grew up helping my mom in the non-profit law center she started and I loved it—everything about it. When I was in Junior High, I'd go in after school and help with filing and things like that. My friends thought I was nuts, and I probably was. As I got older, I helped to prepare the documents and quickly became infatuated with the stories that always came along with each case. I just knew I wanted to follow in her footsteps...help people who couldn't otherwise help themselves. Good legal representation shouldn't only be reserved for the wealthy, and I feel like so many people get penalized in the courts. I don't know; I'm probably rambling."

"No. I get it. I really do," his voice softened. "It's really refreshing to meet someone who knows what they want out of life."

I laughed and took a sip of my wine. "Career-wise, yes. Every other part of my life is still up for debate."

He laughed, but his eyes wore something else behind his expression.

"What about you? I know you work for your father, but I have no idea doing what or where you've been for the last ten years. Gabby mentioned that you and Jason met in the military?"

Aaron nodded and shifted uncomfortably as he debated what to tell me. I could tell his mind was running a mile a minute, and I hoped I'd be able to crack through at some point, someday.

"We did. We both were at a point in our lives where we needed to see the world, really experience it, and the military provided that." He let out a sigh. "And more."

The server placed our plates in front of us and asked if there was anything else we needed, which there wasn't.

"It was a wake-up call for me. I had a pretty easy life up to that point, and I don't think I really thought everything through when I joined..."

"Yeah?"

He nodded and his eyes darkened with his admission. "But it gave us both the start we needed," he continued. "One thing I knew for sure when I got out was that I didn't want to re-up. We had come up with an idea for civilian surveillance using an app, and it turned out to be something that was missing in the marketplace, so we got several lucrative offers. The last one being from my father. Jason wanted the cash and out of it completely. He was never really into the company past the idea. But I wanted to stay on and see the business through. I was able to negotiate that into the sale, and the rest is history."

"So what do you actually do now that it was brought into the fold of your father's company?"

"I oversee development and manufacturing."

I pulled my phone out of my purse and swiped the screen until I came to our home security app.

"Are you telling me that this is yours?" I asked, pushing it in front of him.

He nodded.

"Well, then that explains why Gabby's father was so quick to put it in our condo. It's pretty cool. Except that it doesn't work." I flashed a smile.

"What do you mean? Are you filing an official complaint?"

"No. I think it's user error. We screwed it up somehow a few weeks ago and haven't been able to connect since."

"I'll check it out sometime," he said, finally grabbing his fork and loading it with pasta.

"So you're more than just a pretty face?"

He cracked a smile and shook his head as he continued eating. I glanced down at my plate and tried to get up enough nerve. As I wound the linguine around my fork, avoiding most of the shellfish, I took a bite and was completely blown away by the flavor.

"This is delicious," I said.

"I told you I wouldn't lead you astray."

"Yet."

He flashed a grin but his eyes caught something behind me. My stomach knotted at the thought of him being incapable of having one meal without scouting the female selection surrounding us. Fighting the urge to look behind me, I took another swallow of wine and hoped it would help relieve the jealousy that so easily swept in. I had to get over this if we were only friends.

Aaron quickly glanced at me and then back behind me. Unable to hold it in any longer, I waved at him.

"I'm over here."

His lips broke into a smile. "Yes, you are, and you're very hard to miss."

"Then why don't you tell me what's so interesting behind me? Or should I ask who?" I raised a brow.

He grinned as his eyes relayed some sort of internal victory.

Damn him!

This friend thing wasn't going to work. I was an all or nothing kind of girl.

He leaned in close and whispered, "It's getting late. We should probably get you back home. We can't let this night turn into anything more."

And with those words my hidden hope of being more than friends with him were shattered. I nodded and followed him out the restaurant.

CHAPTER ELEVEN

Gabby and I piled out of the elevator into our hallway, groceries in hand for our delicious dinner tonight after a grueling workday. I was making chicken fajitas and couldn't wait. We both worked out at lunch in anticipation of tonight's meal, and I was just thrilled to have Gabby at home for the night. Since she started seeing Jason, she'd spent most nights there, which was fine since all I seemed to do was study. As we neared our door, I saw a little box on the floor.

"What's that?" Gabby asked.

I slid the key into the door and stepped over the tiny box, putting the grocery bags on the foyer table.

"I'll grab it," I told Gabby as she stepped over it, trying to balance her purse and groceries.

I picked up the box, which was wrapped in

gold foil and had a black ribbon crisscrossed on top.

"Looks like chocolates," I said, grinning. "I guess Jason misses you already."

Gabby turned around beaming as she held a bag of tortillas. "He's so sweet."

I handed her the box and she lifted up the tag.

"Um, Brandy. These aren't for me. It's addressed to you and there is no sender."

My blood turned ice-cold as I shoved the grocery bags onto the counter.

"Please tell me you're kidding."

"No. Why would I be?" she asked, unwrapping the foil.

"Don't eat them," I almost barked.

"Why?"

"I'm probably being paranoid, but some weird things have been happening."

"And now you're telling me?" Gabby rested her hand on her hip, clearly not pleased.

"You know those flowers I got?"

She nodded.

"I really don't know who they came from."

"I thought Shane, your ex, sent them?"

I shook my head. "And I've been getting really weird texts and phone calls. At first, I thought maybe it was someone playing a trick on me, but I'm not so sure anymore."

"Should we go to the police?" Gabby asked.

"And say what? Someone sent me flowers and left a box of chocolates. Can you help?"

Gabby laughed and shook her head. "Good point. But the messages and texts seem like something to report."

"The messages have been completely nonsensical and never actually addressed to me so it could just be a fluke. Maybe it's Shane messing with me."

Gabby's expression relaxed. "Maybe it is."

I searched for my cell in my purse and quickly texted Shane, but after I sent the message I knew it made no sense.

"Why would he go to all the trouble to either borrow people's phones I don't know or get disposables? That doesn't make any sense."

"Well, maybe it's two separate issues. Maybe he's trying to get your goat by sending the flowers and candy, and maybe the other is just nothing at all."

I liked that idea and was busily putting away the groceries, enjoying the release of tension, once I decided that's what had to be happening.

And then my phone rang.

"It's Shane," Gabby said, tossing it to me.

"Hey," I answered.

"Is everything okay?" Shane asked, his voice concerned.

"So I take it that you're not the one sending me the messages."

"I wouldn't do that to you," he said, his voice softening. "I know I was totally immature in college, but I wouldn't stoop to that. And I have changed, which if you'd meet me for coffee, you might find that out for yourself."

"I'll keep that in mind," I laughed but knew I couldn't lead him on. He had been a good boyfriend—attentive, loyal, sincere—but there was something missing between us. I never felt that spark that I'd heard about, longed for. It was more like a friendship with benefits. I never found myself daydreaming about Shane, not the way I had about Aaron.

"Seriously though. What's been going on?"

"I've been getting all kinds of random texts and calls. And someone sent flowers to my work and chocolates to my condo." Once I said it aloud to Shane, the uneasiness rushed through my body, squashing all of my attempts to explain it away.

"And you don't have any idea who it might be?" he asked.

"I was hoping it was you. Only not," I said. Our breakup wasn't horrible, but it was more one-sided.

"I actually don't even know where you work," Shane confessed. "So even if I wanted to, I couldn't."

Why didn't I think of that? That's right. I never told him where I got a job.

"Have you reported it?" Shane asked.

"I don't think there's anything to report. But if anything else weird happens, maybe I will. Well, thanks for calling me back."

"It was nice hearing from you. I miss you," Shane said, his voice hopeful.

"It was really nice of you to call me back," I repeated. "Maybe we'll grab coffee sometime."

"Sure," Shane said, his tone falling. "Talk to ya later."

And he hung up.

"Well, that was great. I just added salt to the wound there." I tossed my phone on a cookbook and let out a deep sigh.

"Maybe we should get the security cameras hooked up again," Gabby suggested.

"That's probably a good idea. Actually..." I hesitated and started slicing the chicken and caught Gabby looking at me suspiciously.

"Is there anything you want to tell me?" she asked, her brow raised.

"I think your brother mentioned something about being able to fix them."

She turned around, brow raised. "Really and when was this?"

"Just that day at the hospital," I said, which wasn't a complete lie. It did fall during that twenty-four hour period.

"That's a good idea."

"I thought so, and it would save us some money. Plus—"

"What?"

"Nothing."

"I know you're holding some stuff back so spit it out."

"I'm sorry. I think I've been preoccupied with studying. I'm kind of freaking about starting law school. I've been planning this forever and I just don't want to screw it up."

And I can't stop daydreaming about your brother who apparently got my message about being only friends and hasn't called or texted since.

"You'll do amazing. You always worry and stress and then by the end of whatever you set your mind to, you soar."

"Thanks. I hope so."

"How many of the incoming students do you think got a chance to volunteer all through high school and college at a law firm?" she asked, slicing the peppers.

"It wasn't a law firm. It was at my mom's non-profit law center."

"Same difference and you know what I mean. But, regardless, I think what you need is to completely let loose this weekend at your brothers. It sounds like it will be so much fun, and I can't wait to finally get to take part."

I laughed at the thought. Every year my brothers hosted a weekend long party at some property they owned. I would always invite Gabby, but in the summer she was always off on some luxurious vacation with her stepmom. This was the first summer that they didn't tour Europe or something because Gabby was working at the office.

"Don't get your hopes up," I teased. "We're talking about a cabin owned by two guys who love to party, and tents propped up all over the place by fellow partiers."

"It sounds like something we both need," she said, tearing up as she moved on to the onions.

"I'm so happy Lily gets to come too. I think she was starting to get really sad that she never got to see you when she drove up here."

"Which is why part of me is super sad that

Jason can't make it and the other is relieved. I wouldn't want Lily to think I completely ditched her for a man, again."

"If anyone would understand, I think it would be Lily." I dropped the chicken into the skillet and began adding seasoning and stirring quickly.

Gabby brought me over a glass of wine as I made dinner.

"Well, here's to a fun girls' weekend," she said, smiling and texting. "Aaron said he can come over next week to fix the system. Does that work for you?"

I nodded.

"I'm just gonna give him your cell number so he can text you the details."

"Great." Just what I needed. Now he had an excuse to text without Gabby getting suspicious.

Within in seconds the first text came over.

So whachya doing?

I texted back

Not much. Just got done texting an old boyfriend

I waited for a reply and realized Aaron obviously couldn't take a joke. My phone remained silent the rest of the night.

CHAPTER TWELVE

"How long have we been in the car?" Gabby whined. She was sitting in the backseat, handing out goldfish crackers and M&Ms to Lily who was sitting in the front. "It feels like forever."

The music was on a constant turn between Lorde, Imagine Dragons, and Capital Cities, and the air conditioning was blasting. We had officially made it to the other side of the state, which meant hotter temperatures and not much scenery beyond wheat and hay fields and the occasional gas station. Or at least that was the road we chose to take. I remember seeing prettier scenery when one of my brothers drove.

"You are worse than my four year old cousin," Lily laughed, unfolding her hand for more goldfish.

"We've been driving for a little over four hours, but that counts the multiple snack stops you needed," I said, looking at Gabby in the rearview mirror.

"Whatever. All you brought was trail mix and fruit leather. When have I ever been a granola kind of girl?" Gabby narrowed her eyes at me and threw a couple M&Ms at me, and they bounced off the center console before hitting the floor.

I shook my head and started laughing as the GPS instructed us to turn off the road we were on. Flipping the blinker on, I took a left and spotted another country store with a half-burned out sign for a café.

"We've only got ten more miles, but the road looks a little sketchy so who knows how long it will be," I replied.

"I thought you'd been here before?" Lily asked, scanning the playlist selection.

"I've been here a few times, but I was never driving." The road led us to more greenery and I instantly calmed. This was the scenery I remembered, not all the brown everywhere. I had obviously taken a different route than my brothers.

"I wonder if there will be any hot guys there," Lily mused, looking out the windows.

"You can only hope," Gabby chimed in.

"I'm not hoping. I'm praying," Lily laughed.

"Hey, aren't your brothers single?" Gabby teased, catching my look in the rearview.

I nodded and grinned at Lily. "Yep. Both ready for the taking, Lily."

Lily shot a devilish grin at me and then at

Gabby. "I never wanted to mention the obvious, but they are pretty fine."

I rolled my eyes and shook my head. "I'll be sure to pass on the message."

"You better not," Lily quipped, throwing a goldfish at me.

"You guys are both going to owe me a car detail after this trip. I swear you're worse than toddlers."

"It's not us," Gabby laughed. "You're the neat freak."

I spotted the glimmer of water in the distance between the pines that were sparsely scattered along the road.

"So I know we brought a tent, but are we really going to have to stay in the tent?" Lily asked.

"We don't have to, but the cabin is like a frat house. Ayden saved us a room to share, but I have a feeling you'll learn to appreciate the tent as soon as you see—"

"Is that it?" Gabby interrupted, pointing at the one cabin in sight situated next to the water. It was about the size of a pencil eraser from our distance. There were miniature-sized people already on the lake in Jet Skis, and my heart began to beat a little faster. I needed this break.

"That's it. Looks like the party has already started." I turned the car onto the road that would take us directly to the cabin and immediately felt close to home.

I had been stuck in such a rut of studying and working that it was nice to think about letting loose. And if anyone knew how to throw a weekend-long party, it was my brothers.

As the road snaked along the lake, the people on the lake came into better view as well as the makeshift campsites peppered along my brothers' property.

"This is going to be phenomenal," Lily exclaimed, turning in her seat to watch the jet skiers.

"I wish Jason could've come," Gabby groaned.

"Doesn't the idea of a girls' trip do it for ya?" I teased.

She stuck out her tongue and started rolling up the M&M bag.

"The nights are going to be cold and spooning with you guys isn't the same. Sorry." She pretended to pout and I grinned. It was awesome to see Gabby so happy.

Watching the jet skiers gave me the jitters and I shook my head. "Please promise me you guys aren't going to go out on the water on those."

"Please promise me you aren't going to stay on the shore," Gabby mimicked.

"Really?" I asked. "You want to do those?"

"Hell, yeah," Gabby said. "It's like a bike on water."

"Exactly my point," I replied.

"You've never been on one even with all the times you've been over here?" Lily asked, perplexed.

"Nope, and I don't plan on it. I don't have to feel like my life is on the line to have fun, you know."

Approaching the long, gravel driveway I hugged the left side so I didn't knock off anyone's side mirrors. This party looked bigger than any of the others they'd held over the years, and I was kind of nervous about it. I didn't want anything to go wrong as the weekend went on. I couldn't even guess how many people were here. The liability always worried me, which in turn, was why I was meant to be an attorney. At least, I could turn my worries into something useful.

I saw two orange cones with pink and silver balloons tied to them with a large sign written in a sharpie.

"Guess that's your parking spot?" Lily said, laughing. "I'll get out and grab the cones."

"Thanks." Leave it to my brothers to keep a watchful eye out for me. They always treated me like a princess but not in a bad way. I had come to expect certain things from men because my brothers always put me first, and I was grateful for it. My standards were set high because of them. But maybe that's why I was so leery of Aaron. Maybe it really had nothing to do with him being Gabby's brother, but what if he could never be that perfect person or offer me that imaginary life? Maybe no one could. I thought back to the chemistry with him. Everything felt so right.

I let out a sigh, which Gabby caught as soon as it slipped.

"What's up?"

"Nothing."

"Come on. Spill the beans."

"Honestly?"

Gabby nodded.

"I was just wondering if my brothers ruined me for ever finding the perfect guy. They have always treated me like—"

"Like you deserve to be treated," she finished for me. "Don't lower your standards. The right guy will appear and when he does, you'll know beyond a shadow of doubt that he's the one. He might not be perfect, but he'll be right for you."

What if that someone was your brother?

Lily took the orange cones and held them out in front of her chest as if they were attached to her, and I couldn't help but laugh. I doubted that she'd ever grow up.

"Nice," I hollered out my window.

"You like?" she laughed.

And that was why the guys flocked to her. A tall blonde began making his way over to her with a beer in hand, and Gabby busted out laughing.

"She never ceases to amaze me," I muttered, as I pulled the car forward and watched Lily joke with the newcomer. Putting the car in park, I watched Lily work her magic and wondered if I should start adopting Lily's carefree attitude.

"He's a cutie. Do you know him?" Gabby asked.

"Nope." I opened the door and stretched as Gabby followed my lead.

"Hey, knucklehead," Ayden called from the stoop.

Gabby started laughing and waved at my brother. "Some things never change."

"Tell me about it." I crinkled my nose and waved back at my brother.

Ayden walked down the stairs and glanced at Lily. "Be careful of that one," he shouted in her direction.

"Is he that bad?" she teased, smiling at the blonde.

"I wasn't talking about him," Ayden chimed back.

The guy next to Lily started laughing as she crossed her arms in front of her and flipped my brother an evil look.

"I've got the master saved for you three," Ayden said, spying the tent tied to the roof of the car. "Why'd you bring that?"

"Brandy said we probably wouldn't want to stay in the cabin. It was what... like a frat house?"

I nodded.

"Well, we've got new rules in place, so I'm sure it will be just fine. Let's at least haul everything up there and if you still want to tent it, then fine." He began untying the straps on the roof and released the tent. Gabby opened the trunk and grabbed her bag and Lily's.

"I'll get Lily's stuff."

"Hey, where'd she go?" I looked around the driveway, noticing Lily's absence. "That didn't take long."

"I'm sure she's just getting us some drinks," Gabby chuckled.

"When pigs fly," Ayden muttered.

"Hey, now," I warned. "She's my friend."

Ayden winked and grinned as he hauled the

tent bag and my duffle bag off the roof just as Mason walked along the side of the house.

"There you are," he called. "I saw Lily and knew you couldn't be far behind."

He came up and gave me a big hug and then switched to Gabby. "How are you two doing? Ready to party like it's—"

"Don't say it," Gabby said holding up her hand. "You'll make us feel older than we already are."

He laughed and grabbed the cooler out of the trunk. I'd brought some meat for the grill and some drinks. It was kind of a do-it-yourself setup, and I knew my brothers had already footed the bill for most of it.

"Off to see your room?" Mason asked.

"Sure."

Gabby and I followed my brothers through the cabin, and it was just as I remembered it. The exposed timbers on the inside of the cabin gave it a cozy vibe. The wood-burning fireplace in the corner of the great room had logs stacked neatly next to it. The two dark green couches had been pushed back to the walls to provide more seating with the foldout chairs. As we followed my brothers toward the back of the house where the staircase was, I started laughing as I saw what they had done. Two yellow caution tapes had been crisscrossed at the bottom of the stairs.

"We knew you didn't like all the commotion upstairs so we think we found a fix," Ayden said proudly, unpinning the caution tape so we could move through.

"This way we can keep an eye on you three as

well," Mason said, grinning.

"That was very sweet of you," I said laughing, climbing up the stairs.

There were two bathrooms upstairs. One was to the right of the stairs in between the two guest bedrooms, and the other one was connected to the master.

"See. There's no one sneaking around upstairs now," Mason said, completely enthralled with his bright idea.

I pushed open the master bedroom's door and was completely shocked. They had redone the room. There was a large pine four-poster bed that was jetting out from the corner of the room. A chaise was under the picture window that overlooked the lake, and my brothers had blown up a full-size air mattress that was tucked in front of the closet.

"Do you realize how much you two spoil me?" I asked, dropping my backpack down.

"We try, knucklehead," Ayden said.

"This is great. Forget the tent," Gabby said. "I'm staying in here. I don't care if someone's doing beer pong outside the door. This is where I'm staying."

"Agreed," I said, watching her plop both bags down next to the air mattress.

"It's so freaking hot on this side of the mountains," she said, looking toward the bathroom. "I think I'm gonna shower and suit up."

"Awesome. I'll do the same, but first I'm gonna get the scoop from my brothers," I told her as we three exited the room.

Gabby closed the door and my brothers, and I walked back down the stairs.

"Okay, guys. I've kind of got a surprise planned for Gabby."

"Yeah?" Ayden said, his brows raising.

We reached the bottom of the stairs, and I followed my brothers to the kitchen. It was a bright and cheery space, and every surface was covered with either chip bags, cracker boxes, or cookie tins. We would not be going hungry this weekend.

"So you know the bike builder she's been seeing?"

My brothers nodded.

"Well, I invited him over here for the weekend. He had some delivery today, but was planning on getting here tonight. I gave him both of your numbers in case he needed directions."

"I thought it was a girls' weekend for you three," Mason said, grabbing a bag of potato chips.

"It is, kind of. But she's so happy with him, and I thought it would be an awesome little getaway for them. And that's why I brought the tent."

"What was his name again?" Mason asked.

"Jason. He's so sweet. I think you guys will really like him."

Ayden and Mason both shook their heads. "We've heard that before," they said in unison.

"Well, whatever. Just keep it a surprise and if you get a call from him, let me know. I was also kind of hoping with a pretty please and a cherry on top, that you'd maybe sneak up there and grab the tent bag and put it up somewhere for them."

"Anything for you," Mason said, pecking the top of my head with a brotherly kiss right before he shoved me away. "Now go suit up and start to have some fun you worrywart, and no, we didn't make any of our guests sign waivers."

"Hardy-har-har." I grinned and ran up the stairs.

This weekend was exactly what I needed.

CHAPTER THIRTEEN

The afternoon had turned to early evening, and the temperature was beginning to shift. I was lying on a towel by the lake, reading one of my favorite authors as Lily and Gabby took turns riding one of the Jet Skis. We had gorged on hot dogs and potato salad for lunch, but my stomach was already responding to the smells from the grills lighting up around the property. It had been a wonderful afternoon, and my skin was already turning a nice shade in the ninety-degree weather. Lily had ditched the blond but was still keeping her eye out as she showed off on the watercraft. I wasn't sure when Jason was going to be able to get across the mountains, but my guess was early evening. I hoped it was before it got dark so he could find it easier, but there wasn't anything I could do about it. Even on a mini-vacation I managed to worry. How annoying.

"Hey, girl. I'm freezing," Lily said. Unfastening her life vest, she tossed it on the grass next to me. "I think it's time for me to get in my sweats."

"Me too," Gabby seconded, towel drying her hair.

"Sounds good to me." I snapped my book closed and sprung up.

We grabbed our towels and headed for the cabin. I saw Ayden's ex-girlfriend and waved. She gave a friendly wave back, and I noticed there was a guy standing next to her, his hand on her shoulder. I was always amazed with how my brothers handled break-ups. Granted, I wasn't as extreme as Gabby where she'd switch her phone number and call out the national guard, but I don't know that I'd ever be inviting them to parties I hosted.

Opening the front door, I saw the fire roaring and knew it was going to be a wonderful, cozy night. Even though the days were warm over here, the nights cooled off tremendously. My brothers had already stopped by while we were at the lake to let us know about the three different bonfires that they were setting up along the waterfront. Mason also managed to whisper to me where they had set the tent up for Jason and Gabby, which was so sweet.

Before running upstairs, we stopped in the kitchen and each of us filled a bowl with tortilla chips, and I grabbed the guacamole.

Gabby grabbed the entire bag of chips. "Just in case we need more."

We ducked under the caution tape and jogged up the stairs, excited to change into something warmer. I grabbed a pair of pink sweats that I could roll up and a white hoodie. I didn't bother putting on a shirt and just zipped up the hoodie. My bikini top would be fine. Lily slid a pair of jeans on and an oversized sweatshirt. Gabby grabbed a pair of black, baggy sweats and a grey sweatshirt. She pulled out a face wipe from her bag and began wiping off all of the sunblock and makeup from her skin.

"There. Now I feel all ready to snuggle in for the night next to the bonfire. Which one should we hit up?"

"Whichever one doesn't have Dustin hanging around."

"Dustin?" I asked, confused pulling on my sweatpants.

"Yeah. Dustin," Lily replied, exasperated.

"Oh, the blonde," Gabby chuckled.

"I say we do the fire closest to the house." I eyed Lily and she nodded, once she realized I wanted Jason's entrance to be caught by Gabby.

I scooted back on the bed and grabbed my bowl of chips as Gabby and Lily piled on top. Tossing them each a throw blanket we settled in and munched on our chips quietly for a few minutes.

"So how's everything going with your brother?" Lily asked, scooping a huge pile of the guacamole on her chip.

Gabby crossed her legs underneath her and let out a deep breath. "Surprisingly good. I kind of figured I had two ways to go about it. Keep him out of my life forever and hold a grudge or just accept the past as the past and move on. I mean, truthfully, I couldn't hold a grudge against my brother and not hold one toward my dad. And then what? Have no family? My dad was equally to blame, if not more so. I'd have no family left if I didn't just accept it. Aaron's not a bad guy. In fact, from what I've seen and learned about him, he's done some pretty incredible things."

Lily glanced at me quickly and I dropped my gaze.

"It sounds like you've really done some thinking about it," Lily said. "I'm proud of you. It's like we just might be becoming adults after all."

"Well, some of us," I interjected, repositioning my pillows.

Lily tossed a pillow at me, and it narrowly avoided the guacamole bowl.

"I think it's really amazing how mature you're being about it. I was just thinking about your family the other day, and I thought about how angry I would have been at my brothers if they just took off without a trace for ten years," I said.

Gabby bit her lip and nodded slowly. "What really hit home for me was the fact that, sure I didn't have my brother for ten years, but I *did* have my family. He had no one. Imagine holidays and birthdays passing year after year with no family around to celebrate. I at least felt loved. My father basically banished him. I couldn't even imagine."

The moment the words escaped Gabby's lips, a knot formed in my stomach. The thought of Aaron without anyone, family or loved ones, made my heart hurt just thinking about it. And it also explained his inclination to stay that way, alone.

"I mean I know it had to have screwed with him. Look at his dating life. He obviously doesn't trust women so he just keeps them at a distance."

"Has Jason ever mentioned anything?" I asked, tracing the pattern of the comforter. It was the one tip-off this house was owned by guys. The sheets and comforter cover were a Christmas pattern full of snowmen and miniature Santas in the middle of summer.

"A little bit. He tries not to put himself in between anything, but he's mentioned a few things that had happened over the years, and it tore me up. When they were in the military together they formed a bond really quickly and became one another's family. He did tell me that he doesn't think Aaron has ever been in love before. Can you imagine?"

My heart started pounding and I felt Lily's gaze on me.

"No. I can't imagine," I managed to say.

"Everyone deserves love," Gabby continued on. "I hope he finds it sooner than later rather than continue on with those meaningless relationships. Actually, I don't think they'd even qualify as relationships. I googled him, and I don't think I've ever seen him with the same person twice."

Exactly what I found. My cheeks began to burn, and I prayed the fresh tan would disguise my embarrassment at thinking that I had a shot at changing him.

"If only he could settle down with a nice girl like Lily," Gabby teased. "That would certainly give him a run for his money."

"I doubt you'd be fine with any of your friends dating him," Lily scoffed.

"I wouldn't care. If that made him happy or whoever... Who am I to say who people can or can't date?"

My pulse quickened with this confession, and I suddenly wanted to blurt out that I had been Google-stalking her brother, but I kept quiet. Voicing that she doesn't care who her brother dates was far different than actually witnessing it with her best friend.

"What sucks is that I think he can't trust women because of our mom. Like he wants to punish women or beat them to the cheating thing."

"That would make sense," I agreed.

"Although, I don't think he actually cheats on anyone because he doesn't date anyone long enough for it to qualify as a relationship."

"Does anyone want any more guacamole?" Lily asked, sliding off the bed.

If she thought that now was the time I was going to confess my love for Gabby's brother, she was quite mistaken.

"I don't need any," I said, raising a brow.

I knew her tricks.

"Yeah, I'm fine too. I'd like to fit in my bikini tomorrow," Gabby laughed.

Lily reluctantly climbed back on the bed and sat quietly. I glanced out the window and saw flames beginning to roll as the bonfires were started. I hoped Jason would get here soon.

"It's funny where people find love," Lily said, jolting me out of my daydreams. Her tone had softened, and this was a side of Lily that didn't come out much.

"That's so true," Gabby said, pulling the blanket around her a little tighter. "I never thought a guy who we crashed into would turn out to be..." her voice trailed off and she blushed.

"The love of your life?" I finished.

She nodded.

"The way Jason looks at you is beyond lust. It's pure love. He adores you," Lily said.

"You think?" Gabby asked.

"Totally."

"Have you ever been in love?" I asked Lily. We'd all been best friends for years, but there were a couple unwritten rules, and one of them included not getting too deep on the subject of love with Lily.

Lily looked down at the comforter, and the words that fell ever-so-quietly from her lips took both Gabby and me by surprise.

"Yes. I've been in love. Once." Lily looked up, and I swore I saw tears in her eyes. Gabby reached over and grabbed her hand.

"At the time I thought I was too young, and it

was impossible to love or be in love like I was. But I was wrong. I know that now, but it's too late." She glanced out the window and back to us.

"It was in high school, and in senior year he asked me to marry him. It wasn't official. There wasn't a ring, but the look in his eyes told me he was serious. He meant it."

"What happened?" I asked, completely surprised Lily was finally allowing us into this part of her life.

"I accepted. And the last few weeks of school before graduation were amazing. It was like right out of a storybook. But my parents began interfering, telling me that I was too young. That there's more fish in the sea...blah-blah," she laughed bitterly. "He was so attentive. Completely wise beyond his years. I knew my parents were wrong. We lived in a small town and everyone's business was every one's fuel. I remember going to get my haircut a few weeks after graduation, and that's when I heard the first of many rumors."

"What do you mean?" I asked.

"That he had gotten some other girl pregnant. That he had planned on proposing to her to fix it and make it right. All sorts of things. The funny thing was that we had spent every waking and non-waking moment together so my logical side should have weeded the gossip out as gossip. But I didn't. I fell right into the trap and believed everything. I was stupid. I was young. I boxed all my belongings up and shipped them off to college early and made my way soon after where

I met you lovely ladies."

"Did you ever talk to him?" Gabby asked.

"I called him and told him everything I heard and then before he even had a chance to say something, I hung up on him. Of course, both of my parents were delighted and helped move me right along. I was just a heartbroken barely eighteen-year old. That is the biggest regret of my life. So when I say that I know what love looks like, I mean it." Instead of looking at Gabby she looked directly at me. "It's not something to dismiss, no matter what complications might come with it."

I nodded and smiled, privately thanking Lily for sharing something so personal with us.

"Did you ever find out the truth?" Gabby asked.

Lily shrugged. "I think I always knew the truth. I just took the easy way out, pleased my parents, and left the love of my life—potentially. I mean who knows what really would've happened."

"You do," I whispered.

Lily nodded in agreement.

The room was full of quiet tension. All of us slowly letting go of our secrets. Gabby telling Jason about her heart transplant, Lily admitting to herself why she bounces from guy to guy, and me wanting to confess that I might be falling for Gabby's brother. But this was why we were friends. We never held anything against one another and when the time was right, we'd confess our sins.

"Ready to drink our hearts out?" Lily interrupted the silence. "I'm not big on confessionals and think I need to wipe it away."

I threw the comforter off my legs and shot Lily a sympathetic grin. "Absolutely."

I snagged one of the throw blankets to take outside with us in case the fire didn't do its job, and we all trundled downstairs. And to think we managed to get to the heavy subjects before the drinking even started.

As we reached the porch and closed the door behind us, I heard a faint rumble in the distance and grinned at Lily. It had to be Jason. We walked down the steps, toward the closest bonfire. We could see the long drive from our vantage point, and the adrenaline pumped quickly through my veins. I loved surprises as long as I was throwing them for someone else.

"Do you hear that?" Gabby asked, as we wandered toward the flames. There was already a group gathered, passing around sticks, marshmallows, chocolate and graham crackers as we made our way to the fire pit. "That sounds like a mean machine."

"That it does. A mean, dangerous machine," I added, standing next to the fire but trying to get out of the smoke drift.

Gabby started laughing. "Actually, it sounds like more than one."

"Seriously?" I asked, straining my ears. Maybe, it wasn't Jason.

The laughing and hollering around the flames got louder just as the roar of the bikes' engines began to hit the driveway. She was right. It wasn't the roar of one engine I was hearing. It was two. Gabby grabbed a marshmallow out of the bag and passed on the graham crackers as she poked the marshmallow onto the end of the stick.

"Hope whoever it is, lets me take a peek at their bike."

"Isn't it enough that you already own one," I sighed, just as I saw the first bike come into view. It was definitely Jason. He was dressed in black leathers and a matching black helmet. Another bike followed right behind him down the drive.

Gabby glanced up and gasped. She turned around to look at me and hopped up and down. "You got him to come? Seriously?"

"Seriously."

Gabby dropped her marshmallow on the ground and ran toward Jason, who was leading the other biker down the drive.

I watched as the second biker pulled right next to Jason's bike. It was obviously a man driving it. His broad shoulders filled out the leather jacket. He was dressed in black leathers too, but his helmet was matte black. His sunglasses looked familiar, and then suddenly my heart started pounding.

I turned to stare at Lily but no words would come out.

"Aaron?" she asked, reading my mind.

I nodded. "Think so."

"Well, surprise, surprise."

Chapter Fourteen

I watched the mystery biker pitch his leg off the bike and begin to unzip his jacket. Lily gently nudged me toward the driveway where Gabby was already wrapping her arms around Jason's neck, and he was swinging her around.

"I can't go over there," I hissed.

"It would be weird if you didn't," Lily said. "Trust me. I'll come with you."

I heard murmurs behind me as some of the guys in the crowd admired the bikes from a distance. Jason whispered something into Gabby's ear, and she giggled and waved at me.

As Lily and I walked over, I glanced at the biker who had now completely taken off his leathers, and my heart was pounding. It had to be Aaron, especially since he was leaving the helmet on for drama.

Typical. I tried to force the smile off my lips as

my eyes ran over his tight fitting shirt and low slung jeans.

Once in earshot, I hollered to Gabby, "See why I brought the tent?"

She laughed and wouldn't stop hugging Jason even as he attempted to secure his helmet to the handlebars. They had parked directly behind my car. Once we arrived, I leaned against the trunk and crossed my arms.

"So who is the guy who doesn't want to remove his helmet?" I asked Jason.

Jason gave me a large grin, and I saw a twinkle behind his eyes that told me he knew something about Aaron and me. Not that there was much to know. But maybe Aaron had at least mentioned me and that I would take as a positive sign.

"That's my brother," Gabby laughed. "He thinks he's too cool to show his face right away."

Aaron reached for his helmet and loosened it before tugging it off his head.

"Hope you don't mind that I invited him along," Jason said, smiling a wicked smile.

"Not at all. I'm sure there's a tree we can plop him under or something. We've got extra sleeping bags."

I glanced at Aaron and was thankful I was already leaning against the car. The spark in his eyes as I mentioned sleeping bags about undid me. His hair was completely disheveled from the helmet, and his smirk was directed solely toward me. Thankfully, Gabby was all swept up in Jason, and Lily just enjoyed the show, doing her best not to laugh at the scene unfolding.

The longer Aaron stood there, the more I became less aware of everyone else standing around. The day had almost completely traded for night, and the remaining shadows traced along his cheekbones and jawline, which made him appear even more sensational than normal. This wasn't part of my weekend plan.

"I bet you guys are starving," Gabby said, as Jason slid his hand into hers. "We've got hot dogs we can go burn on the fire over there."

Lily already wandered off toward the bonfire, which if I was to make an educated guess meant someone caught her eye.

"Sounds perfect," Jason said, kissing her cheek tenderly.

I felt Aaron's gaze on me as I watched Gabby and Jason interact. Embarrassed, l looked away and started toward the house.

"Why don't you show Aaron around," Jason stopped me. "And Gabby can show me the grounds."

"Sure," I said, realizing Gabby had absolutely no clue, which put me at ease.

"That'd be nice," Aaron said, walking up behind me. Feeling the familiar tingle between us made my stomach twist as I remembered what I was missing.

He gently placed his hand on my waist, sending a jolt up my spine. I turned to look at him, a complete mistake. His eyes connected with mine, and yearning spilled between us as the space diminished.

"It's nice to see you," I said softly, my voice

catching.

"Is it?" he asked. "I wasn't sure it would be."

"Just testing out the waters?" I teased.

We climbed up the steps, and I turned around to face him. Seeing Gabby and Jason off in the distance laughing and teasing one another, made me realize I needed to stop the complexities between Aaron and myself.

"It is. And I'm sorry I've sent such crazy signals. I didn't want to hurt the one person who'd always been there for me."

He nodded, placing his hand on my shoulder.

"I know. And I should've respected that. But I couldn't." He lightly caressed my cheek and grinned. "You haven't been easy to forget."

"You haven't either," I said quietly. "And I tried."

"I bet," he laughed a deep-throaty laugh, and dropped his hand.

I could sense that he was trying really hard to be reserved and respect the time and space between us, but I wasn't sure that's what I wanted any longer.

I turned back to the front door and swung it open. Ayden was sitting near one of the card tables they had unfolded for some friendly rounds of nightly poker.

"Hey, knucklehead," Ayden said, standing up quickly.

My cheeks reddened, and I wanted to run a fist into the side of my brother. It felt like high school all over again.

Before I even had a chance to take a step

forward, Ayden was in front of us extending a hand toward Aaron.

"I'm Brandy's brother and you must be?" Ayden was one of the few people who could match Aaron in size and demeanor.

"Aaron. Aaron Sullivan. I came with Jason. I think Cole's floating around here too?" He nodded and gave a firm shake to Ayden.

"Oh, the famous Aaron. Gabby's brother, Aaron?" Ayden raised a brow and glanced at me, smirking.

"Famous or infamous?" Aaron joked.

"Good catch," Ayden said. "Yeah, I think Cole's coming up tomorrow."

"Ugh," I groaned. "I was hoping he wasn't going to show up."

"Nasty breakup?" Aaron teased.

"Would you please inform our visitor that I never dated Cole, regardless of what Cole's been telling people?" I crossed my arms in front of me and waited for Ayden to say something.

"It's true. He's tried hard to get her over the years, but I think she'd rather join a convent. And I don't blame her. He's a bit rough around the edges."

"Anyway, I wanted to show Aaron around so that he can use the inside bathrooms rather than the outhouses."

"Wow. First class treatment," Aaron joked.

"Only if you're nice to me." I smiled.

"You must be higher on her list than I thought," Ayden said. "This is the first year we took measures to stop people from disturbing the princess. She likes order and our parties aren't generally very orderly."

I scowled at my brother. "I'm not that bad."

"Yeah. You are," Ayden said, as he walked by us to go outside. "If you're into poker, the game starts at midnight."

"Thanks, man," Aaron said.

Ayden closed the door softly and the house was left quiet. I wondered if anyone else was inside.

"So this is the main room. There's a bathroom over here," I said, motioning for him to follow me. We walked down the hallway toward the kitchen.

"It's only a powder room so if you want a shower, you'll need to go upstairs. This is the kitchen. Would you like a beer or anything?" I was talking nonstop as my nerves ramped up.

Aaron took a step closer and wrapped his arms around my waist, sending a frisson of delight up my spine.

"Don't be nervous," his voice was low as his eyes locked on mine. "There's nothing to be afraid of."

"I'm not afraid. I'm..." my voice trailed off.

"You're what?" he asked, his voice gentle.

"Okay. I'm terrified."

"Don't be." His arms dropped from my waist, and his familiar smirk surfaced as he took a step back. I couldn't help but laugh as I shook my head.

"So about that beer?" I asked, opening the fridge. "There's Redhook ESB, Pyramid

Hefeweizen, and Elysians Dragonstooth. Or we could wander off to one of the kegs floating around..."

"The ESB's fine," he said laughing.

"That's what I'll have too." I pulled two bottles out and sprung the caps off.

Taking a swig, I hoped the liquid would calm me down, but I was certain it would take more than one bottle. My emotions were running wild having Aaron here.

"So what's up with the caution tape over there on the stairs? Is this place safe to be in?" he laughed.

"That's what my brother was talking about. They put up caution tape to stop people from going up there. I'll show you around. Not to worry."

Aaron walked with me toward the staircase, and I ducked under the tape. He unpinned the tape and reattached it rather than use my technique.

"This is a really great piece of property," Aaron said.

"Yeah. It's pretty cool. My brothers started saving for a cabin right out of high school. They bought it together, and it's been a party pad ever since. Although, I think my mom's hoping that someday it will become a nice place for their families to come up to. However, that would involve them settling down, and I don't see that happening anytime soon."

We reached the top of the stairs, and I pointed to the main washroom and to the linen closet.

"That's where you can shower."

"Thanks." I could tell he wasn't really paying attention to the grand tour. Instead his gaze fell to mine and a faint smile traced his lips.

"My brothers set up a tent for Gabby and Jason. Since I didn't know you were coming I—"

"I brought a small tent. It's on the bike," he interrupted. "I'm set. I don't want to be an imposition."

"I doubt you'd ever be an imposition," I said, walking toward the master bedroom to finish the tour.

He followed me, his stride matching mine as the proximity between our bodies closed quickly. I stopped in front of the door and turned to face Aaron. He was only inches away, and the reaction he caused inside of me was explosive. Every nerve in my body was buzzing with electricity as my eyes fell to his lips. His hands quickly clasped my face, tracing his thumbs along my mouth. My breath hitched as he ran his fingers through my hair. Bringing my head back, he lowered his mouth to my neck, gently guiding his lips down my skin. His breathing changed as he brought his lips up to mine, pressing the weight of his body against me. I felt the need growing inside of him as our hearts pounded together.

I wrapped my arms around his neck, feeling the softness of his kisses turn more determined as the craving between us grew. Slowly, he moved his hands down my spine as his mouth dove deeper into mine. My body stiffened with the realization that I couldn't stop the feelings pulsing through me. Whatever this was between us was unstoppable. My mind and body was completely at his mercy as I reached under his shirt. My hands skated across his firm chest, and I allowed the warmth of his skin to direct me as my body desired so much more than this one kiss.

His lips broke free of mine as he bumped us up against the door, his mouth falling along my jawbone, bringing his mouth close to my ear. A parade of chills ran over my skin as his breath danced lightly off my flesh. He parted his lips, gradually bringing his mouth to my ear, his teeth softly catching my lobe, sending a wave of pleasure all the way though to my bones. I gasped as his lips continued down my neck, his tongue sliding over my skin, going dangerously low.

"You smell so good," he whispered, resting his fingers on the zipper of my hoodie.

"You feel so good," I whispered, allowing the strength of his body to hold me up.

He began softly kissing me once more when I heard Lily's voice shout my name from the hall. She was upstairs. No!

My body went rigid and my mind emptied. What was I doing? Aaron smiled and took a step back, dropping his arms to his side.

"Later?" his voice low.

I nodded unable to speak from the flood of emotions crashing down on me.

CHAPTER FIFTEEN

The intense morning sunlight sprayed onto my skin, warming it only slightly as the chill of the outdoors awoke me. My head was pounding, and I quickly scanned my surroundings. I gasped feeling the slick material of a sleeping bag wrapped around me, along with another pair of legs. I shot up and out of the sleeping bag, trying to regain some sense of reality. The sunlight filtered in through the canvas of the tent, and my heart began pounding to match my head as I looked to my right and saw Aaron sleeping next to me. The light danced off his bronzed, bare skin as I slowly brought my hand up to my mouth. What had I done?

His eyes slowly opened, and a slight curl of lips appeared as he watched my reaction. I grabbed my portion of the sleeping bag and tugged it to my chest when I realized I was without my hoodie and sweatpants. At least I had my bikini on.

"Hey, gorgeous," he said, his eyes combing over my bare shoulders.

"Are we...did we?" I asked, completely mortified that I couldn't remember anything from the night before.

"Believe me when I tell you that if we did...you'd remember."

I rolled my eyes and laughed, completely relieved. "Sure about that, huh?"

His eyes flashed a mix of mischief and wonderment as his grin grew wider.

"Absolutely," his voice was low and sent a burst of shivers through me.

I ran my hand through my hair, combing the strands as best as possible. My hair was a tangled mess and my headache wasn't letting up.

"So how did we wind up in your one-person tent?" I asked.

"You really don't remember?"

I shook my head.

"You really were in bad shape."

"I think we can make that present tense," I confessed.

And then the memory of his kiss crashed into my mind, his hands skating up my body as his mouth traced along my flesh, but I could remember nothing beyond being upstairs with him. So how did I get here and where did my evening go?

"We kissed," I whispered.

"We did." Aaron sat up slowly, trying not to

knock the condensation off the tent.

I rubbed my temples and sighed.

"Are you okay?" he asked, his voice tender. "I think the kiss was what sent you over the edge, actually."

"Of course you do. But yeah, I'm fine...just utterly confused. Should we tell Gabby?"

"What's there to tell? We kissed and then you made it absolutely clear that we can't be anything but friends." His eyes watched mine for a reaction. "And you were even on the fence about that."

"I did?" I cringed.

He nodded.

I bit my lip, trying to grab hold of the memories from the night before. Only none came.

"I should probably get showered, and I desperately need to brush my teeth," I relayed, suddenly self-conscious.

He reached over and tugged on the tent zipper, opening the flap.

"I expect to hold you to your promise," he said, as I attempted to crawl out of our shared sleeping bag.

"And what was that?" I asked, turning to face him.

He looked absolutely amazing in the morning, a grizzled shadow appearing along his jawline and his dark hair a mess.

"You promised you would go on a Jet Ski with me."

"No way. Absolutely not. Anything I said

wasn't binding. I was drunk."

He started laughing a deep, masculine laugh and began zipping the tent back up as he muttered something I couldn't hear.

I looked around the property and saw people beginning to emerge, rubbing sleep from their eyes and massaging their heads reminding me that I was in good company. After all, that's what this trip was all about, letting loose and forgetting the stresses from home.

I walked toward the house and saw the front door swing open, with Mason peering out the hole.

"Hey, sleepyhead. Looks like you got a nice rest," he said, laughing. "Ready to hop on that Jet Ski?"

"How do you know about that?" I narrowed my eyes at him, climbing the stairs.

"Are you serious? You don't remember?"

I let out a sigh and shook my head. "No. Afraid not. But I don't care what I said or did last night, I'm not hopping on one of those machines."

"Aaron and Lily guessed you'd say that so they had me take this." He reached into his back pocket and whipped out his phone. "Here's the video."

He tapped the screen with his finger and turned up the volume and sure enough, there I was standing in front of the fire with a beer in each hand, giving a speech about facing my fears and flying fancy over the water. Aaron was in the background, telling me not to promise anything I'd regret and the next thing I saw, I was hopping on him giving him explicit instructions to drive me around on the piece of equipment, telling him it was part of the buddy pact. I couldn't see Lily in the footage, but I heard her laugh echoing throughout the video. My parting words were that if I didn't get on a Jet Ski on Saturday, I would be leading a skinny-dipping expedition Saturday night. The crowd was cheering right before the video went blank.

I looked up at Mason, completely horrified. "That couldn't have just been the beers."

He nodded. "You drank out of the Keg on our porch here, right?"

"Yeah. I think so."

"Well, that's the strongest beer there is. Every cup was probably the equivalent of one and a half of the lightweight stuff you're used to."

"Kill me now," I said, walking past him.

There was no way I would ever go skinny-dipping. Ever. So if to save myself from the horror, I had to putt around on a Jet Ski, fine. I could handle that. I bent under the yellow caution tape and quickly ran up the stairs and into the master. Lily was already showered and dressed and flashed me a huge grin when I entered the room.

"Well? How was everything with your friend or wait...I mean buddy?" she teased.

"Everything was just fine with my friend, and I'm looking forward to my ride on the water later today," I said, pushing by her to get to the bathroom.

"You don't remember a thing, do you?" she

called through the door.

"Not a single thing."

I turned on the shower and grabbed a towel. Once the steam was rolling over the top of the shower curtain, I tested the water and stepped in. Feeling the water droplets penetrate my hair snarls, I let the warmth trickle down my scalp as I tried to do a recap of the previous night's events. A buddy pact? What the hell was that? Did drunk Brandy gravitate to first grade? Was Gabby anywhere around when I was acting like a fool and did it even matter? It didn't sound like she cared if one of us turned out to be interested in her brother. Although, I was sure she would never suspect it would be me out of the bunch.

"So where'd you sleep?" Lily popped her head into the bathroom.

"I think you know exactly where I slept and sleeping was all I did."

"I don't doubt it. You really put Aaron in his place," she laughed.

"How so?" I asked, unsure of wanting to hear the answer.

"It started with you explaining the first Google search you conducted on him, which led to the next Google result and then the next. I think by the end of it, you made your point clear that you never wanted to turn into one of his bimbos and all the sweet talking or not-so-sweet talking—as you put it—would ever convince you to look at him as more than a friend. You were more responsible than that and had more respect for yourself than anyone he's ever been out with.

And then I think that was about the time you sat on the stump and fell asleep."

"Oh. My. God." I turned off the water and grabbed the towel from the rod, drying myself off quickly. "Was Gabby around?"

"No, she and Jason were long gone. He doesn't drink so I think they had plenty of other things to keep themselves busy."

"I think by the sounds of it, I should stop too," I confessed, wrapping the towel around my body.

"Don't be hard on yourself," Lily said. "I know what's really happening here and I think once you admit it, you won't keep trying to run from it. Or I mean him."

Lily sat on the bed as I quickly dressed and twisted my wet hair into a clip. I grabbed some mascara and lip gloss and decided that was good enough.

"I think the best part of the whole show was the fact that you had all of the Google sites, you showed, bookmarked."

"Oh, Lord."

"On the bright side, you weren't the only one who was completely blitzed so it's doubtful anyone else will remember."

"Maybe, I should just admit that I can't stop thinking about him and act like an adult."

I heard the shower turn on down the hall and then the sound of someone rummaging through a closet, the wrong closet. It must be Aaron.

I darted to the hallway and sure enough, it was him.

"Hey, friend. The towels are in the other

closet." I pointed in the other direction and he turned around, grinning.

"Thanks," he said, opening up the other door.

"I guess I'll meet you at the water later?"

"You saw the footage?" he asked.

"That I did." I smiled, feeling the warmth spread through me as he looked at me with those beautiful eyes.

"I wouldn't mind if you reneged on your agreement there," he said, his eyes holding promise.

"I bet you wouldn't. But I hate to break it to you. I'm not a skinny-dipper."

He grabbed a towel and nodded as he went into the bathroom.

"I hope you don't blow it, Brandy," Lily whispered from behind.

I turned to Lily and nodded. "No more beer for me this weekend and I think I'll be fine. But I do need some coffee to get this pounding headache gone."

"I think it will take more than coffee but that's a start."

I followed Lily down to the kitchen and watched her prepare her special brew, which never worked but we didn't have the heart to tell her. I slowly sipped the mixture of Gatorade and Alka-Seltzer, grinning and nodding as I did.

After the last gulp, I placed the mug on the counter and Lily smiled.

"You've got it bad."

I shrugged, dismissing her comment and wandered onto the property toward the lake. I spotted Jason holding Gabby on the makeshift pier as they stared at the water. That was what I wanted, someone to hold me in an embrace and just enjoy what the world had to offer, together. I glanced back at the house to see Lily and Aaron walking down the steps. He caught my stare and gave a quick nod as he listened intently to Lily.

Gabby called my name and waved me down to where they were standing, and I gladly took her up on the offer.

"I heard you had a pretty interesting night last night," Jason teased, letting go of Gabby.

"Word certainly travels fast," I said, glancing over at her.

"Well, I'd say either Aaron or Jason would be the best to drive you around, and I already claimed Jason." She gave me a wink and hugged Jason, who was beaming down at her.

"You'll be fine. Aaron'll take care of you," Jason said, grinning.

"Are you ready?" I heard Aaron call down to us.

I spun around just in time to watch him tug his shirt over his head. I nearly died right then as the length of his torso extended toward the sky, exposing the v-definition leading down to his swim trunks. He tossed the white t-shirt onto the ground and looked up, catching my gaze.

Nodding, I looked back at Jason and Gabby, who ushered me forward, and Lily, who was already picking out a life jacket for me.

"This ought to do," she said, shoving the hot pink and black vest in front of me.

"Thanks," I said, grabbing it from her.

I slipped my arms through the holes and began adjusting the straps. But before I had a chance to tighten any of them, Aaron's fingers slipped over mine, and he began pulling and tugging on the black straps.

"It has to be tight or there's no point in wearing one," he instructed. His fingers sliding in between the nylon fabric and my skin. The trail of goose bumps his touch left behind was a dead giveaway that he did more to me than I wanted to admit. The thought of wrapping my arms around him—even with the life vests creating a barrier—completely warped my insides as my mind flashed back to the kiss.

I looked up into Aaron's eyes and simply muttered a quick thank you before half-waddling-slash-walking to the shore.

Gabby came up to stand beside me as Jason and Aaron walked out into the water, untying the Jet Skis and bringing them back in for us.

"You will love it," Gabby whispered. "I promise."

"I'm scared spitless."

"Why?" she challenged. "What's the worst thing that could happen? If you fall off, so what? You're landing on water and you've got a life jacket on. You'll pop right back up. Plus, we're in fresh water not salt water so if water goes up your nose, it's not that bad."

"You might want to stop while you're ahead," I teased.

But, she was right. It's not like I'd be landing

on cement. I felt my arms steady as I slid my hands out from under the vest and watched Aaron bring the Jet Ski as close in as he could get it.

"You think you can reach up and slide on?" he asked, quickly maneuvering onto the front portion of the seat. "You can grab onto my hand."

I nodded quickly and reached for his hand, giving a little hop as my chest hit the back of the seat. Without even realizing what was happening, he hauled me into position and I was upright.

"Woohoo," Lily yelled from the shore as a crowd gathered, including my two brothers. "No skinny-dipping for my girl."

A chorus of male boos from the shore boomed into the air as Aaron started the engine. I caught both Ayden and Mason smirking on the beach next to Lily, and I wondered what they were thinking.

"Ready, babe?" Aaron asked over his shoulder.

My heart skipped a beat, and I slid my arms around his waist.

"Yeah, but go slow."

"I'll try, but I can't promise anything."

We slowly began to move through the water, and I was no longer able to distinguish the source of the butterflies. I had no idea if they were from taking off on the Jet Ski or being so closely wrapped around Aaron. The firmness of his body as it flexed with the rhythm of the machine created an internal distraction. I barely noticed that we had sped up until the cool water began splashing on my legs.

"How are you holding up?" he asked over the crashing sound of water.

I looked around to see the trees and shrubs whipping by as we followed behind Jason and Gabby. My muscles slowly began to relax. The tension in my shoulders and arms dissipated as I realized how truly fun this was.

"I'm kind of glad I made the bet," I admitted.

I felt his body shaking slightly and wondered if he was laughing.

"I still don't remember much of the bet or last night actually, but the only other time I was close to that amount of drinking was right after I met you. I made poor Gabby go out to a club, telling her it was so she wouldn't think about Jason."

"Is that so?" Aaron's body shuddered as the laughter left his lips.

"The real reason I dragged her out was so I could try and forget about you."

Aaron's body stilled and his laughter went silent.

"I hope you won't try to forget about me anymore," he said, his words almost inaudible over the beating wind.

"I don't think I could no matter how hard I tried."

He slowed the Jet Ski to a stop and let Gabby and Jason get far ahead as ours bobbed in the wake. Turning slightly on the seat, so that his eyes locked on mine, made my entire body tense up.

"I hope you meant that," he said, gently

tracing his finger along my jawbone.

"I do."

He leaned forward slightly, and it felt like he was going to kiss me. But he stopped short and smiled.

"I think we need to go slow. We've had a lot of false starts," he said.

Disappointment was quickly filled with relief when I spotted Jason headed toward us. I might be ready to start contemplating an us with Aaron, but I wasn't sure I was ready to let Gabby know just yet. I gave a quick wave to Gabby as Jason made a quick turn on the Jet Ski, drenching us completely with spray.

"Okay," Aaron yelled at Jason. "It's on."

He slid back into position, and I held on tight as the watercraft took off at a high speed.

"Hold on, babe," he hollered, and I nestled in feeling freer than I had in a long time.

For once in my life, the fear completely dissolved as I felt the breeze running over my wet skin and blowing my hair in the wind. If riding a motorcycle felt anything like this, I could see why it would be so tempting. Maybe with Aaron by my side, there would be another side to life. One that I never thought I'd want to explore.

CHAPTER SIXTEEN

We pulled up to the shore, greeted by my brothers and Lily and a few others waiting to hop on the Jet Skis. Jason and Gabby were coming in behind us, and she looked about as happy as I felt.

"How was it?" Lily asked.

"Amazing," I said, sliding off the Jet Ski into the water. "Thanks to him."

"I don't know how you did it, man," Mason said, looking over at Aaron. "We've spent our entire lives trying to get her over her fears."

I glanced up toward the cabin and saw Cole and some girl attached at his hip.

"Cole's here, huh?" I asked, blocking the sun out of my eyes. "I was hoping he and his car would get stuck on the side of the road somewhere."

"Yup. But luckily for you he brought his own

entertainment."

"Poor thing," I said, grinning as I looked back at Aaron who was tying up the Jet Ski.

Lily walked over and handed me a green towel, which I wrapped around my chest tightly. The light breeze was causing my skin to prickle now that Aaron's body wasn't acting as my shield. We had been on the water for hours and every minute was glorious. Holding on to Aaron, feeling his body next to mine was amazing, like I was in heaven.

Aaron walked out of the water and stood next to me, his body still glistening and dripping from the lake. I unwrapped my towel and handed it to him. "Since I'm a nice person," I teased.

He grabbed the towel from me and began wiping off the water droplets. I was slightly jealous of the terry cloth that was running along his body instead of me and began to chuckle.

"What's so funny, knucklehead?" Mason asked.

"Enough with the knucklehead stuff."

"You know you'd miss it."

I rolled my eyes as Aaron laughed and handed me back my towel. My fingers touched his, and another spark ignited in me just as Jason and Gabby pulled in. The others waiting for the Jet Skis hurried into the water to take both of ours out, and I knew I needed to keep my thoughts and hands to myself as I quickly tied the towel back around me.

"Is that Cole?" Jason asked, blocking the sun with his hand.

"Yup," I replied.

"Who's that with him?" Jason asked.

"Some poor soul. I'm sure he'll introduce her since it looks like he's coming this way," I said, noticing Aaron staring straight ahead, his jaw tightening.

I glanced at Lily who noticed Aaron's gaze and quickly came by my side. Aaron's eyes were pinned on Cole and his date as they walked down to us. Something was definitely off with this encounter. I could feel the tension rolling off of Aaron and couldn't figure out what had changed so drastically since we were out on the water.

"How's it going?" Cole hollered from the bank. His date was gorgeous. She had long black hair and was dressed in a miniscule pink bikini that showed off her tiny waist but otherwise ample curves.

Cole was holding her hand helping her down the hill, stopping right next to my brother when he looked at us all.

"Looks like my timing was perfect," he said, grinning. His eyes bored into Aaron. "Everyone, this is Nina. But I think you already know her, if I'm not mistaken?" He was staring directly at Aaron.

I glanced at Aaron whose eyes were on fire. My insides were churning as I looked over at Nina who was staring at Cole, horrified. What was going on here?

"You didn't tell me he would be here," she whispered, glancing quickly at Aaron.

Cole looked over at me and flashed a wicked

grin, and Lily slid her hand into mine for moral support.

"It's nice to see you, Nina," Aaron said, his voice low.

She turned to face him, her eyes blazing. "Is it? I wouldn't have known. I gave up waiting for your call months ago. My mother said you were still alive, so I figured it was just you being you."

I wanted to grab Aaron's hand, wrap my arm around his waist, anything to claim him as mine, but I couldn't because he wasn't mine and because Gabby was only a few feet away. So instead I just stood in place feeling completely insignificant as the blissful memories and hopes for something more faded away.

"You are a total creep," Nina said, turning to Cole.

"What?" he asked, throwing his hands into the air. "I thought you two—"

"Why don't you come with us to the house," Gabby offered looking over at Nina.

"Who are you?" Nina asked snidely.

"I'm Aaron's sister."

I wasn't sure that was actually a selling point at the moment, but she seemed to soften a small amount. Nina shot a glance to Aaron and he nodded. So whoever she was, they were close enough to know about him having a sister.

Wonderful!

Gabby moved from Jason and marched over to a very hostile Nina. Once reaching her, she grabbed her hand and started hauling her up toward the house with Mason right behind.

Leave it to him to swoop in and help clean up the mess. I knew I was supposed to follow, but I couldn't. My legs felt like they were bolted to the beach, and I wasn't sure I wanted to hear her side of things, especially if it involved Aaron.

"What do you think you're doing, man?" Aaron asked, his eyes narrowing on Cole.

"Honestly, I didn't think it would be a big deal," he said, glancing at me. "How was I supposed to know you and Nina had some sort of messed up history?"

I felt Aaron's eyes on me, but I couldn't look at him. This was exactly why I couldn't get involved with him. There was just too much of *this* floating around waiting to come in and spoil otherwise perfect moments.

"And to think I thought you were kind of cute," Lily said, squeezing my hand as she looked at Cole.

"No, you didn't," I blurted.

"Don't you think it's only fair I show Brandy what she's getting into with you?" he asked, ignoring Lily's comment. "After all, I went to school with her brothers, and it's partly my responsibility to look after her."

"Do you really think bringing one of Aaron's exes to my brother's party is going to bother me?" I asked, my heart pounding. "He's twenty-seven years old. He's bound to have had relationships. And we aren't even together anyway."

"Could have fooled me. The way you two were out there together, straddling him like your life depended on it," Cole replied, taking a step toward me. His eyes narrowed.

"What's that supposed to mean?" I asked.

"Your hands were all over him out there."

"I was holding on to him for dear life." And then I remembered. Last year, Cole tried everything under the sun to get me on a Jet Ski with him and I refused.

"Whatever. If you want to waste your time with someone who has no respect for anything without a dick, have fun."

That was it. I leapt toward Cole and pounded my fist into his chest. "Take a hike, Cole. You're no better."

He fell backward onto the shore, bringing me with him. His arms circled around my waist as I tried to get away, but he only squeezed harder.

"Let me go," I said, pounding on his chest.

"Not until you say you're sorry."

"Let me go, Cole, or I'll have my brothers make you sorry you ever showed up."

Within an instant, Aaron's arms swooped around my waist and pulled me off of Cole. Cole scrambled to his feet, but it was too late. Aaron landed a swift punch to the side of Cole's cheek. Jason quickly responded by hauling Aaron away from Cole, and something told me this wasn't the first time these two had to intervene for one other.

"That was kind of hot," Lily whispered, and I looked at her with a huge grin on my face.

"Tell me about it."

"I'm sorry about all that," Aaron whispered.

"There's nothing to be sorry about. You're allowed to date."

"Yeah, but the accusations that were—"

"That's all they were. It's not my business. It's not like we were together at that time in your life." Even as I spoke the words that's not how I felt. At all. The jealousy that bolted through me was insane when I realized there was a connection between Nina and Aaron. That kind of connection.

"And according to your plan, it's not like we'll be together anytime soon..." his voice broke off.

"People are allowed to change their mind," I whispered, sliding closer to him.

The night's temperature was dropping quickly, and I heard the loud shouts from the nightly poker match beginning, which meant it was midnight.

"You tired?" he asked.

I shook my head. "Not at all."

"That's good." He stood up from the steps and grabbed my hand, hauling me to my feet.

"What are we doing?"

"You'll see."

"I don't think we should..." My heart rate accelerated at the thought of where he was taking me, and I couldn't finish my sentence. I didn't want to finish my sentence. I wanted him to take me anywhere he wanted, do anything he wanted.

Aaron held me close as he led me away from the house toward the wooded area along the lake. Darkness led the way as the houselights reduced to nothing, and the moon's glow was our only splintered source of light through the trees.

"Where are we going?" I whispered.

"Far enough away where we won't be bothered." He stopped and stared down at me, his fingers tracing along my cheek as my pulse quickened. "But we're not quite there yet." His voice was so low, seductive. Just as I had imagined it so many times before. The images of him this afternoon cascaded through my mind as he began leading me deeper into the woods. Normally, I would have been panicked. But somehow being with him made it all right.

He led us down closer to the lake to a small clearing where the moonlight splashed more freely. There was a blanket rolled up and tucked underneath a thicket. Confused, I pointed at my find and he smiled, reaching for it. "You're not the only planner." He unrolled the blanket and tucked inside were two plastic cups and a bottle of wine.

"I saw this place when we were on the Jet Ski and had to check it out," he said, handing me the cup. "It was a good diversion to cool off from Cole."

"Thank you for that, by the way."

I took a step closer and tossed the cup onto the blanket.

"I can't keep fighting the feelings I have for you," I whispered.

His mouth parted slowly, and all I could imagine was his lips on mine.

"Then don't." He placed the unopened wine back on the blanket and drew me into him.

I looked into his eyes and saw the passionate, kind soul I wanted to unravel, and my insides were barely holding on for the ride. I leaned up against him as he kissed my neck, sending waves of heat rippling through me.

"I've been dreaming about feeling those lips on me since last night," I murmured, feeling the moistness along my flesh.

My body shuddered as he wrapped his arms around me, pulling me against his firm body.

"I've been dreaming about it since the moment I saw you at the winery," he said, his eyes locking on mine. "And every time after that."

I ran my hands through his hair and brought his mouth closer to mine.

"Feeling your body wrapped around mine on the water..." His lips trembled as I softly kissed his lips. It felt amazing knowing I could do this to him. I felt his hands slowly glide down my sides, resting on my hips as our bodies pressed up against one another. An uncontrollable heat ran through me as his mouth parted and our kisses deepened. Feeling the warmth of his lips on mine became my drug, but as our kisses deepened, the warmth was traded for the cold flick of his metallic tongue ring, sending my insides into a spiral.

Better than I imagined!

There were no words for what he was doing

to me with each kiss. My legs weakened as his tongue dove deeper. I leaned into him more as my body failed me and felt his firmness press against my stomach.

My breathing caught as his hands worked their way up my back, skating over the bikini straps that he quickly released. I felt my bikini top fall to the ground, but my t-shirt was still on.

"We should wait," I murmured.

"For what?" he asked, his breathing ragged as his fingers traced along my shoulders.

"Until we're sure about us."

"You have doubts?" his voice lowered.

"A few," I confessed and saw his expression fall. I backed away and sat on the blanket where he followed soon after.

I leaned my head against his chest and felt the beating of his heart begin to steady as I wondered what I was trying to stop between us. Or maybe that was the problem. There was no us, but I desperately wanted there to be. Falling asleep in his arms, I dreamed of a carefree relationship with Aaron and hoped that when I woke up, I'd be able to remember some of the pieces to make it a reality.

CHAPTER SEVENTEEN

Curled up by the fire in our condo, I was reading over the differences between real property and personal property. It had been so busy at the office this week I could barely believe I'd ever been on a weekend trip. It was almost like the entire weekend escape never even happened. And regardless of my drunken "buddy only" proclamations to Aaron, it was really nice to get to know another side of him. He still vowed that he wasn't the one who sent the flowers or chocolates, but I had my doubts. I was so excited to tell him about the lessons I had signed up for. I doubt he'd even believe it. The truth was that I was somewhere between terrified and elated at the thought of my first motorbike lesson on Saturday, but after getting a taste of riding the Jet Ski, I wanted to face my fears and take some motorcycle lessons. I even got Jason on board, and he's building me a small bike to begin on, and he swore he wouldn't tell anyone.

Meeting Nina definitely wasn't a highlight of the trip, but if anyone knew he hadn't been celibate, it was Google and me so I didn't completely understand Cole's intentions. But that was his past, not his present, and now I just wanted to focus on the remaining weeks of summer before law school.

I grabbed the fireplace remote and checked the temperature. Even though it was the middle of summer, the weather was as cold and rainy as mid-November. The thermostat read sixty-five, but it felt chillier than that so I grabbed another blanket for my lap.

I was looking forward to meeting up with some of the other students who were entering law school this quarter and had a little bit of time before I had to leave the house. Some of them had gotten a jumpstart on the reading like I did, and a few of them didn't bother. Must be nice to be so confident. I always got good grades through school, which was why I wasn't too worried about getting into law school, but I always had to earn my grades. I wasn't one of those who naturally floated by. I had to study, memorize and study some more.

My phone buzzed, and it was a message from Gabby letting me know she was going to spend the night at Jason's. I already figured as much and planned on inviting Aaron over tonight. I wanted to cook for him and try to make things as normal as possible for our first official non-date

date.

I texted back a smiley face and decided I had completed enough reading. I walked to the kitchen and pulled out the marinating chicken and stirred it once before placing it back in the fridge. I picked a meal that had absolutely no garlic in it just in case I was lucky enough to experience a repeat performance from the weekend. Aaron was working late tonight and had planned on coming directly here from the office so he was probably going to be exhausted but a girl could hope. If this turned into something, I promised myself that I would tell Gabby. But I didn't want to complicate anything now. I had done enough of that.

I glanced at the clock and decided to head for the coffee shop. I picked up some of the schoolbooks I'd been reading and stuffed them in a bag. I flipped off the lights and locked the door. As I waited for the elevator, excitement crept over me. I couldn't wait to see Aaron. The kiss we had shared was impossible to shake and conquering my fear of the Jet Ski was pretty intense as well. The elevator opened into the lobby, and I gave a quick wave to the doorman as I stepped out onto the street. I hadn't brought an umbrella with me and was thankful the rain had let up on my walk.

The coffee shop was full and I quickly scanned the crowd, trying to find a group of strangers that looked like they were about to enter law school. I had no idea what that would look like but hoped for the best. I saw a woman toting a large bag of books, grabbing her drink off the bar and beelined toward her. She had to be part of the group.

"Are you here for the study group meet-up?" I asked the woman. She had short, wavy blonde hair and green eyes. She had a small frame, and she looked like she was going to be swallowed by the books she was hauling. Relief spread through her face and she quickly nodded.

"I'm Brandy. And you are?"

"Teresa," she said. "I'd shake your hands, but I don't have any left."

I started laughing at the awkwardness of everything and glanced toward a large table in the back of the coffee shop.

"Must be everyone over there?" I asked.

"I think so," she replied.

"Okay. I'll be back there in a sec. I'm gonna grab something to keep me going."

She smiled and nodded before turning toward the group of people. They all looked innocent enough. There seemed to be an equal divide between men and women, and the ages were just as varied. I stood in line to place my drink order and watched a couple of the guys glance in my direction, making me chuckle internally. Not a chance. The giddiness of getting to see Aaron tonight was almost unbearable. I couldn't imagine this lasting more than an hour. Placing my drink order, I felt the buzz of my phone.

By the time I got to the end of the counter, I felt another buzz.

Looking forward to seeing you I might come early.

Oh, shoot!

I wouldn't do that. You'd be very lonely since I'm not home. I'm meeting with some class members to form a study group.

The reply was almost immediate.

Well that sounds fun :/

I laughed and texted back.

Law school is known for being a blast. You should stop by and see how the other half lives.

He didn't waste a second.

Don't tempt me. Maybe I'll swing by. Which coffee shop?

My heart started pounding at the thought of him making an appearance, and I had absolutely no idea why.

Fifth and Pine

I shoved my phone in my bag, grabbed my latte and started walking toward the table of strangers. They seemed pleasant enough. Teresa waved me over and pointed to the seat next to her. I smiled and wandered through the packed coffee house, landing my books on the chair with a thud.

"With the sound of those books, you're definitely in the right place," a guy at the end of the table said. He stood up and reached over to shake my hand. He had wavy brown hair and hazel eyes, which were a little hard to see behind the glasses. He was dressed conservatively in a pair of khakis and a button-down pink and white shirt with a yellow sweater draped around his shoulders. Just like the movies, I thought to myself, trying not to laugh. I'm sure to some he'd be attractive, but he looked like he took this new world he was attempting to enter a tad too seriously.

"I'm Jeff," he said, giving me a limp shake.

"Brandy."

Greetings from around the table circulated as I shoved my bag to the floor and took a seat. I felt Jeff's eyes on me for most of my chitchat with the others, but didn't want to think about it.

"Can you believe how many books we have?" Teresa asked.

I shook my head. "I knew I had to get a head start."

"Me too."

The group was naturally forming into smaller groups as the discussion turned away from law school and toward summer vacations and interests.

"What is your focus?" Jeff's voice boomed over the group. I glanced up and realized he was staring directly at me even though Teresa and I were in a conversation of our own.

"Civil Advocacy and Family and Juvenile Law," I said, turning my attention back to Teresa.

"You're one of those," he continued.

"One of what?" I asked. Teresa snapped her head in Jeff's direction as well.

"A fancy do-gooder who's too self-righteous to make a penny."

This guy was a complete prick. I felt my pulse quicken and glanced around at the now silent table as they waited for my reaction. This wasn't how I wanted to start off the introductions. Growing up with Mason and Ayden allowed me to voice my opinions articulately and perfect how to channel my temper, especially around males. But I didn't really want to go down that path. Not today.

Instead, I smiled at him, but I knew my expression was full of pity, which only infuriated people like him, men like him.

"Exactly what I thought," he scoffed.

I took a sip and looked around the table at the shocked faces. They were just as confused as I was about this guy.

"Do I look like someone you dated back in high school who dumped you or something? I'm really not sure what set you off."

He leaned back in his chair and stretched, smiling.

This was really creepy. I actually did hope that Aaron showed up.

"Hey, man, chill out," a guy sitting across from

me said. I think he said his name was Dan. He looked about thirty and completely unimpressed with Jeff's attitude.

"I'm just pointing out the obvious. Mark my words. She's going to be a real pain in the ass."

My blood was burning, but I didn't want him to think he had that kind of power over me. As if on cue, my phone buzzed and I grabbed it out of my purse.

"Oh, Jeff. The eighties called and they want their shirt back," I said, smiling as I glanced over Aaron's text. He was only a couple blocks away.

The group busted into skittish laughter, but I caught a glimpse of something behind Jeff's eyes that burned of hollowness and something much deeper. He grabbed his cup of coffee and continued staring at me as he drank.

"You going to be okay?" Teresa whispered, as she turned her head in my direction.

"Yeah. I think so. But it certainly doesn't give me a warm and fuzzy feeling for when classes start up."

"Judging by the sounds of it, you won't have to worry about any of your classes crossing over."

"Hope not."

A shiver ran up my spine as I felt Jeff's eyes still on me. There had to be something more here. And then the thought of the random texts and voicemails entered my mind, but that was completely ridiculous. I had no idea who this person was, and he would have no idea how to get my home and work address. We'd only just met. I was sure of it.

"So I was thinking that with a couple of our core classes each quarter, we could have a Sunday night meet-up for those who wanted to discuss our readings and assignments. Would anyone be interested?" I asked, avoiding Jeff's gaze.

"I wouldn't miss it for the world, doll," Jeff laughed.

I turned to him, my blood pounding in my ears. "Listen, jerk. I don't know what your problem is, but I can guarantee that you don't want to mess with me."

"Why? Will your two big, bad brothers come and hurt me?"

My blood curdled when the words fell out of his mouth. In an instant I jumped up and darted toward him. Before I knew it, I was fisting his sweater and pulling him out of his chair. He reeked of alcohol so badly my eyes burned.

I felt others congregating behind me as I stared into Jeff's cold eyes.

"I suggest you take your things, go home, and sober up. And when you run into me at school, I don't want a word said to me and not even a glance. You got it?"

"What's going on?" Aaron's voice thundered through the crowd.

My hand unclasped Jeff's sweater just as Aaron pushed his way through the group.

"This guy's got some sort of problem with Brandy, and none of us can figure it out," Dan said, from across the table.

My hands were trembling, and I was forcing

the tears away that suddenly wanted to overtake me. My heart still pounding, I turned toward Aaron whose eyes were blazing as he stared at Jeff.

"She's got it coming to her," Jeff mumbled, as the alcohol continued to settle into his bloodstream.

"What did you say?" Aaron's voice was deep and determined as he took a step forward.

"She's got it coming," his voice trailed off.

Aaron grabbed Jeff's sweater and twisted it in between his knuckles, yanking Jeff toward him. Jeff's body was only inches away from Aaron's, almost hanging like a ragdoll, when Aaron punched him right in the stomach. Jeff let out a wheeze, and the group quieted as Aaron tossed him back in the chair. The wooden chair skidded backward a foot but stopped with Jeff still eyeing us.

"Let's get out of here," Aaron whispered, grabbing my hand.

I nodded quickly, completely shaken, and grabbed my bag. Out of the corner of my eye, I saw the other guys in the group attempting to pick up Jeff and haul him out of the coffee shop. I hoped they would dump him on the street like the trash that he was.

"Do you know him?" Aaron asked, taking my bag from me.

"Not for the life of me that I can remember," I said, my voice on the verge of hiccupping. "He just went off on me, and I don't know why."

"A lot of help your classmates are," Aaron's

voice was gruff.

"They're all wannabe attorneys so any kind of criminal blemish that could result in—"

"That's not comforting," he interrupted. "You having to defend yourself with a group of people only watching…"

"I could have taken him," I teased, glancing at Aaron. His expression softened, and he pulled me into him as we walked down the sidewalk toward my condo.

"I'm so sorry you had to get involved," I said.

"Don't apologize. You didn't do anything wrong." The harshness reappeared in his voice.

We arrived at my building and I glanced at the pizza place across the street.

"I don't feel much like cooking anymore. Would pizza be okay?" I asked.

Aaron looked down at me and nodded. "Are you all right?"

I drew in a breath as everything settled and shook my head. We walked into my building, but a lingering feeling of being watched stayed with me. I looked up at Aaron as we stood in the elevator and wondered what all I should tell him, if anything. This night wasn't turning out anything like I'd imagined.

The elevator stopped on my floor and we walked to the door, but my hands were now trembling.

"Why do I get the feeling you aren't telling me everything?" he asked, his voice full of concern.

I opened the door and threw my keys onto the table.

"You know when I asked you if you sent me flowers?"

He nodded.

"Well, I still don't know who did, and then I came home to a box of chocolates outside our door."

"Could those be from any ex-boyfriends?" he asked.

"You might be pleased to know that I don't have that many, but no. I've also been getting weird text messages and voicemails."

"Can I see them?" he asked.

"I've deleted quite a few of the texts because in the beginning I thought it was just a mistake."

"We can get them back if we need to," Aaron replied. His demeanor had completely changed.

I handed him my phone and he went through the texts before listening to what few voicemails I kept. He handed me the phone and we walked toward the family room. I followed behind, my heart pounding but not for the reason I had hoped.

"Those aren't random messages."

"What do you mean?" I asked.

"They're code."

"What do you mean code? Like for software?"

He nodded and sat down on the couch, quietly thinking as his gaze was fastened to the floor. "It looks like source code. Jason knows more about that than I do, but I think that's what it is."

"Really?"

He nodded. "Are you sure you don't know who that guy was?"

I sat next to Aaron and shook my head. "I honestly can't remember him. Not from college...high school. I just really don't. But he mentioned my two brothers, and I don't know how he would know about them. Our class profiles are listed on the law school blog, but I didn't list my brothers on there."

Fear began to spread as I thought about just how much this guy might know and how he found out the information or how he found me.

"I'll have you copy everything over for me, and I'll see what Jason or I can come up with."

I nodded and grabbed the remote for the fire, suddenly chilled with the new information.

"This wasn't how I wanted tonight to go."

His eyes connected with mine. "What did you have planned?"

The familiar smirk replaced concern as he scooted closer. He was still wearing his jacket and I motioned for him to take it off. I flipped on the television, wanting background noise to make me forget about the run in at the coffee shop.

"I was hoping to pick up where we left off on Friday or Saturday," I said, smiling.

"Purely platonic, of course." His brows rose as the smug expression settled on his features.

"Obviously," I said, running my hand over his chest. "I've got a surprise for you, but I can't tell you until I'm all done."

His brows shot up and he laughed. "And when will you be done?"

"In a couple weeks." I curled into him on the

couch and placed my head on his shoulder.

I felt his warm breath ruffling the hairs on top of my head, and I imagined how wonderful it would be staying like this all night, curled in his arms.

"I could get used to this," I murmured, feeling the stress of the earlier events begin to dissipate.

"I try to take good care of my friends," he mumbled, as his hand slid down my arm.

"You don't let Jason curl up like this, do you?"

Aaron started laughing, and I couldn't shake the image of the two snuggled together on the couch.

"Only when it's cold outside."

"That's something I'd like to see."

"Is that so?"

I started laughing uncontrollably and felt him pull me onto his lap.

"You know, I never really thanked you for helping me to get over one of my fears."

"The Jet Ski?"

I nodded. "I didn't actually think about how many things I don't like doing because I'm scared. I just manage my life so that I don't encounter them."

"I have to thank you for something as well."

"What's that?" I asked, looking into his eyes.

"Busting my balls."

"When did I do that?"

"That morning I wanted to talk to you about Gabby, you told me to grow a pair."

"I totally forgot about that," I chuckled and shook my head. "No one messes with my Gabby."

"I gathered that." He grinned. "But that was something I needed to hear."

"Glad I could help."

Now kiss me please!

"So what is it about this surprise or—"

"Nice try. I'm not saying a word, but it has to do with the whole fear thing."

"I thought you weren't saying a word?"

"I don't keep secrets well. They eat me alive."

His lips were so close to mine, and when his gaze fell to my mouth I closed my eyes, expecting to feel the softness of his lips. But I didn't. Instead, I opened my eyes only to have him smiling at me, studying me.

"You're a hard one to figure out."

"I don't mean to be."

"I don't doubt it. I just think you're wired that way."

"Possibly." I shrugged and a thought occurred to me.

"My parents are celebrating their anniversary by going to Ireland, but my brothers and I are throwing them a surprise party before they leave."

"Yeah?" he asked.

"Would you maybe want to go with me and just hang out?" I asked, suddenly uncertain why in the world I brought that up to him. We weren't dating yet, and that was probably the equivalent of dragging him to a wedding.

"I'd love to come with you and meet the two people who could spawn such an odd creature."

"Really?"

He nodded.

"You don't even know when it is."

"I'll make sure to be available." He picked up my hand and kissed it gently. The feeling of his warm, wet lips against my skin sent my world spinning, and I secretly begged him to be kissed elsewhere. Instead, my prayers were answered by a text.

My cell buzzed, nearly jolting me out of my own skin, and Aaron picked it up and handed it to me. I looked down hoping it wasn't anything that would add to the night's drama.

"Oh my god. Gabby's on her way up. She doesn't have her keys, but she left her medicine here and needs it. You've got to hide," I said, hopping up.

Aaron started laughing and grabbed his coat.

"If we're just friends, what does it matter?" He shrugged his shoulders.

"My room," I said, quickly pushing him toward the bedroom.

"Wait. Would it be so bad if..." His eyes sparkled as I managed to wrestle him in there.

"Go to the closet," I said. "There should be plenty of room. You're not supposed to be here until tomorrow, and she can read me like nobody's business. She'd know if I was lying to her."

The knock on the front door rattled me even though I was expecting it. I glanced around the family room and down the hall, making sure there weren't any clues left around.

"Hurry up. Jason's waiting downstairs and we

don't want to miss the ferry," she said, through the door.

"Okay. Okay." I opened the door and laughed as I saw her flushed cheeks and huge smile. She was in a pair of jeans and a tight black shirt. "You're just lucky I'm home from the study group."

"My lifesaver, yet again," she said, pushing her way past me as she headed to her room. "How was the study group?"

"Not what I expected," I said, not wanting to slow her down. "But I'm sure it will come in handy. I'll fill you in when you have more time."

She reappeared with her little baggy of pill bottles that rattled as she shook them at me. "Got 'em. I've got some pretty big news. I can't wait to tell you," she gushed.

"Thanks for leaving me hanging," I teased.

Gabby gave me a quick hug and walked out the door. I was left with an uncomfortable feeling as I realized what all I was hiding from my best friend. After locking the door, I leaned up against it for a few seconds to calm my nerves and heard Aaron walking down the hall.

"All clear?" he asked, his eyes twinkling.

I nodded slowly as the guilt flooded through me. He stood in front of me, pulling my body into his as he wrapped his arms around my waist.

"What's wrong? Why are you so quiet?" he asked.

"I don't think we should do this," I said quietly. "It's not fair to Gabby."

The playful expression fell from Aaron's face,

and his arms unlocked from my waist.

"Do what, exactly?" His eyes focusing on mine.

"This." I motioned to us both. "I can't just be friends with you, and I don't want to sneak around."

"So don't. Let's tell her," he said, his voice restrained.

"I just..."

"Is this what you did all through college? Played games?" he asked, his voice rising.

"I'm not playing games."

"You are. We've been on a handful of dates, and we keep circling around to the same problem. A problem you're creating." His gaze pierced through me as I allowed his words to sink in.

"I'm trying not to hurt your sister."

"Hurt my sister? Who said she'd care one way or the other. There's something else that's making you do this. And I think you might want to figure out what it is before we get in any deeper." His jaw tensed, and I watched his gaze land on the door behind me.

I backed against the door, shaking my head.

"Please don't leave. We should talk about it."

His fingers wrapped around my upper arms and moved me aside like I was a cabbage patch doll.

"There's nothing to talk about. You need to decide what you want to do. The ball is in your court. Remember to keep the door locked with that weirdo."

And that was it. He slipped through my fingers

just like that. I felt the first of many tears trail down my cheeks.

CHAPTER EIGHTEEN

It had been two full weeks of silence from Aaron. The first week I didn't attempt to reach out. I felt foolish and absolutely childish, and I never liked to admit when someone else was right, especially if it highlighted that I might be wrong. Hopefully that would pay off in my chosen profession, but it didn't bode well for my personal life. It was a trait I was going to work on.

By the second week, I had my apology to Aaron all worked out, and I even wrote a letter to Gabby about my feelings for her brother. It stayed in my jewelry box until the time was right. Or now I should say if the time would ever be right. I had left several messages on Aaron's voicemail, sent texts, and emails, and he didn't respond to any of them. Of course, that pulled me to the wonderful interwebs where I searched and searched to see if any new images of him with someone else were posted online. Thankfully there weren't any, but that didn't mean anything necessarily. I think he had plenty on quick dial. The thought made me queasy.

But I had to get in the zone because today was my final driving class on the motorcycle, followed by my endorsement test, and it was the first time I'd be using the bike that Jason built for me. It wasn't anything fancy. I wanted a basic bike to learn on, and I felt the safest knowing Jason rebuilt it for me. It felt odd going through the motions when the person I started to do it for might possibly not be in the equation any longer or maybe he never was.

My phone buzzed and it was Jason, right on time. He was downstairs waiting to show me my new two-wheeled wonder. Shaking the disappointment away, I took off for the elevator and hoped it would put me in better spirits.

When I made it downstairs, Jason was standing on the curb with a plate of baked goods.

"Is this what she's been up to?" I asked, giving Jason a big hug.

"Indeed. Hopefully, you have someone to share them with."

My insides twisted at the realization that I actually didn't have anyone to share them with, and why wouldn't Jason know that? Did I become that inconsequential?

"I'll put these on the seat until you go upstairs. Now let's check this baby out. I can tell you Gabby is absolutely going to flip when she finds out you've learned to ride. And Aaron. Hell. He's going to think he died and went to heaven."

A lump formed in the back of my throat and my gaze fell to the sidewalk. Please not now, not in front of him.

"Brandy, you okay?"

My movement went from a slight nodding gesture to completely shaking my head. The tears began to spill down my cheeks and the embarrassment of the situation was almost as stifling. I mean I knew Jason but not that well and here I was bawling in front of him. He took me into his arms and hugged me.

"Whatever's going on...It's going to be okay," he said, stroking my hair.

"I don't think it is. I think I blew it with Aaron before it even had a chance to go anywhere." I sniffed into his chest.

"Aaron doesn't like complication. He's a smart guy, but he doesn't seem to understand that's what relationships are made of—complication. Lots of tiny bits of emotion, history, and dreams all bundled into one big complicated mass that's a ticking time bomb of great passion or great heartache."

"So he didn't tell you anything?" I asked, stepping back and trying to regroup.

"He didn't. He usually keeps to himself when it comes to relationships. I was surprised he even told me what he had about you. He's really struck by you. Frustrated, definitely—but completely enamored. I've never seen him cut himself off from options, if you know what I mean."

"Unfortunately, I know exactly what you

mean, more like who, but I think that might not be the case any longer. He's not answering my emails, texts, calls."

"Listen. Don't give up on him. He's a good guy... a really good guy and once you peel back the layers, you'll see that he's worth fighting for. But he's not used to the relationship thing. You might just have to be persistent and patient."

I drew in a deep breath. "I'm nothing if not persistent. Now let's see that bike so I can get to my last class." I attempted a smile and Jason patted my shoulder before unlocking the trailer.

"Also, we've just about cracked the code on all of those text messages. Once we do, he or I will let you know what we find out. But it's looking really strange so far so be extra vigilant."

"Thanks. Hopefully, it was a fluke. I haven't had anything weird happen for a while."

"Well, just be careful. Things aren't sitting right."

He pulled out the ramp and climbed in. Seconds later he backed out a rebuilt motorcycle, completely fitting what I was looking for.

"It's a 1964 Honda CB 160. We completely tore it apart and rebuilt her from the ground up. She's better than most new bikes and the perfect size for a beginner."

"It's gorgeous," I said, as he backed the beautiful red bike into place.

"You want to take it around the block?" he asked, handing me the matching helmet.

Nodding, I slipped the helmet over my head and fastened the buckle.

"You ready?" he asked.

"I am." I lifted my leg over the seat and settled right onto the leather. "This is really comfortable. Way better than the ones at class."

Jason started laughing. "I bet."

Feeling the lift of exhilaration that I was beginning to enjoy here and there, I flipped the ignition and nodded at Jason as I began to take off. The traffic was light, and I managed to sneak right into the lane as the wind began to beat against my body. There really was something freeing about being so out in the open and connected with the road. I turned toward the water and watched the many admiring eyes as I rode past all the wandering tourists and Seattleites. I felt an itch to keep going, but knew I needed to get to class and felt comfortable enough to ride there on it. Taking the last right to meet back with Jason, I felt a wave of excitement at what I was about to accomplish.

Jason was waving as I pulled up behind him. I was grinning so much, the muscles in my cheeks hurt.

"You're doing amazing. It's like you've ridden for years."

"Yeah?"

"Totally. You'll get your endorsement no sweat."

"Can I ask a favor? I know you've done a lot for me already..."

He nodded.

"Can you give me Aaron's address?"

Jason's expression fell as he thought about

what I was asking. He knew his friend better than anyone, and he knew as well as I did that showing up out of the blue might really blow up in my face.

"Please? I can handle it. No matter what I find."

He let out a deep sigh and nodded. "Yeah. I'll give it to you."

He programmed the address into my iPhone and briefly explained how to get there. Aaron lived closer to the country than the city, which completely took me by surprise. I'd just imagined that he was someone who wanted to be near the action.

"Thanks, Jason," I said, giving him a quick kiss on the cheek. "I'll run the goodies upstairs and be on my way. Wish me luck."

"You aren't going to need any luck. You've got this. And Brandy?"

"Yeah?"

"Don't give up on him. Even if you find him doing something stupid."

My stomach knotted as I took the tray of brownies and cookies upstairs. Jason knew something and he just wasn't telling me. That much I knew.

I passed the driver's test with flying colors and was so unbelievably proud of myself that I did the unthinkable and texted my mom the good news. It only took a few seconds for an immediate response back from her, asking if I'd lost my mind. I quickly texted Ayden and Mason, and they didn't believe me so I sent them a selfie of me on my brand new bike holding the endorsement. Mason wanted me to come over and show off my new bike, and Ayden wondered what drug I was on. This new me felt absolutely amazing, and if nothing else, I wanted to thank the person who helped me get over my fears. The entire time I was testing, I imagined being on the Jet Ski with Aaron. The way he went into the turns, and the first feelings of absolute freedom that crept in.

I texted Aaron and hoped for a response but expected none.

My surprise is ready. I hope you are.

And none was what I got.

I tucked my phone in my leather jacket and got ready for my ride, trying to push the sadness away. I needed to focus on my drive to his house. I only had one stretch of highway and the rest was back roads. The weather was beautiful with the sun blazing in the sea of blue, and I couldn't ask for better driving conditions. As I started the engine and slowly took off from the parking lot, my mind began to wander to different scenarios. Would I show up and some woman would be rolling out of bed behind him or would I get there and find an empty house because he was shacking up somewhere else? And why were all of my scenarios involving other women? I needed to keep myself sane and upright. Those were the two rules I had for myself. And to get home before dark.

The scenery passed in a blur as I kept my speed between forty and fifty before pulling onto the freeway. My pulse began racing as I merged in between two very aggressive drivers, but I didn't panic and continued at freeway speeds that were surprisingly pretty fun and made the bike feel even steadier. I passed several exits, feeling more and more confident and finally hit the exit I needed. My heart started beating faster, and I realized it had absolutely nothing to do with riding this bike, and everything to do with possibly seeing Aaron.

A grocery store sat sprawling at the main intersection where I took a right and began my drive through the rolling hills and country roads where meadows were more frequent than houses. With every mile the anticipation of seeing him was increasing and so was the doubt.

I turned onto the rural road where his driveway was supposed to jet off from. As I drove along, only slowing to read addresses off of mailboxes, the nervousness turned to eagerness. Spotting the correct address painted in silver on a black mailbox, I turned down the private, gravel road and began second-guessing my bright idea of showing up to his house unannounced.

I was a planner. Always had been. But here I was about to drop in on Aaron and hope for the best and with his track record his best day might be the worst day in my life. I drove the bike slowly along the gravel drive, avoiding potholes and large rocks the best I could while trying to focus on where I was driving.

Once his home came into view, I knew I couldn't back out now. The house sitting at the back of the property took me aback. It wasn't sprawling and extravagant like I imagined. It was understated and cozy with a small stoop tucked into its modern architecture. Slowing my speed even more, I drew in a breath as I spotted a small workshop with the garage door rolled up. My heart was hammering as I noticed some sort of light glowing from inside the garage. Was he in there?

I glanced at the house and saw a shadow move across the upstairs window and my insides fell. Aaron couldn't be in two places at once. I spotted a large Cedar tree and parked underneath it, turning off my engine. I let out a deep breath and unfastened my helmet, only to be met with crashing music coming from the garage. He had to be in there. So who was wandering around inside his house? Maybe I imagined it. Hopefully, I imagined it.

I hung my helmet on the handlebars, shook out my hair, and slowly walked toward the garage opening. As I got closer, I realized the glowing light was actually sparks flittering across the cement floor, and I slowed my stride unsure of what I might see. Maybe it wasn't Aaron inside the garage after all.

The music was blaring, and it wasn't at all what I expected. Old Rage Against the Machine transitioned to Prodigy. This wasn't the Aaron I knew, but it certainly was one that I wanted to get to know. As I turned the bend, I saw a large metal sculpture in the corner of the garage and Aaron standing on a ladder, welding along the top of the piece that looked to be the star of the show. Even though the arc was nowhere in sight, I shielded my eyes as I attempted to take in the scene unfolding in front of me. The sculpture was absolutely magnificent. The curls of the metal sprung from a cavity that looked like it represented a mouth opening wide, displaying an intricate pattern of wood and metal pieces intertwined throughout.

Aaron continued to attach pieces, switching between a small soldering gun and a welder, stopping only momentarily to stare at his creation. His head would bob to the beat of the music every so often, and I felt completely conflicted as I stood and watched something so personal unfold in front of me. But I couldn't move. I didn't want to move. Watching him stand on the ladder, his lean body stretching as he attached pieces of metal was beyond exhilarating. It fed something inside me and told me to fight for whatever it was I thought this could be.

The way his body moved and worked with the piece was like artwork in itself. The dull block helmet covered his head, and he was wearing leathers for protection, but the outline of his body was still quite visible and very enticing. Every movement became sensual as he worked the metal harder and harder, forcing it to mold into the vision he saw.

Before I realized what was happening, I saw him turn off the torch and remove his helmet as he climbed off the ladder. He shook his head and ran his fingers through his dark hair quickly, and my heart was in my throat, waiting for him to turn around and see me.

Part of me wanted to hide, like I was witnessing something intimate and personal that I shouldn't have interrupted, but the other half of me wanted to run over to him and strip him bare.

He tossed his helmet into a box and began unbuckling the leather protective gear he was wearing, but he was still facing the back of the workspace. I was paralyzed as I debated whether to walk inside or maybe call out to him. As he bent over and released the last clip, he threw the leathers into a bucket and spun around, staring at the ground, concentrating. Reaching for a bottle of beer, he took a swig and still hadn't spotted me.

Unable to hold anything in any longer, I took a step forward and dug my hands into my jeans. "It's breathtaking."

Aaron's head jerked up, startled, as his eyes locked on mine. "What are you doing here?" his voice was void of any infliction.

Maybe, this was a mistake.

"I texted before I drove out here. You know

that surprise I mentioned a couple weeks ago before everything—"

He didn't say anything and I cringed internally. I really might be too late.

"Well, I completed it and wanted to share it with you," I finished.

He stood in place, his body frozen, and I wondered if it had to do with whoever I might have seen inside the house.

"You haven't answered any of my messages," I continued. "And I got concerned."

"How'd you get my address? Did you Google it too?" He looked at me, but his eyes were in a far-off place.

I shook my head. "I got it from Jason when he dropped off part of my surprise." Even though I was unraveling inside, I tried to keep my demeanor upbeat.

Aaron's eyes flicked to mine and then to the door and my stomach fell.

"I didn't know you were an artist..."

"There's a lot of things you don't know about me, but then you haven't really tried to get to know me at all," his voice was low. "That's one of the many realizations I've had over the last couple of weeks."

I took another step forward.

"I know, and I actually came here to apologize. What you said about treating you or us like a game is...was accurate. I was so focused on the big picture of what it would look like to others that I didn't stop to pay any attention to how either of us felt. I made myself completely ignore what I was feeling inside when I was around you because I was afraid of where that might lead."

Aaron crossed his arms and glanced toward the house, confirming my suspicions that there really was someone inside. "I've got a lot work I want to get finished."

I felt a lump in the back of my throat and gulped it down. One crying session was plenty for the day, and I absolutely wasn't going to lose it in front of Aaron. Jason was bad enough.

"I'm sorry for dropping in. I just wanted to apologize for my behavior, and I couldn't seem to reach you any other way. But Aaron, I truly am sorry. You were right. I was acting immature and apparently the several year age gap between us is more apparent in..." my voice trailed off when I saw a glimmer of a smile appear on his lips. "What?"

"You're really hard to stay mad at," he grumbled, taking off his leather gloves. He still wouldn't meet my gaze.

"Maybe that's a good thing," I offered, taking another step forward.

He let out a deep sigh and ran his hands over his head as he brought his gaze up to meet mine. His shirt tugged up, and I blushed as he caught me taking in his hard stomach.

"So I've got a lot on my schedule today. What was it that you wanted to show me?" he asked.

My pulse started racing as his eyes burned into me. The desire to be held in his arms was making it almost impossible to think straight. The attraction hadn't diminished since we'd been apart. It had only grown, and I was certain he felt it too. Something like this couldn't be one sided, right? I nodded and slid my hand into my back pocket and pulled out my wallet as I walked toward him.

"What are you doing?" he asked.

"You won't be able to see it from far away." I pulled my license, which displayed the temporary endorsement, out of the leather wallet and handed it to him.

His brows pulled together in confusion as I handed him the plastic, and he looked it over, his eyes stumbling to the sticker.

"You got a motorcycle endorsement? You didn't have to do that for me."

Not quite the reaction I was looking for.

"I didn't. I did it for me, but you were the one who opened up that door for me. You taught me not to be so scared of things I haven't even tried so I wanted to share my surprise with you first. Wanna see the second half?"

And that's when I heard the voice. A woman calling out for Aaron from the main house, and my heart and mind sunk to a place I didn't even know existed.

CHAPTER NINETEEN

It felt like my world was closing in and to top it off, the embarrassment that was spreading through me made me nauseous and completely light-headed. How could I have been so stupid and presumptuous to think that he cared enough about me to actually wait for me to figure things out? I began taking steps back, avoiding his eyes and waving my hands at him to stay put. I didn't want any sympathy hugs or anything of the sort.

"I've gotta get going. It's going to be dark soon," I said, stumbling backwards.

Feeling the hardness of the concrete as my body slammed into it only added to the humiliation I felt.

"Aaron?" I heard the voice call again.

Damn it!

Scrambling back on my feet, I quickly looked at him and muttered a quick apology for intruding and took off for my bike. I threw my leg over the seat and started the engine. I knew I was in no way prepared to ride right now, but if I could just get down the driveway and off his property, I could pull over and shed the tears that were threatening to escape.

"Hey, Brandy," Aaron shouted, jogging after me. He was holding something in his hand, waving it at me.

Shit! My license.

I pulled my helmet over my head and secured it quickly, refusing to look toward the house. I didn't want to know what she looked like or, worse yet, who she was.

"It's not what you think," Aaron said, his voice competing against the roar of the engine.

I reached for my license, but his fingers gripped it tightly.

"Please just let me leave," I said, my voice trembling.

"Brandy, please. It's not like that..."

"It is like that and it always will be with you. That's the problem. It has nothing to do with your sister. I've been afraid of you, and I finally just admitted it to myself." And the tears began their parade down my cheeks.

Aaron turned away from me and yelled across the driveway," Not now. I'll come in later. You've done enough for the day."

My fingers were trembling as I attempted to rub the tears off my skin so my strap wouldn't get completely soggy, but I couldn't keep up with the amount of leakage.

"Please just give me my license. I should've taken the hint when you didn't reply back to me. Please. Or I'll just take off without it."

Aaron's gaze softened as his eyes connected with mine. He stuffed the license in his pocket as I drew in a wobbly breath, and he brought his fingers to the straps of my helmet. The roughness of his fingers as they glided across my chin still sent my heart racing, and I cursed the weakness of my body as he unstrapped my helmet.

"You aren't going anywhere. I accept your apology. But you shouldn't be the one apologizing," his words lingered in the air, only to be wiped away by the wandering female behind him. "And I have one for you too."

An apology isn't gonna cut it, buddy.

I spotted the female figure standing on the porch, but I couldn't make out her features from this distance.

"Age hasn't had anything to do with it. I've been just as immature as you." His lips turned up slightly in the corner. "I got all of your messages. Every single one of them, and I played them over and over again."

I brought my attention back to Aaron, my gaze falling to his mouth.

"I was away on business and when I got home you started sending your messages."

"Where did you go?"

"China. But that's beside the point," he said smiling, touching his thumb to my chin. "I've been miserable thinking that I may have lost you

195

because I didn't want to be patient. But patience isn't one of my strong suits."

A strong breeze began to pick up and I shivered. "Now let's get you inside and get you warmed up. It's getting close to nightfall, and I don't think you should be driving back tonight."

"I can't. Not with her in there," I whispered.

A smile touched his eyes as he grinned. "Let me help you off and try this again. We can start in the garage and go from there. I'd love to show you what I do in my off-hours. How I blow off steam."

I nodded slowly and saw the shadow of a woman go back into the house.

"Here, give me your hand." He helped me off my bike, even though I needed none before, and I let him wrap his arms around me. If nothing else, I would enjoy the next few moments before my fantasy blew to the wind.

"So how long have you done this?" I asked, pointing to the garage.

"Jason and I both learned about metal fabrication in the military and I don't know... it just unleashed something in me. I knew I wouldn't be able to make money with it. Or at least not the kind of money I wanted to make, but I've never stopped doing it."

We walked back into the garage, and I felt my tearstained cheeks tighten as I attempted to smile. It was impossible not to be impressed with the large sculpture in front of me. The emotions that were captured in the twists and twirls of the metal and protrusions of wood stirred something deep inside.

"It feels angry," I whispered. "The mouth gaping like that. I feel like it's trying to swallow my soul."

"Then it's doing its job," he said, releasing me from his embrace.

I blinked up at him just as he touched the button on the wall, closing the large wooden doors behind us with a thud.

"I don't know if that should make me scared or not..."

"This is what I felt with the thought of losing you; my nightmares coming back to greet me, swallow me whole. All of the loneliness and feelings of inadequacy I've felt over the years went away when I was around you. The moment I left your condo, they all came flooding back. Instead of going to the places I normally sought out...I began on this." He looked up at the sculpture and then over at me. There was a heat in his eyes, and my heart began pounding as I let the words sink in.

"I'm sorry for saying the things I said outside," I murmured.

"Don't be. I understand why you said them. I haven't had the greatest track record, and I'm thrilled the Seattle magazines have been there to capture it." He pressed his lips together and held out his arms. "Can we start over?"

I nodded, gravitating to the one place I felt the most secure—in his arms.

"What about the woman inside?" I whispered, knowing I needed to face things head on from now on. No more blaming situations or people who were not truly the cause of my discomfort.

His body began to shudder in laughter as his hands ran through my hair.

"That's my housekeeper, Norma."

I started laughing as relief filled my entire body at once. "Seriously?"

I felt him nod as he held me tighter. He smelled of cologne, soap, and fire as I buried my head deeper into his embrace.

"But I should tell you something."

Of course. Nothing was ever simple with him.

"She's Nina's mother. That's how I met Nina, and I'm guessing that's why Norma felt she needed to interrupt us."

I let out a sigh and had the urge to break into hysterical laughter but resisted.

"You do know what that means, right?" I asked.

"Time to get a new housekeeper?"

"Mm-hmm."

"Anything for you," he breathed into my hair.

"Promise?" I asked, tipping my head up.

"Promise," he whispered, running his fingers through my hair.

The sound of an engine starting outside, followed by a car driving away made me giggle nervously.

"We're alone?" I asked, locking my eyes on his.

"Seems that way."

I pushed away gently and let my fingers softly travel down his shirt; the feel of the soft fabric against my fingertips as I watched his reaction made me almost insane. Reaching the hem, I pulled it over his head and dropped the shirt on the concrete floor. Aaron smiled as he watched my eyes wander along the beautiful lines of his body. His olive skin glistened in the soft light of the garage, and I knew what I needed to do. What I needed to feel.

He raised his hands, cupping my face, and I backed away.

"I'm in charge. This time. It's all me," I whispered, removing his hands from my face and holding them in mine as I slammed him against the wall. His breathing caught as I pressed my body against his, holding his hands at arm's length. The warmth of his skin soaked through my shirt, creating an almost frenzied state within me. I slowly began kissing his throat, feeling the coarseness of his whiskers against my lips as I scattered my kisses down to his chest.

Tasting the saltiness of his skin, I lowered my mouth along his abdomen, making his body shudder in anticipation. Running my tongue lightly along his flesh created a tingling sensation throughout my body as I took control of this man who had never let go before.

I gradually moved my hands away from his but still kept his body pinned to the wall.

"You're dangerous," he murmured, his breathing ragged as I teased him with my tongue.

"Without a doubt. But so are you," I whispered, bringing my mouth back to his. The taste of his lips, a mixture of alcohol and sweetness, was addicting. My mind imagined his tongue circling along my body, the metal of the stud creating an ecstasy I hadn't yet shared with him.

His fingers wrapped through my hair as he gently pulled my head away. My hands rested on his jeans as my mind toyed with the idea of unfastening them. I traced my fingers along the waistband, feeling the dips and peaks of his contours as I pictured him on top of me.

He kissed my neck softly as his hands unwrapped from my hair. A moan escaped my lips, and that was when he scooped me into his arms, kissing the length of my exposed skin. He elbowed the button behind him, and the garage doors opened up exposing the night sky.

"Not out here," he whispered, carrying me into his home.

I nuzzled my head into the crook of his neck as I heard the click of the front door. He pushed open the door and carried me up the stairs. My stomach tightened with every step closer to the bedroom as I realized my fantasy was about to become my reality.

He laid me gently on his bed. The only light trickling in from the hall bounced off his beautiful torso. The definition of his chest and abdomen were like a work of art, and I motioned to let me touch him.

A smirk spread across his face as he towered over me. "Now it's my turn."

He placed his arms on each side of my body as I squirmed to be in contact with him. But he wouldn't allow it as he anchored my hands above my head with one of his. I felt a slight tickle as his other hand slowly began to lift my t-shirt up my abdomen. His fingers stopping every so often to trace along my skin, sending shivers up my body. I felt his hot breath against my belly as his tongue ran along my curves, leaving me begging for more.

"You're so beautiful," he whispered, hovering above me now as he pulled my shirt over my head. His eyes held a deep hunger and my body responded quickly. My hands finally free, I moved my fingers across his chest feeling the hardness of his muscles that were etched just underneath his skin.

"So are you," I murmured.

"Do you know how many nights I dreamed about being with you, like this?" he asked as his fingers traced the contours of my body, sending a wave of heat and yearning through me.

Not as many as me!

His touch was driving me absolutely insane and my body was aching for his. He placed soft kisses from my collarbone down to my chest, circling each breast before continuing slowly down to my belly. His fingers unbuttoned my jeans and he pulled them off in one swift motion.

I began to wriggle as he stared down at me in only my bra and panties.

"I need you," I whispered, feeling the burning sensation run through my body the longer his eyes held mine. "I've been dreaming about this moment for months."

He licked his lips and smiled and that's all it

took. I sat up and pulled him down on top of me. The weight of his body falling onto mine was crushing as my body called to his. I kissed him, gently sucking on his lower lip as his fingers traveled down my sides.

I slid my hands between our bodies and unbuttoned his jeans. "I want to see all of you."

He smiled and stood up from the bed, and I followed. He was absolutely gorgeous, and I couldn't wait to see the rest.

"I'm all yours," he said gruffly, his eyes burning with desire.

His words melted me in place as I ran my fingers up his chest. He worked the clasp of my bra undone, and it slid to the floor. The feeling of his bare chest against mine made me almost burst with anticipation. His fingers slowly slipped between my lace thong and my skin as he slowly slid them down my legs. He pressed his left leg in between my legs, and I flushed with a mix of embarrassment and excitement as the roughness of the jeans pressed against me.

"You feel so good," he whispered, gliding his fingers slowly up my thigh.

"Touch me," I moaned.

"Where?"

"Everywhere."

He brushed his hands over my belly, and my tummy clenched as his fingers went lower. His breath hitched as his eyes focused on me, and I couldn't help but reach out and tug his jeans down, leaving him completely bare. I wanted him to use my body however he needed.

I looked up into his eyes and felt the desire running between us. It had always been there. He put his hands around my hips and slowly knelt down in front of me.

Please do!

I felt his lips slowly nipping along my bikini line, his fingers softly circling along my back as his mouth began to open and close around me in a fluid, controlled motion. The chill of his tongue ring shot through me as his tongue continued to swirl in a meticulous manner. My hands fell to his shoulders, and my body shuddered with every flick and movement he made.

"Aaron," I moaned.

His mouth circled up my belly as he slowly stood back up, leaving a trail of warmth along my body.

"Make love to me, Aaron," I whispered.

He moved me slowly to the bed where I felt him slide me up the mattress. I heard the rattle of the drawer as he rustled around and sheathed himself.

Slowly placing kisses along my breasts I felt as he pushed into me, and my world filled with complete ecstasy. The intensity we shared as our bodies came together, tangled in each other's arms, left me with a tingling, buzzing mess of emotions as I dreamed about the possibilities of what tomorrow would bring.

Chapter TWENTY

I was a nervous wreck. My blissful night had been blown to pieces when I arrived at my door this morning. Half delirious from my Aaron escapade, I nearly tripped over a vase that contained a dozen dead roses. I placed a call to Aaron who quickly came over and stayed with me while I grabbed as much of my stuff as possible. Until things got figured out, I had no intention of staying alone at the condo. And to top it off, today was my parents' anniversary party.

My mom and dad had absolutely no idea what my brothers and I were up to, and it was my brothers who were charged with getting my parents to the reception hall. Now I looked around the mostly empty space and started to mildly panic. There was a lot of decorating to do and a short amount of time. Aaron hadn't left my side since the night at his house, and I loved every minute of it.

"Where do you want me to put the arrangements, babe?" he asked, carrying in the first of twelve large floral arrangements. He seemed distracted, but I couldn't really put my finger on it and didn't want to get caught up in my delirious suspicions on such a special night.

"On the tables I haven't set up," I said flatly.

He put the arrangement that was filled with roses, hydrangeas and lilies onto the floor and glanced over at me, looking absolutely adorable. "Where are the tables at? I can get them set up."

"They're behind that door over there," I said, pointing to the far corner of the room. "I think they're just folded in half. They're the circular ones, not the rectangle ones."

Aaron took off on a mission, and I ran the other way toward the kitchen. Carla found out about my parents' party and not only recommended her favorite caterer but insisted on that as an anniversary present. I didn't feel comfortable with such a huge gift, but Aaron told me I had no choice. That was how Carla worked. The way the day was going, however, I was thrilled that I had the extra help. I smelled the delicious garlic and lemon scents drifting from the commercial kitchen and peered into the space, watching everyone slicing, dicing, and stirring.

"I've got the food tables set up. Are these the tablecloths I should put on them?"

The head caterer looked over and nodded.

"We'll take care of that, Brandy."

"That's okay. I need to keep myself busy," I said, grabbing the pile of linens.

"The silver ones are for the banquet tables and the black ones are for the guest tables."

"Gotcha." By the time I got back into the space, Aaron was already wheeling out the last of the round tables and was unfolding it and popping it into place.

"You're beyond amazing," I said, handing him the black pile of tablecloths.

"I'm trying," he said, grinning.

I glanced at the clock on the wall and saw that we only had about forty-five minutes before the guests would start arriving and another fifteen minutes before my parents would arrive.

I quickly placed the tablecloths on the banquet tables and grabbed the bag of rose petals that was leaning against the wall. I opened them up and began spreading them along the tables and turned to see Aaron running the tablecloths out on each dinner table.

He was dressed in one of my favorite suits, and I couldn't stop imagining what it would be like to strip it off him later tonight. How horrible was that? I was preparing for my parents' anniversary party, daydreaming about getting it on with my boyfriend. I completely blamed Aaron.

My phone buzzed, and it was Mason letting me know that everything was going as planned. I quickly texted back that things were looking good here too, and we should be set for the first guests to arrive.

I wandered over to Aaron who was now placing the arrangements in the middle of each table and sliding his hand over each tablecloth smoothing the wrinkles off of it.

"Signs of the military?" I asked.

He started laughing and nodded. "Guess so."

A few of the servers began wheeling out the china and silverware and waved.

"It looks great," one of the servers said. "We've got it handled from here. Go grab a drink from the bartender and relax."

"That sounds like a great idea," Aaron said, sliding his arm around my waist.

"Yeah. It does."

We walked over to where the bartender was placing the selection of beer and wine along the bar.

"Nice selection," Aaron said.

"Carla helped in that department as well. I still can't believe she did all of this. My parents would die if they knew someone did that for them that wasn't related."

"Carla did it for me because of you," he said softly. "She knows how much you mean to me and..." his voice trailed off, as he slid his hand into mine. I felt the blush color my cheeks as the bartender continued to set out glasses, acting as if he wasn't overhearing our conversation.

The bartender turned around, sensing our conversation had come to an end. "What can I grab for you two?"

"I'll take a Jack and Coke. And she'll take a

Royal Washington Apple."

"Are you trying to get me drunk before the party even starts?" I asked, teasing.

"Actually just before I tell you what we found about the messages you've been receiving."

"Seriously?" I asked. "You've got to tell me tonight?"

"Yeah. Unfortunately, what we found out needs to be taken care of immediately. Jason worked his magic. No matter how much the guy says he's not into tech stuff, he sure knows his shit." Aaron grabbed both of our drinks, and we found a couple of comfortable looking seats along the far wall.

I took a seat and sipped my drink, feeling the sting as it touched my lips.

"It's definitely that Jeff guy from your class," he began.

"Are you sure?" I asked. "That's so weird."

"We're positive. Once we figured out who it was, Jason was able to tap into his wireless and connect into his systems. He's been stalking you for quite a while."

"Isn't that illegal?" I asked, staring at Aaron.

"Yeah, stalking is quite illegal."

"No. I mean tapping into his system."

"We have ways around it. Besides, there's enough evidence that was collected to be able to turn over to the police just from the texts he sent you."

"Why?"

"The Jeff guy's nuts. Jason's got a few buddies at the police station he's talking to before he gets here tonight, but you are in definite need of a restraining order and security."

"You've got to be kidding me."

"I wish I were." Aaron pulled out his iPhone and tapped on a link. "Check this out."

I looked down at the screen and watched a video game reenactment that looked all too familiar. It was the inside of my apartment.

My marrow chilled as I continued to watch. A haunting overture played in the background, as I followed the intruder through my apartment, first looking into Gabby's bedroom, going through her things, and then leaning over her while she slept. My heart was pounding so hard and I could barely focus. Granted these were cartoonish images of us, but the point was clear. My palms moistened as I continued to watch where the gamer went next. Into my bedroom. I watched as the items on my dresser were moved and then placed back in their proper places before he spun around to look over at me sleeping in my bed, with the exact replica of my comforter and pillows carefully placed around me.

"He's been inside our house..." I felt numb as my body filled with terror.

"I wanted to wait until after the party, but I figured I couldn't do that. Not if we needed to be on alert with this large group of people just milling around."

I took another sip of my drink and looked back at Aaron.

"He might have stolen some items from my

bedroom."

"What do you mean?" his voice sharp.

"This sounds absolutely bizarre and—"

"What?"

"A while back I noticed some of my underwear went away." I blushed at the thought, at the ridiculousness of what I was saying.

"You're just telling me this now?"

"I figured they got lost with laundry or who knows. It's like the case of the missing socks. I can't go more than a month with perfect matches. There's always a mate missing— always. This is so mortifying." I sighed.

"It's worse than that. It's downright dangerous," he muttered, texting Jason the latest revelation.

"And there was some jewelry..."

"Seriously?"

I nodded.

"You need to be more vigilant, babe. Is there anything else?"

I shook my head. His eyes said everything and more as he looked at me.

"You're not staying at your place any longer. And neither is Gabby."

"Does she know?"

Aaron nodded. "Yeah, Jason just showed her on the way to the police station."

"There's got to be a connection to him that I just can't remember," I muttered, wondering what in the world introduced him into my life.

"Probably. We'll see what Jason says when he gets here tonight."

I nodded, my heart pounding as I slammed the rest of my drink and nervously awaited for the first of many guests to arrive.

The music was pounding and my parents were having the time of their lives. Seeing that kind of love gave me hope. Watching them hold each other as they swayed to the music and the possibilities for decades more together helped to take my mind off of everything that was starting to fall into place about the madman.

Gabby looked pretty petrified, but it was hard for her to hide her emotions. She was as transparent as cellophane as Jason danced with her in the crowd.

I hadn't told anyone about what we had found out, not even my brothers. It could wait until tomorrow, and in the meantime, Aaron was handling everything anyway. There was no reason to spoil my parents' special night.

I turned to face Aaron who had been watching the crowd the entire evening, looking for anything suspicious. I knew both Jason and Aaron were armed and the thought terrified me... not so much that they were armed, but that I was somehow in a position where the people around me felt they needed to protect me.

"I can't believe I didn't recognize him with the brown hair," I said to Aaron, shaking my head. "Derek Bourot gave me the creeps years ago, but

I never suspected he'd be capable of this type of hatred or—"

"Obsession."

The word sent a spike of fear down my spine. The police were granted a search warrant immediately and found far more than the video game reenactment at his apartment. Unfortunately, Derek was nowhere to be found. It turned out he started going by his middle name several years ago about the same time he started watching me, following me. He was the son of one of the law center's clients. His mother was sentenced to time in prison for several petty crimes that added up to a stiffer sentence. I remember feeling so bad when I learned about their story. His father was killed in an accident, and his mother spun out of control shortly thereafter, falling into drugs and alcohol. The law center was her last hope, and my mom and her team were able to get her sentence greatly reduced, but she died in prison. What we've been able to scrape together in a few short hours was that he wanted my family to pay for his mom's death, and I became his target.

"We need to tell my mom as soon as possible, but I don't want them to find out tonight. We've got a hotel suite reserved for them and—"

"I've got a security detail already in place. They won't know a thing is wrong, but they'll be protected. I promise."

"Thank you," I said, pressing my head against his chest. "Who would have known I was such a catch?"

He started laughing and hugged me tighter. "I already knew that. I didn't need some psycho to point it out."

"What does that say about you though?"

He placed a soft kiss on top of my head, holding me closely, and I'd never felt safer than I did in his arms.

CHAPTER TWENTY-ONE

"They got him," Aaron announced, hugging me tightly as he turned off his phone.

"Are you serious?" I asked.

"Yep. They picked him up loitering around your condo."

The moment I heard those words, it was like a big weight had been lifted off my shoulders, and I no longer felt frightened to show up to my classes tonight.

"Just in time," I mumbled, picking up my scattered schoolbooks. "I guess it's okay to go back to my condo..."

His eyes caught mine, and I saw a flicker of disappointment—exactly how I felt. I was sitting at the granite breakfast bar and looked around, surprised at how comfortable I'd made myself in the short time I'd been here. My favorite mugs were lined up on the back counter, and I'd even brought over some of my teas.

Aaron walked over to me and placed his hands gently on my shoulders, massaging the tension away. "I'm going to miss you."

"Me too. Is that bizarre in such a short amount of time?" I asked, feeling his thumbs pressing into my muscles in a rhythmic motion.

"If you count all the back and forth, it's been months..."

I laughed, "True."

I glanced at the clock and knew I needed to take off to get to my first class on time. I had taken today off from work to regroup with everything going on. Now that Gabby bought the bakery and left her dad's company, I magically got transferred to the legal department. I knew Aaron had something to do with it, and I was extremely grateful. The official transfer would take place next week and I couldn't wait.

No more cheese for me!

"I should probably give myself an hour to make it into the city since rush hour's about to start."

"You want me to drive you?" His hands fell away from my shoulders, and I immediately missed his touch.

"You'd do that?" I raised a brow.

"Yeah. Why not?" He smiled, but his gaze dropped to the counter.

"You still worried?"

"I shouldn't be. I know he's sitting in a cell, but it just feels like he's still out there."

"Tell me about it." I touched his chin softly

and smiled. "But I'm perfectly fine. I should be home a little after ten tonight."

"Home, huh?"

I blushed and placed a kiss on his cheek.

"Make sure your weekend is completely clear."

"Why's that?" I slid off the stool.

"Think of it as a new chapter and a way to celebrate."

"I think I can handle that," I said, grabbing my bag that held my books and laptop.

He walked me to the door, and I turned around and gave him one more kiss, this one longer. All it did was make me want to forget about class and stay in for the night, again.

"The new housekeeper is stopping by at eight o'clock tonight to go over everything so don't get paranoid if you see a car in the driveway."

I rolled my eyes. "I trust you."

He held up his hands and shrugged. "I'm just saying."

I started laughing as I walked out the door. I was still a little bit paranoid, truth be told. But I was happy to see that the only new photos of Aaron surfacing on the Society pages were of him firmly gripping me. *Thank you, Google!*

I made it to my car and watched him slowly shut the door and knew we'd never be the same again. We were no longer going to take ten steps back to get five steps forward. I needed him and he needed me, but that was okay. As I pulled out of the driveway, I thought back to my parents and wondered if Aaron and I could ever be lucky enough to have such a wonderful life like theirs. It was so cute when I dropped them off at the airport for their trip to Ireland. With all the hugging and kissing and excitement they radiated, it was as if they were fifteen. I only hoped to be that lucky to live a long, love-filled life.

I wondered what kind of things Aaron had planned for the weekend and got excited just thinking about it. I pulled my car onto the highway and began the stop and go, hoping I'd make it to class on time.

※

What I didn't realize as I sat here in the final class of the night was just how fast news traveled. Apparently Jeff or Derek or whatever he wanted to call himself had made quite the impression with several of the other students. Teresa was filling me in during break that the police had questioned many of the students who were connected with our study group.

"Can you believe he'd go that nuts over everything?" Teresa asked, her eyes wide. "Kind of makes me think twice about becoming an attorney."

I glanced away as a few students were milling around and looking over at us. The classroom was small, but it had stadium seating. I was sitting in the back row at the top, nursing my cup of coffee.

"It shouldn't. There are always crazies out there that are unpredictable no matter what we decide to do for a living."

She shuddered and shook her head. "I always knew I never wanted to be a prosecutor or a defense attorney, but I'm telling you it makes me worry. I'm actually thinking of changing my concentration to legal writing."

"There's nothing wrong with that..." I took another sip of the lukewarm liquid. "But make sure you're making the switch for the right reason. Not just because you're scared."

"So do you still want to work in your mom's law center when you pass the bar?"

I nodded. "Yeah. It's something I've always wanted to do, and I'm not going to let someone else shatter my dreams. Besides, he had a rough life, and while I don't understand why he chose my family as a target, I understand the pain that drove him. At least partially."

"You're a better person than I," she hummed.

I laughed, "Hardly."

The Professor came walking back to the classroom and a few straggling students followed right behind and took their seats. I only had another hour and then I could go home and see Aaron and begin to pack up my things to go back to my condo tomorrow. The last thought made my heart sink a little, but it was for the best. I didn't want to scare him away just yet. It was going to be odd since Gabby basically lived at Jason's house now so she could be closer to the bakery. When she told me that was the reason, it was all I could do to not start laughing in her face.

But anyway, things had been absolutely amazing between Aaron and me since we put the focus on us and eliminated all the second-guessing and worries about others. I was completely ready to hand over my letter to Gabby this weekend. Although, it might have to wait a day or two depending on when we got back from whatever fabulous thing Aaron had planned. I felt confident that she would understand and would be totally supportive. Plus, Jason said he started sharing hints about the possibility, but he wasn't sure she was picking up on any of them, which didn't surprise me.

"Miss Rhodes, you look like you might be able to answer my question," the Professor began.

Oh, no! What was her question?

Teresa scribbled something quickly on a sheet of paper as I sat up straighter in my chair.

The elements required to prove Breach of Contract are examples of what type of law?

Thank God for Teresa! Suddenly feeling as if I were on Jeopardy I answered, "Procedural Law, Professor Loretal."

"Nice work, Miss Rhodes." She shot her stare at another unsuspecting victim and continued her lecture, and I flashed Teresa a grateful smile.

The rest of the class went without any other hiccups, and I was beyond thrilled to pull into

Aaron's driveway, and I was starving, ten o'clock at night or not.

I walked up the steps to Aaron's home and opened the door, my mind wandering briefly to the first time I was brought inside. My heart fluttered at the memories flashing through my mind. I dropped my bag on the slate floor of the large entry and sighed. I really could get used to this place. The walls were a nice taupe and there was a large mirror in front of me, which I happened to glance at. I saw my reflection and started laughing. I looked horrible. If the circles under my eyes were any darker I'd put zombies to shame.

"How was your first night?" Aaron asked, walking into the foyer.

He looked sensational when I left, but even better when I returned. He had traded out his suit for jeans and a sweater, and his hair was still wet from a shower.

"Grueling, but I loved every minute of it."

He wrapped his arms around my waist and lifted me up, scattering a few kisses down my neck. "I made you dinner in case you were hungry." He put me back down on the ground and stood back, grinning. "I had no idea how much I'd miss you. I—"

He stopped himself, and his gaze shifted nervously as he bit his lip.

Oh, please, dear Lord. Was he going to say those three words?

"You what?" I asked, hoping that he'd finish what he started.

"I. Am. Starving."

I looked at him and smiled. "I. Am. Too! Very. Much. So! I enjoy these three word sentences."

He laughed once he realized I wasn't really planning on letting him off the hook. Seeing the beautiful candles that he'd lit on the kitchen table, along with a vase full of autumn-colored flowers and place settings for two filled me up with feelings of affection and adoration. Why rush something that can always wait until tomorrow? We already knew that those three words were on the tips of our tongues. I looked over at Aaron, his eyes searching mine for a reaction, and knew I already loved him and had for some time.

"This is so sweet of you. I—" Smiling, I bit my lip and chuckled.

"You what?" he asked, his brow arched.

"I. Am. Starving."

"It might be a little light if you're starving," he said, walking into the kitchen.

He opened the door of the large stainless fridge and grabbed a metal bowl and a jar of dressing.

"What's in there?" I asked, sliding out the chair.

"Salad with pepper steak strips," he grinned, placing the bowl on the dining table.

"I'm impressed."

I glanced up at Aaron and his eyes locked on mine. "I really like having you here."

"I love being here...especially if I could look forward to this kind of treatment," I laughed as he plated the salad.

"I thought making you a latte every morning would make you want to stay."

"I don't want to wear out my welcome," I teased.

"You never would."

I shrugged, unsure of where this was heading.

"I mean it. Waking up with you next to me is—"

My body stilled as I saw the sincerity pouring out of him, but he stopped himself.

"I'm probably freaking you out."

"Not at all, but things have been so amazing I don't want to rush things or scare you off," I said, smiling.

"Nothing you could do would scare me off." He grabbed my hand and the familiar tingle of electricity shot through me.

"You say that now, but I'm sure I could prove otherwise." I glanced over to the family room where the fireplace was flickering its brilliant orange and yellows in the darkened room. The room was beckoning, and the soft music he had playing made me think of things other than finishing this meal.

"You know what I'm looking forward to?" I asked.

"What?"

"Spending the holidays with you."

He stiffened slightly and his gaze shifted to his plate.

"What?" I asked.

"I've never actually celebrated the holidays

since I was back at home."

"You haven't celebrated Thanksgiving or Christmas for ten years?" I asked.

"Only if you count felt trees and takeout as celebrating," he laughed.

"Well, I'm going to change that this year," I said, spiking a few of the lettuce leaves on my fork as he did the same.

Something changed slightly in his expression as he looked at me, and I wondered what about the holidays bothered him but not wanting to ruin the streak we were having, I let my question slide.

"I'm going to get everything packed up tonight, and I'll just crash at my condo for the rest of the week."

He nodded and stood up, grabbing our plates and the salad bowl. "Want any dessert?"

I smiled and hopped up. "Definitely. I'll grab the whipped cream and meet you upstairs."

His laughter filled the air as he shook his head. "You never cease to amaze me."

"And I hope I never do."

CHAPTER TWENTY-TWO

It was Saturday morning, and I had spent the night at my condo. I woke up to the awful sound of my alarm clock but bolted right up once I remembered that Aaron was on his way over to pick me up. I glanced out the window and was thrilled with the beautiful clear skies. It wasn't every day that the sun shined in Washington during the fall.

Since Aaron wouldn't tell me much about what was happening this weekend, I packed two pairs of jeans, two sweaters, one dress, plus a pair of slacks.

I turned on the faucet and ran warm bathwater into the tub. I poured two capfuls of the bubble bath that Aaron had bought me under the running water and turned toward the mirror. Stripping off my clothes, I turned around in the mirror and noticed that between Gabby's baking and spending so much time at Aaron's house, I seemed to have filled out a tiny bit, but my clothes still fit so I wasn't going to worry about it. I quickly brushed my teeth and let out a sigh as I thought about how much my life had changed and how little of it I had shared with my best friend. But this weekend that was going to change. Okay, maybe Monday that would change. Right now, I just wanted to focus on my weekend with Aaron and much needed relaxation. Between working full time and attending law school, I was exhausted—thrilled! But exhausted.

As I slid into the warm bath water, the bubbles spread out in several directions, and I scooped as many back toward my body as I could capture and sunk in deeper as the warmth hit my bones. The scent Aaron picked out was so light and florally, and I absolutely loved it. Every day when I was staying with him, he somehow managed to spoil me with some little something. I took a deep breath and slithered under the water, feeling my hair float around me. Running my fingers through my hair, I daydreamed about Aaron being in here with me, and just when I was running out of air, I slowly emerged to the chill of the room.

I heard footsteps coming down the hall and my heart began pounding.

"You here?" Aaron's voice called into my bedroom.

"In here."

"I should probably give your key back now that—" Aaron stuck his head around the corner and his expression completely lit up. "Or not."

"I thought I was meeting you downstairs."

"I wanted to surprise you with some fresh baked croissants," he said, holding up a brown sack. "From Gabby's Goodies."

"Sounds delicious."

"Not as delicious as you."

I rolled my eyes but reveled in the compliment.

"I also wanted to grab the keys to your bike."

"They're hanging by the door. Is it coming with us?"

He nodded and I glanced at the towel next to him.

"Mind bringing me that?"

Aaron tossed the bag on the counter and grabbed the grey towel, holding it open for me. "I'll just help you out."

"I'm sure you will."

His eyes locked on mine as I stood up from the water. The way his eyes fell along my body made me feel like the most beautiful woman in the world. His lip curled up slightly as I stepped out of the water onto the bathmat and reached for the towel, which he immediately dropped to the floor.

"I don't think you'll be needing that," he murmured, pulling me into him.

"You're going to get completely soaked," I objected.

"Fine with me," he said, as his fingers drifted along the droplets on my arm.

I looked up into his brown eyes and saw the

familiar glow of desire. Knowing that I could unleash that in him made me feel amazing, powerful. I draped my arms across his shoulders, leaning into him as his mouth slowly parted. His kiss was slow, deliberate, and delicious as my fingers tangled through his hair. His hands glided along my body, stopping at my hips as I felt his firmness pressed up against my bare body.

I delighted in what the morning held for me, but he drew away from me and grinned as I let out a moan. Thinking I held any power over this man was laughable as I stood here feeling absolutely powerless in his embrace.

His grin turned to a smirk, and he slowly dropped his hands from my hips. "There'll be more of that later, but I should go load up your bike on the trailer."

He grabbed the towel off the floor and threw it gently at me, but I was too much of a mess to even attempt a catch.

"You play so dirty," I laughed, picking up the terrycloth from the floor.

"Can't let you see all my tricks, babe."

<hr />

We had been driving for two hours, and I had completely sprawled out in his car with several half-read magazines and my Kindle Fire recharging.

"Almost there," he said, glancing at me.

"Really?" I looked out the window and only

saw the long country road that we'd already been on for half the journey.

"It's my other place," he said, putting the blinker on.

The Mercedes SUV bounced along the gravel driveway as the trailer hopped along behind.

"What's wrong with the one you have?" I asked, teasing as I peeked out searching for our destination. "I thought it was pretty spectacular."

Through the trees ahead I spotted a river, and as we rounded the corner, I saw a beautiful log cabin with a red roof.

"Is that the place?" I asked "It's huge."

"It is," he confirmed.

I glanced at the cabin and saw two other structures; one that looked like a garage and another that was possibly a shop. "Do you work out here too?"

He nodded and slowed our vehicle as the garage door opened and we drove right in. This garage was absolutely huge. I looked behind me and saw the entire trailer come in with us.

"What made you want a place like this?" I asked, glancing at him as he turned off the ignition.

"It's just nice not to be bothered. The reception is kind of spotty out here. Once the snows come it's a pretty great place to be." He pointed to the other side of the garage where a couple of machines were covered.

"What are those?" I asked.

"Snowmobiles."

"Really? I can't believe I'm saying this, but I

can't wait to try those out."

"I think the first season, you should just wrap yourself around me. You know, learn the ropes."

I laughed and opened the car door, nearly falling out with the magazines. I stretched and continued looking around the garage. "So that other building is the shop where you work on your sculptures?"

He nodded as he lifted our bags out of the SUV and dropped them on the ground.

"Do you have any completed pieces in there?"

His mouth turned up into an almost sheepish grin. Something that was completely unlike Aaron. "One."

"Yeah?"

He nodded. "I actually built it when—"

"Enough said." I grimaced not wanting to go back to that time. It seemed so long ago. "Let's untie these bad boys and get riding before the good weather goes away. I haven't been riding since that whole stalker thing happened. I'd like to get at least one more ride in before the weather turns horrible."

"You've read my mind. Let's go get changed."

I picked up my bag but Aaron quickly grabbed it from me. "I got it."

As we walked toward the log cabin, I took in the beautiful surroundings. It was so quiet and peaceful. I heard a constant whooshing in the distance, which was no doubt the rushing river and imagined spending the holidays here one day. Most of the leaves had already fallen off the maple and oak trees, creating a golden brown and red carpet leading to his front porch. I glanced at Aaron and held in a chuckle. If he knew the thoughts that were running through my head, I was sure he'd take off running for the mountains, never to return.

He unlocked the front door and pushed it open, displaying a huge great room with a cobblestone fireplace in the corner. Rustic furniture complimented the brown leather sectional that was situated in front of the television.

"Looks like you could hold your own weekend party here," I said, laughing.

"I'm too picky. You're the only person who's ever been here, besides Jason."

His admission made my heart flutter as I wondered if the possibilities of a happily ever after with him were tangible.

In the far corner, a large kitchen was home to a beautiful granite island and breakfast bar. All of the wired lights were a mix of antler replicas and wrought iron. It felt completely cozy. Next to the kitchen I saw an opening to a long hallway.

"The bedrooms are down here," he said, as I followed him down the corridor.

"How many are there?" I asked.

"Four," he said, pointing at the first.

"Wow. That's quite a few for a single man's cabin."

He shrugged. "Well, not really with a family and all someday."

Did he just say that?

Please let me be part of that equation. Please.

"I never figured you for that type, Mr. Sullivan."

His eyes caught mine as he flipped on the light to the first guest bedroom.

"Once the right person falls into your life, anything is possible."

A surge of excitement ran through me as he softly pressed his lips to mine in a quick kiss before beginning the tour again. He showed me the remaining two bedrooms before we entered the master at the end of the hall.

It was mammoth and had its own cobblestone fireplace, along with a jetted tub in the actual bedroom that overlooked the river outside. I guess we wouldn't have to go far from the bed that way.

Nice...

"This is a special place," I whispered, taking in the pine furniture and pair of green chaise lounges. I ran my finger along the fabric of one of the chaises and glanced at him. "So no one but Jason has been up here?"

I found it hard to believe, especially as I stood here staring at two chairs strategically placed in front of the window that overlooked the woods.

"I actually just got those delivered." His brow arched. "I only recently started thinking in pairs." He smirked as he watched my expression change from caution to satisfaction.

"Is that so?"

"The right person will do that..."

"Even to a guy like you?"

"Especially to a guy like me."

I smiled knowing that what we had was special, unexplainable, and worth all of the heartache and confusion that led us to this place. I unzipped my bag and grabbed my protective gear for riding. I was already wearing jeans and a Henley so I wasn't planning on changing.

"You ready to get back on?" he asked, slipping on his leather-riding jacket.

"I am. I'm really excited. It's like my secret addiction. Besides you, that is."

Aaron's laughter filled the space as I zipped up my jacket and pulled my hair into a ponytail.

"I'd almost bet money that you like the whole secrecy thing." His brow raised slightly as he waited for my objection.

"Is that so?" I asked.

Truthfully, I kind of wondered the same thing. I'd had ample opportunities where I could have told Gabby about her brother and me; yet I chose not to and put it all in a letter, which still sat in my jewelry box. "Well, it is kind of fun this way."

"I knew it," he said, shaking his head. He grabbed my hand and pulled me back through the hallway. "We better enjoy it while we can."

He locked up the house, and we walked over to the garage where he unhooked his bike and mine, rolling each off the trailer.

I buckled my helmet into place and swung my leg over the bike.

"You look insanely hot on that thing," he said, laughing. He slid his phone out of his pocket and took a picture.

"You're not so bad yourself," I laughed, as he

sat on his bike.

We both started our engines, and he motioned for me to follow him down the gravel drive. My pulse quickened as I rode over the divots and lumps in the gravel, taking extra caution with each increase in miles-per-hour.

Grateful to hit the end of the gravel drive, he waved me over and I pulled up next to him.

"You go in front of me. I want you to feel comfortable with the speed and don't want you to be pressured to go faster than you want. If you just stay to the left, we'll wind up back here eventually," he yelled from under his helmet.

I nodded and took off slow and steady, hearing the wind whip against my helmet. I began giving it more throttle and felt my pulse quicken at the thought of feeding my bike more speed. It was a beautiful day for a ride, and I couldn't imagine being anywhere else with anyone else in the world. I followed the road as it bent slightly to the left and dipped down. I squeezed on my brakes gently but the bike didn't slow down very much, if at all.

That was odd. Trying not to panic, I began to steady my bike, hoping the speed would let up.

Just as I was about to try my brakes again, a deer hopped onto the road in front of me. My fingers instantly gripped the brakes, but my bike didn't stop.

I cautiously turned my wheel slowly and to the right, barely avoiding the deer as it hopped away. I let out the breath I'd been holding in just as I heard Aaron holler from behind, right when my front wheel hit a large rock.

My entire life went into slow motion as the bike stopped instantly, throwing me off the front of it. I felt like I was flying through the air, weightless, as I prepared myself to land hard. I could take it. I grew up with two brothers, after all. I heard Aaron yelling as his bike stopped behind me. I even saw him pulling off his helmet just as my body slid across the gravel on the side of the road.

I lifted my head up to unfasten my helmet. Or I thought I did. But my helmet was still on. Aaron was already on the phone to 911. I heard the operator on speakerphone as he came running over to me. I smiled at him as the warm pool of liquid continued trickling down my back.

"Baby, stay with me. You're going to be okay. I'm here. Everything's going to be fine...." His eyes were full of tears as he took instruction from the operator.

"You're gorgeous. Absolutely gorgeous. Do you know that?" I muttered, but he didn't hear me. I tried again, louder this time, but he paid no attention. I felt another trickle of warmth running down my forehead. It tickled. I tried to wipe it away, but my arms wouldn't move.

This was ridiculous. What was happening?

"I don't think she's conscious. She's breathing, but it's shallow. Her eyes are closed," he spoke into the phone.

"No, they're not. My eyes are wide open, and I'm looking right at you, dork. Granted there's a pink hue to everything, but I guarantee you I'm staring right at you."

"No, I haven't moved her. I'm afraid to. There are tree limbs all around her. I'm afraid she might have landed on one."

"Well, now you're just being dramatic. I'm fine, silly. A little stiff...but fine. Maybe thirsty?"

The sirens in the distance became a distraction as I glanced over at my bike. It was tipped on its side, but it didn't look that badly damaged. Thank God. I wanted to finish our ride today.

"Baby, please hold on," Aaron cried next to my helmet. His fingers touched the tiny bit of exposed skin on my forehead. He removed his bloodstained hands and wrapped them around my gloved hand. "Please, baby. I love you. Open your eyes."

His cries startled me as I watched him kneeling next to me, praying.

"I love you too," I whispered, but he still paid no attention.

"Just open your damn eyes. Show me you're here. Show me you're listening," he murmured, his hand ran along my arm, finally gripping my fingers.

My eyes are open.

Was I the only one awake right now? Was this just some bad nightmare?

The wails of the sirens startled me. They were almost here. I turned my head trying to reach for Aaron. I needed to be held. The temperature was dropping and everything seemed to be getting dark very quickly.

"They're almost here, my angel. They're almost here. Hold on for me. I promise, I'll never leave your side. Just hold on for me. I love you so much."

Please just hold me.

Two ambulances pulled in right behind Aaron. The doors flew open and before I realized what they were doing, Aaron was being dragged away.

"Sir. Sir. You have to calm down. We can't help her unless we can get to her."

"He was helping me," I shouted.

Everyone ignored me.

I watched Aaron fighting the medics, trying to get a glimpse of me, and I didn't understand why. I was fine. I had my helmet on, my protective gear.

A strange hand ran down my back, near the pool of liquid that was now turning chilly. I liked it better when it was warm.

"Please don't," I said, turning to the man next to me. He was dressed in a white short-sleeve shirt and navy pants. He looked official, but he, too, ignored me.

"Her pulse is dropping," a female hollered right next to me.

"Jesus! Where'd you come from?" I glanced at her severe demeanor and wanted to reprimand her for looking so stern.

Aaron was being led back to the ambulance. He was holding his head in his hands.

"We've got a limb through the lower lumbar region of her..."

"Wait. Are you sure?" I asked.

Again no one responded.

"She's gonna need a medevac."

I heard Aaron frantically calling someone. Why wasn't he over here with me?

Please come back.

"ETA on chopper?"

"Fifteen," the female said.

"I don't know that we have that kind of time," the man muttered, who was pulling apart a paper bag.

"Heeelllo. I'm right here. I can hear you. And that type of negative thinking will never get a person very far."

"The limb is half embedded in the subcutaneous..."

They're moving me.

Please don't move me.

Please don't move me.

Oh my God.

The pain.

Please stop.

It hurts so badly.

Two very strong hands gripped under my armpits as someone else grabbed my ankles, scaring me as I looked around. They quickly moved me to some sort of hard platform and kept me on my side as they continued pressing against my lower back. I spotted Aaron coming toward me as two medics attempted to keep him away. He pushed through them and knelt right in front of me.

"Can she hear me?" he whispered.

"We don't know. It's always better to proceed

as if she can," the female said.

"For the last time, I can hear all of you. I can see you too."

I felt a quick pinch on the top of my hand and glanced at the IV that the medics ran.

I hate needles.

"Baby, I'm going to be with you the entire time. I called Gabby and Jason. They're on their way to the hospital. Your brothers too."

"Hospital? I'm not at a hospital. I'm in the middle of nowhere."

"I'll be in the chopper with you," Aaron's voice trembled as I looked into his eyes. "Just give me some sign you hear me, baby. I love you so much."

"Her blood oxygen level is dropping. We need to intubate," the female's voice was almost a whisper. Everything was almost a whisper. What was happening now?

They turned me on my back and a drilling pain shot through my spine. Two hands pressed on my forehead, bringing it toward them as my mouth automatically opened. I felt several fingers unstrap my helmet and switch it for something that they fastened around my neck.

"What's that?" Aaron asked.

"It makes her muscles relax so she doesn't fight it."

Fight what?

A man was unwrapping some sort of tube, a long tube. Aaron didn't take his eyes off the clear plastic and once they opened my mouth, positioning my head so my throat would open up wide, I understood why.

I tried to swallow as they snaked the tube down the back of my throat, but I couldn't. Every second that ticked by felt like an hour as my chest deflated more and more with every shove of the tube deep inside my body. Why couldn't I breathe? What had they done to me?

Just when I felt I was running out of air, they attached some sort of blue pump to the end of the tube and began squeezing it.

"Aaah. I'm alive. I can breathe again."

Aaron turned away, wiping away the tears, and all I wanted to do was hug him and tell him everything was going to be all right.

"She's fully restrained," the woman whispered.

"No, I'm not," I said, whipping my head to face her.

A thumping began pounding through the air, and I saw Aaron put his hand up to shield the increased wind. I craned my neck to see what was going on and that's when I noticed a helicopter on the road. *Now that's something you don't see every day.*

I felt whatever platform I was on swiftly being moved toward the chopper. I also noticed that the woman was NOT keeping very good track of squeezing that little pump. I needed air. I needed air more than I needed this damn helicopter.

Give this pump to someone who can count, please!

Three men dressed in red jumpsuits were now hovering over me. One of them finally taking over the blue pump from the woman, giving it a quick squeeze.

Thank God!

"Sir, unless you're family, we can't allow you on the chopper."

"I'm her fiancé," Aaron said, his tone convincing. He pressed his fingers along my cheek and bowed down to my ear. "That's right, baby. You're mine forever."

I heard the slamming of the chopper door and felt Aaron's touch fall away. I looked around, but everything was dark...everything was quiet. There was no chopper. There was no Aaron. I no longer knew where I was, but for the first time since the accident I was afraid.

I was alone.

CHAPTER TWENTY-THREE

"I can't imagine he's the type to stay by someone's side when..." my voice trailed off as I looked at all the tubes leading from my body to make my point.

My head was pounding, but that was nothing compared to the rawness in my throat. It felt like it was sliced open and with every swallow, a pound of salt was ground freshly into the wound. The nurse had assured me that was normal after the ventilator tube was removed and that it would feel better soon.

Yeah, right!

Obviously our ideas of 'soon' differed greatly.

"Well, you better start believing it because Aaron hasn't left your side from the moment the accident happened," Lily explained, touching my hand. Her touch didn't actually feel nice. My nerves were on end, and the slightest contact seemed to set off a nerve-ending revolution. But I didn't want to hurt her feelings so I stayed still, focusing on the flowers surrounding me.

"I made him leave to clean up...about ten minutes before you woke up. We have all tried to get him to sleep at home, but he wouldn't hear of it. See that chair? That's where he's spent his days and nights. He's probably been away from you two hours at the most and that counts this little excursion."

I squinted at the object in the far corner that Lily was pointing at, but I couldn't bring it into focus. It just looked like a light beige blob. Everything looked like a beige blob. And I felt like a beige blob.

"Really?" I whispered, hoping that would lessen the pain in my throat.

It didn't.

"Yeah, really."

"Where are my parents? Are they back from Ireland yet? They didn't cut their trip short, did they?" I asked. "My brothers, do they know?"

Thoughts were flooding through my mind at a rapid pace, and I felt like I couldn't sort them quick enough.

"They're on their way," she assured me. "They've been here with Aaron most of the time, but they'd at least go home to sleep and eat. Your parents were here this morning but left to take care of their dogs."

"How dare they," I teased, trying to lighten the mood.

I looked around the hospital room and even

though everything was fuzzy, I could tell that I had been here too long. There were flower arrangements on every surface that was available, along with balloons, stuffed animals, and chocolates. I also spotted three of my favorite blankets, two folded over the chair and one across my hospital bed. I shifted in the bed and my body ached all over. Maybe more meds would be on the way.

"What day is it? Shouldn't you be at work? I need to get back to class."

"It's Sunday."

I caught tears surfacing in her eyes as she squeezed my hand once more.

"I'm going to be okay," I told her.

Truthfully, I had no idea what okay was at this point. I had several specialists in and out of my room, and I didn't think they expected me to be able to hear or comprehend anything. But I did. And it scared me. Their idea of okay and mine were vastly different. I was reminded of this as I attempted to move my legs.

"How's our girl?" Gabby asked, entering the room. I moved my head slowly, in an effort to make the pounding lessen. Jason was with her, holding her hand and guiding her through the maze of tables and chairs.

"Spectacular. I can't wait to try to ride again," I said, smiling.

Jason laughed. "I'm not sure Aaron would love to hear that."

I noticed Gabby taking in the extent of everything from tubes to cords to casts before

Jason's hand moved to the small of her back, interrupting her trance.

"I was so worried," Gabby said, releasing Jason's hand. She placed both hands on the railing and leaned over to kiss my cheek.

"I thought Aaron would be here," Jason said, looking around the room.

"I forced him to go home and change," Lily explained.

An overwhelming feeling of anxiousness began to waft through my body. The room felt extremely stuffy, and the tubes and cords anchoring me to this bed made me want to scream. Was this normal?

"Brandy, what's wrong?" Gabby asked, brushing my hair from my face.

"Would one of you guys take a pic of me on your phone and let me see it?" I asked.

"I don't think that's a good idea," Lily answered, shaking her head.

"It probably is a horrible idea," I confirmed, "but I still want it done. I want to see what you all are seeing."

Lily and Gabby traded glances before I saw Gabby slowly remove her cell from her purse. She let out a deep sigh and went to the foot of the bed, trying to hold the phone just right.

"I'm not tall enough," she said, glancing at Jason.

His jaw tightened as he looked at her and then looked at me. He was over six feet tall so I knew he'd be able to get the angle just right.

"Please, Jason? It was me who helped you in

the beginning with Gabby. Remember the bikini accident? You wouldn't have gotten such a wonderful image to forever hold dear without me." I turned my head to Lily who was chuckling lightly. "Don't you think he owes me?"

Lily nodded in agreement and Jason's face lit up.

"You're right. Definitely right," he said, grabbing the phone from Gabby.

He took a quick pic and showed it to Lily and Gabby, who nodded slowly.

"Let me have it," I said, moving my arm to clasp onto the phone. A slight tug of the IV in my hand reminded me not to move too quickly.

"Here you go, hun," Jason said, smiling.

Grabbing the phone, my curiosity turned to shock. I imagined what I might have looked like lying here, but it never looked this bad. My left cheek was scraped, but a scab had lightly formed across the new flesh, and my other cheek was bruised, but it wasn't purple. It had now made it to the yellow-green phase. Instead of seeing all of my hair, I saw some of my hair and a white strip of gauze wrapped around my head. I spotted a few of the strays that Gabby had pushed away. Seeing this puzzled me considering I didn't feel any pressure around my head. It didn't feel like there was a wrap there at all. My head pounded, but that was an internal sensation not an external one. There was also a tube leading to a bag, which no doubt explained why I didn't have to get up to use the restroom since I awoke.

Lovely!

I looked tiny in the narrow, white hospital bed for the most part, but the large bulge around my waist was a dead giveaway. The blanket from home was laid on top of my feet, but that didn't account for the large mound.

I gave Gabby her phone back and lifted my blanket to see the light blue hospital gown stopping at the knees where the cast on my right leg was visible.

"This sucks," I sighed, dropping the blanket back down.

Lily and Gabby laughed nervously as Jason shook his head.

"We're just so happy you're here," Gabby whispered. "You gave us all a scare."

A melodic female voice cut through the air as Jason stepped to the side, letting her through. "How are you feeling, sweetie? Nice to have you up and in the world."

I watched the nurse make her way to my bed with a solution bag and syringe in hand. Her red hair was pulled back into a severe ponytail, and her yellow scrubs had blue stars all over them. She was about forty and her features were soft, kind. But my heart rate quickened as I watched her begin to reach for one of the tubes to inject the syringe solution into.

"Please. I don't want to go back to sleep. Please, let me stay up," I pleaded.

"Oh, sweetie, I think the worst is over. This," she said, showing me the syringe, "is only to keep the inflammation and swelling down. And this is how you get your nutrients." She dangled the bag in front of me.

"Sorry," I muttered.

"You have nothing to be sorry for, my dear." She removed the cap off the syringe and pushed the liquid into the opening. "I should have explained as I went. Now, how are you feeling?"

"Groggy. My head's pounding and my nerves feel like they're ready to explode. But other than that I'm doing really well. Will I get to leave soon?" I asked, smiling.

The nurse shook her head and laughed. "I have to leave that up to the doctors, but I will tell you that since we removed you from the ventilator, your progress has been amazing. We just need to keep the swelling going in the right direction," she told me as if I was supposed to know what she was referring to. And the frustrating part was that I think I was supposed to know. I felt like someone mentioned it, but I just couldn't pull it out of my memory.

"Groggy. My head's pounding and my nerves feel like they're ready to explode. But other than that I'm doing really well. Will I get to leave soon?"

The nurse stiffened, and I caught the glances between Lily and Gabby. What was the matter? Did I say something wrong? The nurse quickly wrote something in my chart, and my anxiety level was about through the roof. I obviously did something worrisome, and no one felt the need to tell me what it was.

"How's my baby girl?" I heard my mother's voice ring out into the room, and I had never been more relieved to have an interruption.

"Mama," I squealed, seeing my dad right on her heels as they came to my bed.

She pressed her palm gently to my forehead just like when I was a little girl.

"Daddy," I whispered, as he stood right next to my mom, watching me.

I watched the nurse exit the room, and Gabby and everyone began to follow her out into the hallway to give us time.

"You, baby girl, sound absolutely beautiful, your voice is a miracle to hear," my father replied.

"How are you feeling? Is there anything I can get you?" my mom asked, her eyes cascading down the hospital bed as if she was checking everything out.

"My throat hurts. And my head. And I'd like to get the hell out of here."

"That's my girl," my dad said, taking a step back. "Where's that fella of yours who wouldn't take a hike?" A smile spread across his lips as he watched my expression change to embarrassment.

It was always so weird to me that no matter how old I got my dad could always make me feel like a little girl. It was puzzling.

"You mean the one she brought to our anniversary party?" my mom teased, gently reminding him that I'm not twelve any longer.

"Lily said she forced him to go home and change," I said, feeling a warmth spread through me. Maybe what Aaron and I had really was special. Maybe it would last.

"Can you tell me what all is going on?" I asked, searching my mom for answers. "I know doctors have been in and out making notes and doing a mess of things, but I can't remember everything I heard."

"Your body's been through a lot," my mom said, pulling up a chair. "If you hadn't been wearing a helmet..."

"What your mom's trying to say is that you've been through a lot, but the prospect is looking really good. You're looking really good."

"I appreciate the vagueness, but I'd really prefer particulars. I'm not guaranteeing I'll remember them anyway. I'm guessing I broke my leg."

"Yeah, that you did. And your pelvis." My mom sighed and shook her head. "Your body was thrown off the bike resulting in a head injury that produced extensive brain swelling. You also had internal bleeding that wasn't easy to track down. You had a puncture wound in your back that was very difficult to treat. It's healing now..."

My mom looked over at my dad as tears filled his eyes. "They had to relieve the swelling of the brain so...."

A horrified gasp escaped my lips as I tried to formulate everything that they were telling me.

"The bandage?" I raised my hand to my head. "That's why it's..."

"You were kept in an induced coma until enough swelling had gone down in your brain," my father replied.

I'd had enough for the moment. I didn't want to hear anything else. I slowly craned my neck to see through the opened curtains. The gray sky reminded me it was fall.

"My school?" I asked, swallowing hard. Law school was never known for being kind to individuals. In fact, anything that could help weed out the weak in their mind was doing them a favor. I was sure this qualified. "Have I missed much?"

My lids were getting tired, and my eyes were going out of focus even more than before as I thought about the heaviness of everything.

"We'll let Aaron tell you about that," my mom smiled. "You look like you need some rest. We're going to go down to the coffee shop. We'll be back."

I smiled and slowly nodded, my eyes closing, just as I saw an image come into my room. But it was too late. Sleep found me first.

CHAPTER TWENTY-FOUR

I awoke suddenly, feeling like the room was spinning, and I was about to lose it. My pulse was off the charts as I tried to calm my breathing. My head no longer pounded, but I was completely disoriented as I looked around the space trying to place exactly where I was. I looked down, recognizing the familiar tubes and hospital blanket and immediately began to calm.

I was safe.

It was dark outside and the lights had been dimmed, and from what I could see, the room was empty. I slowly reached my hand up and felt the gauze still wrapped around my head and let out a deep sigh.

"Baby, you're up," Aaron's voice was soft, tender as he quickly rose from the seat he'd called home since I'd been admitted. "You're drenched."

He gently touched my arm, his fingertips running down the length of it. His touch felt nice, and I was relieved that no pain followed.

"I think I had a bad dream."

"Let me get you a cool washcloth," he replied.

I watched him wander off to the restroom and heard the water running for a few seconds before he returned with a bright white washcloth. He began patting it along my forehead and down my cheeks to my neck.

"Does that feel better?" he asked.

"It feels nice," I whispered, looking at this shell of a man. He was still the most attractive man I'd ever laid my eyes upon, but this accident had definitely taken its toll. He had circles under his eyes, and it looked as if he'd lost a few pounds.

"I thought I lost you, baby," he whispered, tracing the pad of his finger along my jawline. "I didn't know what I was going to do..."

The desperation in his voice sent chills through me.

"I'll never let another minute pass by without telling you how I really feel. I love you, Brandy. I've loved you since the moment you told me to grow a pair."

I started giggling and looked up into his eyes. "I love you too."

"I have never been so scared in my life," he said. "And I've seen some shit."

I smiled and nodded slowly. "I kept telling you I'd be fine. Do you remember?"

His brows pulled together. "When?"

"After I fell off the bike, I told you I loved you and that I could see you even though you kept telling me to open my eyes. I told that to everyone who was there, but you all ignored me. I remember getting so frustrated because everyone acted as if I wasn't aware and talking."

Aaron moved the washcloth along my collarbone. "Honey, you were struck unconscious instantly. You weren't awake."

"I heard you tell me you loved me. I heard you asking me to hold on. I saw everything that was going on. There was a medic dressed in a white button-down and blue pants who initially treated me, and then there was a really scary-looking female tending to me."

Aaron pressed his lips together for a moment and nodded. "That's all true. I should have given you more credit. It makes me feel better knowing you heard me talking to you. And you're right about the female. She was quite something."

"I'm still surprised you stuck around," I whispered, barely teasing as I looked up at him.

His eyes focused on mine as a smile spread across his lips. "What faith you have in me."

"I'm just familiar with your track record," I muttered, reaching up to grab his hand. "I'm a realist."

I attempted to squeeze his hand, but my fingers felt so weak in his that I let him hold my hand instead.

"You had me so worried," he repeated, leaning over me. "But it's nice to have your feistiness return with a vengeance."

Even in my sorry state, I couldn't help but feel the charge from him. How I had resisted him for so long I'd never understand because right now all I could think about was being in his arms.

"I'm so sorry. I don't know what happened. I tried to brake, but—"

"Don't apologize," he scolded me, his eyes tender as he took me in. "I never should have let you ride in front..."

"Since when have I ever asked for permission?"

"True," he acknowledged, spotting something out in the hall. "Looks like you've advanced to solid foods."

"Great. I can't even imagine how horrible the food is going to be." I glanced at the male aide who was bringing in a brown tray with a covered plate and chocolate milk. I tried not to laugh as he placed it on the adjustable table.

"Good evening," the aide said. "The menu for breakfast and lunch is under the plate. You can fill those out to order. Tonight's meal was chosen for you since it's your first one."

"Yay me. What delicious meal do I get to look forward to?" I laughed.

The aide smiled and turned around, leaving the room. "I'll let you be the lucky one to find out."

Aaron lifted the metal lid off the plate and tried to hide his grimace. "Looks good. It looks to be a fish of some sort... with a sauce," he said, smiling and grabbing a fork. He pushed the prongs into the meat, and scooped up a pale glop and took a bite. "Okay, maybe not fish but chicken. Definitely chicken. And it's not bad."

"That's just what all you visitors say to make us poor souls feel better," I joked.

He grabbed the milk and quickly guzzled it down. "I'm sorry. I can't do that to you. I'll go check with the nurses to see if they have a sandwich you can have instead. They usually keep a stash in the fridge."

"That bad, huh?"

"Worse, actually." He half smiled and headed for the nurse's station.

I watched him walk up to the counter, waving and smiling at the three women who were stationed there. He had the same effect on them that he had on just about all women. There was no doubt. He would get the sandwich, and I was quite relieved not to have to eat the slop on the plate in front of me.

He returned victorious, sandwich in hand. He slowly unwrapped it and placed it on a napkin and slid the table toward me.

"I need to tell you something," Aaron said.

"Uh-oh."

"I'm taking it no one has talked to you about what caused the accident?"

I shook my head.

"Your brake fluid had been drained."

"Derek err I mean Jeff?" My stomach rolled with nausea. "How could that be? He was in custody."

"He did it before they picked him up."

"When he was at my condo," I mumbled.

"Yeah. He confessed."

"Why would he do that? Confess, I mean."

"I don't know. I'm guessing a plea bargain. Your mom knows the details. Instead of attempted murder, attempted manslaughter, maybe?"

I nodded completely disinterested in the sandwich sitting in front of me.

"I can't believe it, but I do. When I tried using the brakes absolutely nothing happened and then when the deer jumped out..." I shivered as the memories flashed through my mind.

"I didn't want to upset you, but I knew you'd want to know."

"You know me well."

"They also found more code. The finale of sorts."

"What do you mean?"

"Well, you know how he recreated the images of him lurking in your apartment?"

I nodded.

"The rest of the game was a chase," Aaron's eyes filled with anger.

A surge of fear pulsed through my veins.

"And you were the target."

"So I guess I should be thankful that this is all that happened to me?"

"He's a sick son-of-a-bitch."

"I'm just glad they have him in custody. I don't know what I'd do if he was still on the loose."

"I don't either."

An uncomfortable silence filled the air between us as I thought about everything. I took a bite of the sandwich and Aaron was right. It wasn't that bad.

"I've arranged for you to come back to my home once you're released," he began.

"What?"

"I've got the best physical therapists lined up and two nurses who'll help you with anything that's needed. Your parents aren't very happy about it. But I'm telling you right now, Brandy, I'm not having it any other way. They can't take care of you like I can. They work during the day. This is the best option and it's all squared away. I had a special bed delivered for the guestroom that's on the main floor so stairs won't be a problem and—"

"I can't accept that." I shook my head. I was torn between being horrified and being flattered. My parents were proud people, and I can't imagine them taking a liking to anyone offering help. I let out a deep breath and closed my eyes.

"It's not up for negotiation. It's the best thing for your recovery."

"Well, then, I guess a thank you is in order," I said, smiling. "Has anyone heard how much longer I might be here? When I get to go home?"

"I've been talking with the doctors and because of the facilities I have arranged for you, I think we're looking at really soon." His eyes sparkled. "You know, I wanted to ask you to move in, but this wasn't exactly what I was thinking."

I started laughing and noticed my appetite crept back up.

"Everything you're doing for me means so much. You don't have to do this. You're not responsible."

"It has nothing to do with that. I'm doing this because I love you and I want the best for you. You mean everything to me."

"For you to say that when I look the way I do…"

"You look gorgeous."

"You're not as hot of a liar as you think you are. Gabby showed me a picture of myself earlier today."

"What'd she do that for?" he asked, his voice angry.

"Don't be mad at her. I begged her and you know how I can be."

Aaron calmed down and laughed. "True. You actually look a lot better than when you were first in here."

"You don't have to be that honest."

He leaned over and gently kissed my cheek. "I'll get it right one of these days."

CHAPTER TWENTY-FIVE

Voices arguing woke me up, and I slowly raised my head and opened my eyes to see my brothers and mom on one side of my bed and Aaron on the other.

"She's not going to your house," Mason said. "She's going to mine."

"Don't be ridiculous, Mason. I'm her mother. She's staying with me," my mother said, her eyes flashed to Aaron's. "But she's definitely not staying with you. You're the one who got her into this mess. It's your fault she's in here."

I glanced at Aaron, his jaw tightened. I could tell he was holding everything in.

"Excuse me," I said, clearing my throat. "This isn't exactly how I dreamed of waking up."

"I'm sorry, dear," my mom said, grabbing my hand. "We've got good news for you."

"What?"

"You get to go home today," Ayden piped up.

"That hinges on where she'll be recovering," Aaron said, his voice steady and determined.

"Listen, man. You got her into this whole mess. She never would have touched a bike if it hadn't been for you. Just because you're feeling guilty doesn't mean you should swoop in like a hero now."

"Hold up," I said, raising my free hand. "Don't I have a say in this?"

My mom nodded at me and said, "Of course."

She wasn't going to like what I had to say.

Oh well!

"I want to stay at Aaron's," I began. My brothers began to shift uncomfortably, and their gazes dropped to the mattress. It was moments like these where it was quite apparent just how deep the twin thread ran. "You both work nonstop, and mom, you're probably worse than both of them combined. Get your emotions out of the mix and really think about it. Do you have the time and resources to make sure I can wheel myself into the restroom or get taken to therapy appointments?"

None of them said anything.

"I didn't think so." I reached for Aaron's hand. "And blaming anyone for this accident besides the person who drained my brake fluid is absolutely asinine. If it wasn't the bike the guy tampered with, I'm sure it would have been my car or who knows what. If it hadn't been for Aaron, I probably wouldn't be alive. I decided to ride bikes because I wanted to. End of story. And if I ever hear anything like this coming out of any of your mouths again, I won't be speaking to you. Ever."

My mom's eyes filled with tears and she glanced at Aaron. "I'm sorry. I don't know what's come over me. You didn't deserve that. We know it's not your fault and I'm just awful for suggesting it."

"We've all been under stress. Forget about it," Aaron said. "If you guys would like to see the arrangements I have at the house for Brandy before she goes home, you're more than welcome. She'll be on the main floor. The physical therapists will be coming to the house, and I have two nurses who will help with anything else that may arise during her recovery."

My dad wandered in with a cup of coffee and smiled. "Ready to come home?"

We all started laughing, and my dad just looked around the room, completely confused.

"Here we go again," Mason whispered.

"Dad, I'm actually going to begin my recovery at Aaron's house."

"Over my—"

"Don't bother," I interrupted. "It's already been decided."

He let out a sigh and shook his head. "Story of my life."

"So can someone tell me about law school? Is there a way I can catch up for the semester?"

Aaron traded looks with my mother and drew in a breath.

"You won't be going back this semester," Aaron said softly.

"You've got to be kidding me. I have waited my entire life. I can guarantee you that I can get caught up."

"I know, babe. I tried to explain that to them, but they wouldn't reconsider."

Blood was rushing to my head. I was furious. As hard as I'd worked all through undergrad and then studying for the LSATs and finally getting admitted into law school, this was how I was going to be rewarded?

Aaron let out a deep breath. "I was able to get them to defer your enrollment until next semester. They wanted to drop you from the roll all together." He shifted uncomfortably as my brothers stared at him. "I had to remind them who helped fund the new law library that opened last year and then they were more willing to listen."

Typical of schools.

"So they're letting me back in?" I asked, my voice hoarse.

He nodded and my eyes filled with tears.

"Thank you, Aaron."

"We'll leave you two alone," my mom said, rounding up the males in my family.

I watched my family walk out of the hospital room and looked back at Aaron. "You've done so much for me. I don't understand—"

"I love you, Brandy. I haven't done anything that you wouldn't have done." He leaned over and gave me a soft, tender kiss.

"Honestly, I think this actually works better. You can focus on rehab and by the time the next semester rolls around you'll be better than new."

I laughed and glanced at the clock. It was ten minutes to nine o'clock.

"So when do I get some crutches to hobble out of here?"

His eyes focused on mine as he squeezed my hand. "They'll be wheeling you out at around noon."

"Wheeling me out?" My eyes widened.

Aaron nodded and slowly pulled down my blanket to reveal a brace encircling my waist...as if I needed reminding what was going on down there.

"How am I supposed to fit in a wheelchair like this?" I asked.

"You know? I have absolutely no idea," he started laughing. "But I guess we'll find out soon."

I groaned as my head fell back to the pillow. "This is so not my idea of showing you a good time."

"Showing me a good time, huh?" his eyes sparkled as I burst into laughter.

I heard a light tap on the door and looked over to see a nurse pushing in a large wheelchair. "Shower time."

Thank God!

"Fun's starting already," Aaron murmured.

I rolled my eyes and giggled as the nurse came over to my bed.

"I'm going to take out your IV and your

catheter."

I looked over at Aaron, completely mortified. "I think that's your cue to exit stage right."

He gave me a quick kiss on the cheek and headed out of the room as the nurse began preparing me for home.

Aaron was taking things very easy on our drive home, changing lanes like he was ninety years old and turning corners so slowly I swore I could've gotten out and pushed us faster.

But I appreciated it. I appreciated him.

I was sprawled out in the back of his Mercedes SUV. My right leg was anchored straight out in front of me, taking up the entire back seat. I was as close to feeling like a mummy as humanly possible. I watched the scenery go by at a snail's pace and had to laugh.

"I promise I won't shatter," I teased.

"I just don't want your leg to fall off..."

"The seat?"

"No, just off. You look like you're barely pieced together."

I started laughing. "Well, thank you for that." We were only a couple of minutes away from Aaron's home, and anxiety started to pulse through me as I thought about what was ahead for me, for us. I felt absolutely helpless and completely powerless. I wasn't used to depending on anyone but myself, and here I was having my brand new boyfriend take care of me in a way that I wasn't sure either of us would be able to handle.

I let out a sigh as he turned into his driveway.

"Someone's overthinking something back there," he said.

"It's how I was wired."

I saw two cars in the driveway and my heart started pattering faster. "Guess the therapy is starting already."

The front door opened and a friendly-faced, older woman waved at us.

"That's Jackie, the new housekeeper."

"Good choice," I said wryly.

"I thought you'd approve." He turned off the engine and got out of the car just as two more strangers piled onto the porch.

Jackie came over to the far side of SUV and opened the door. "Hi, my dear. Welcome home. I'm Jackie."

I blushed and glanced over at Aaron who was taking charge like this sort of thing happened every day.

"Thank you. It's good to be home," I said, realizing how very dependent I was in this moment. I couldn't even get out of the damned car.

"This is Austin behind me," Aaron said, ducking his head into the car. "He's one of the best physical therapists in the state."

I looked around Aaron and noticed that Austin was quite good looking and couldn't help but smile. He had dirty blonde hair and was completely built.

"Don't go getting any ideas," Aaron teased.

"Right. I'm sure he'd be all over this ass," I whispered, rolling my eyes. "Nice to meet you, Austin."

"You too, Miss Sullivan."

My eyes flashed to Aaron's. I liked the way it sounded, even though it wasn't a reality.

"My last name's Rhodes, but you can call me Brandy," I said, smiling at Austin who had managed to set up the wheelchair.

"Your chariot awaits," Aaron said, grinning.

"Lord," I huffed.

"I'm going to come from behind you and open the door your back is resting on, and then we'll just work you into the chair," Austin instructed.

"Sounds like a plan."

"Aaron, if you could just carefully crawl in there to ensure she doesn't fall out backwards that would be great."

"Yes. That would be great." I started laughing at the absolute horror of what had become a day in the life of Brandy.

My hot, new boyfriend was crawling in through the SUV, maneuvering around my mummified leg and metal encased torso, and reaching his arms out in front of him like he was rescuing a stray cat.

"If this doesn't scare you off, I don't know what will," I teased, feeling Austin's arms wrapping under my armpits as he began hauling me from behind.

"Okay. One. Two. Three. Lift," Austin gently

placed me in the wheelchair and Aaron came tumbling out of the vehicle.

"That was graceful."

He flashed me a smile as Austin began pushing me to the stairs.

"Oh, I've got a ramp," Aaron said, glancing at Jackie. "Do you know where it went?"

Jackie nodded and pulled it out from behind the rhododendron. "Didn't want anyone to steal it," she muttered.

Aaron attached it the porch and Austin wheeled me up to the waiting nurse. I see how it worked. I got Austin and Aaron got...

"I'm Kristy," she said, reaching down to give me a light hug. "I'm one of the nurses Aaron hired."

I couldn't help but chuckle and turned to Aaron. "Is she one of the best in the state too?"

Aaron's eyes flickered with amusement. "Why, yes she is."

Thankfully oblivious to what we were joking about, Kristy took over wheelchair duty and wheeled me into the home.

"You'll be walking again in no time," she whispered. "He spared nothing when it came to this setup. You're one lucky woman."

"Thank you. I really am."

She wheeled me through the large foyer, straight through the family room and down the hall to the guest room. There were silver and pink balloons hovering all over, and a huge sign that read "Welcome Home". The nightstand was covered in flowers and so was the dresser. The sleigh bed that had originally been in the room had been replaced with an adjustable hospital bed. There was also a twin bed right next to the hospital bed. There were several newly attached poles and posts hooked to the far wall.

"Are you planning on me taking up ballet again?" I teased.

"My work is done with you once you can lift your leg on that bar," Austin said, smiling.

"And how long do you think that will take?"

"Different for every patient."

"Where's our girl?" Gabby hollered from the foyer.

"She's in here," Aaron called out into the hallway.

"I've got her favorite treats," Gabby gushed, coming into the bedroom. "Welcome home."

I spotted a platter full of cookies and fruit bars and couldn't help but smile.

She cleared off a place on the dresser and set the tray down before giving me a big hug.

"It's so nice to see you out of the hospital. And your hair smells so good."

"Amazing what a shower will do for a person."

"I hate to bust up the party, but the sooner we start on rehab the quicker she won't need it," Austin said, glancing at Aaron.

"Sounds good to me," I said, smiling.

"I'll be out in the family room with Aaron," Gabby said. "And Lily's on her way up too."

Jackie and Kristy followed everyone out to the living area, leaving Austin and me alone.

"I can't promise that this won't hurt or that

you'll like me by the end of it. But I promise by January no one will ever know you were even injured."

The fear of pain was quickly replaced with adrenaline. "Whatever we've got to do, let's hit it."

Austin helped me to the flattened bed and as I felt my body stiffen and pull with pain, I knew I was going to be in for a long, grueling process of recovery.

But nothing would prepare me for the pain I'd endure with Aaron. I just didn't know it yet.

CHAPTER TWENTY-SIX

Four weeks had gone by, and I was feeling more and more like myself every minute. I had transitioned from wheelchair to crutches and from plaster cast to bootie. At this rate, I'd be snowboarding by January. Although that goal made Austin cringe every time I mentioned it.

But a person's only got one shot at life, right?

Thanksgiving was four weeks away, and I'd been secretly planning a holiday menu with Jackie. I couldn't wait to surprise Aaron with his first holiday at home with family and friends. Austin was going to be coming over in the afternoon for more physical therapy. He was completely blown away by my progress. What he didn't know was that I was working morning, noon, and night on the non-assist exercises. I was down to one nurse, Kristy, who only came in the mornings to help me shower and change. We'd actually become really good friends, and I looked forward to her visits.

I hobbled down the hallway, with only the knock of the crutches as they hit the floor. Jackie was out shopping and Aaron was at work. Tomorrow was Halloween, and I couldn't wait to carve our pumpkins tonight. Gabby and Jason were going to come over, and my plan was plenty of drink, candy, and scary movies. Even though I couldn't wait to get back in law school, I was actually enjoying this temporary freedom. I was on short-term disability through work and even though it wasn't much, I was happy to have it. I tried several times to offer Aaron something, anything, but he wouldn't take a dime so my goal was to repay him in other ways.

I reached the kitchen and flipped on the espresso machine. Even though I had adjusted to things pretty well, the one part of my life that I missed more than anything was my daily morning Starbucks.

Aaron had treated me like a princess from the moment I'd arrived. It turned out the twin bed was where he planned on sleeping, but after two nights of him being so close but so far away, I made him promise to sleep in bed with me. Which he did every single night.

My next milestone was stairs. I managed to get halfway up our staircase yesterday, but I wouldn't be able to get rid of the hospital bed until I could reach the top of the stairs without assistance. The thought of getting to snuggle with Aaron in his bed was incentive enough. I hoped this week would be the week.

The green light on the espresso lit up, and I began packing my grounds when the front door opened.

"Baby, I'm home," Aaron's deep voice rang through the house. "And I've got a Pumpkin Spice Latte for you."

I squealed and spun around on one foot and grinned as he walked into the kitchen. He looked amazing in his suit, and the Starbucks cup he was holding made my heart melt. This side of Aaron was one that I hoped existed under his cocky façade many moons ago. I think my heart knew it had all along, but I was just thankful my mind finally followed, allowing me to embrace this side of him.

"You look gorgeous," he whispered, handing me the cup of the glorious liquid.

I glanced down at my outfit and blushed. I was wearing jeans and an orange sweater with an oversized neckline. "I don't look too much like a pumpkin?"

He laughed and softly kissed the crook of my neck. His mouth slowly trailed lower over my collarbone and down to my chest before he took a step back.

"I love pumpkins."

"I love you."

"Love you too, babe. So what's the plan for the night?"

"Well, since you're home early..."

His grin widened as I ran my hands along his back. "I've been fantasizing about what I was going to do to you all day," he growled.

"Really," I purred, bringing my lips close to his ear.

"Mm-hmm."

"That makes two of us," I whispered, nipping his lobe as his body stiffened.

"You drive me absolutely crazy."

"Then I'm doing my job." I ran my fingers through his hair as my lips wandered along his jaw, feeling the roughness rub against the softness of my lips. He let out a large sigh, his warm breath tickling my already sensitive skin. His hands began to glide along my waistband when I let out a trembling breath.

"You like that?" he murmured.

Nodding, I felt his fingers run beneath my sweater as they followed the dips and contours of my body. Aaron's breathing was charged with heaviness as his fingertips slid my bra up. Feeling the tightness of my skin pucker as the tips of his fingers slid along my flesh was almost unbearable.

Unable to take my eyes off Aaron, I watched as he slowly lifted off my sweater and took me in, all of me. The desire ran through me at a quickened speed as he lowered his lips down to my breasts.

My breath stuttered as he continued teasing me with his mouth.

Jackie opened the front door, and I almost didn't even care as Aaron continued to canvas kisses along my breasts.

But then it really hit me, and I quickly patted

his shoulder to get him to stop so I could slip my top back on.

He took a step back and licked his lips as I pulled the sweater back over my head. I was completely disoriented and needed so much more from him.

"Upstairs?" I whispered.

Jackie rounded the bend carrying two bags of groceries and Aaron went to help her out.

"Your friends just pulled in behind me," she said. "I'll get some appetizers going before I head home."

Damn!

"Thank you, Jackie. That's so sweet of you."

"I'm just happy to see you hobbling all around, dear. And your sweater's on backwards."

My cheeks turned fire red instantly as I worked my arms through the holes and slid my top where it belonged.

"Thank you," I muttered, taking a sip of my latte.

"Happy Carving Time," Gabby shouted from the foyer.

Jason and Gabby walked into the kitchen holding two huge pumpkins.

"Oh, how cute! You dressed like a pumpkin," Gabby gushed.

I turned and scowled at Aaron who was cracking up as he put the milk in the fridge.

"Thanks," I said, rolling my eyes. "Mind taking this to the table after you dump off your pumpkin?" I wiggled my brows at the Starbucks cup that I'd just put back down so I could crutch it to the table.

"Totally," Gabby said, placing her pumpkin next to ours.

"Once the timer goes off, your snacks will be done. Gabby, I'll put you in charge of that, and I'm going to take off for the night. Have fun."

I waved and watched as Jackie grabbed her purse and coat and wandered off toward the door.

"Anyone thirsty?" Aaron asked, grabbing a beer and popping the top off.

"I'll take one of those," Gabby said, pointing at the bottle.

"Me too. I haven't had any pain medicine for two days."

"Two beers coming up. Jason, you want a seltzer?"

"Perfect," Jason said, as he arranged the pumpkins and knives on the table.

"So you look amazing," Gabby gushed. "How are you feeling?"

"Almost like normal. I just can't wait until I don't have to use those things," I said, glaring at the crutches I had propped against the wall.

"I bet. By Christmas?" Jason asked.

"Forget that. I'm hoping by Thanksgiving."

"Never one to waiver under pressure," Gabby laughed.

"I'm hoping we can go on a fun ski trip this winter too," I said, smiling.

I glanced over at Aaron who shifted his gaze to Jason. What was going on between them?

"Don't you think that would be fun, guys?" I

tried again.

"I'm totally in," Gabby said. "What about you, Jason?"

"Sounds like a plan to me." He nodded.

"Well, that just leaves Mr. Grinch. You in?" I asked Aaron.

He smiled and his eyes locked on mine, but I recognized something that I didn't want to see.

"I love you, babe," he laughed, and shook his head.

Something was off. I glanced at Gabby who noticed it too, but Jason quickly turned the topic to making the first cut into the pumpkin.

"I'm going for a Dracula look," Jason said.

"That's awfully fancy," I said.

Aaron stood up abruptly and glanced in my direction but wouldn't make eye contact. "I've gotta make a call. I'll be right back."

"Okay," I replied, trying to shove off the worry.

But it was too late; the first seed had already been planted.

CHAPTER TWENTY-SEVEN

It was another beautiful Saturday with the crystal blue skies out, and the crisp air just calling for the last of the autumn leaves to drop. Aaron had left to run some errands, and Jackie had the day off. Gabby would be here any minute, and I was really looking forward to spending time with her. I needed some pick-me-up girl time. I tried to ignore a few of the recovery hiccups that I'd encountered, but there were some that were harder to ignore than others. My hair had started growing back in the areas where it had been clipped, but I still wasn't necessarily feeling as fabulous as I wanted. Aaron made me feel like the most beautiful thing to walk the planet, but many mornings—and this was certainly one of them—I felt less than human. I wasn't sure which scars from the accident were going to be harder to heal, the external or the internal ones.

Wandering into the kitchen, I opened the fridge and laughed. I told Jackie I had everything covered for my impromptu lunch with Gabby, but she apparently didn't believe me. She had a plate of various cheeses sliced, a plate of sliced fruit, and a platter full of meats. I was sure Jackie's plan was to fatten me up before I left this place, and I was pretty sure it was working. I grabbed each plate out of the fridge and placed it on the island. Grabbing crackers and chips out of the pantry, I spread them out on a plate when the doorbell rang.

I walked at a pace that was slower than pre-accident, but faster than last week and that's all I could ask. I opened the door and Gabby ran in, hugging me tightly.

"Oh, girl. It's so nice to see you, especially at my brother's house." She let go and took a step back. "I can't believe the progress. First no crutches and now no cane?"

"What can I say? I'm Wonder Woman."

"Are you off pain meds?" Gabby asked.

"For the most part. I think the last time I took one was a few days ago."

"Score," she hollered, pulling out a bottle of wine from of her purse.

I started laughing as we walked into the kitchen.

"I'm getting so excited about the holidays with Aaron. Everything feels so right, Gabby. It's been so easy...Like the bubble is going to burst any second."

Gabby grabbed a plate and began choosing various cheese and meats to decorate her crackers.

"That's one way of looking at it." She grinned. "But most people wouldn't look at a near-fatal accident as easy, but you also fantasize about law school so beats me." She shrugged.

"Haha." I rolled my eyes. "You know what I mean."

"I do." She grinned wider. "And I have to say the thought of your becoming my sister legally is pretty sweet."

"Do you know something?" My eyes wide.

"Nothing, but my hunch is that it's gonna happen someday."

I grabbed a plate and piled cheddar on a couple crackers and pulled a few grapes free.

"Do you mind sitting on the patio? Aaron turned on the heaters for me. I just want to enjoy the last few days of sunshine."

"Totally. I'm bundled up," she said, following me outside.

"So how are you taking the news?" Gabby asked, bringing me a glass of red wine.

We were sitting on Aaron's patio with the heaters cranked on full blast. I had a blanket wrapped around me, but I was determined to squeeze in the last few blue skies we had left, regardless of temperature. Being cooped up so long hadn't done wonders for my spirits.

I took a sip and looked over at Gabby, perplexed.

"I know I've been a little bit out of it lately, but

I'm actually not sure what news you're referring to."

Gabby was drinking her wine and stopped mid-swallow, her eyes widening.

"Oh, nothing then. I probably got my wires crossed." She set her glass on the table and looked out toward the pond.

"Nice try," I said, repositioning the blanket to cover my ears. "What news is flying around our circle that I don't know about?"

"Oh, god...Brandy. I thought Aaron had spoken to you already. He said last night he was going to talk to you this morning."

"Spit it out."

Gabby shook her head, her ponytail bouncing all over the place. "I can't. It's not my place."

"Does he need me to move out? I totally understand if that's what it is. I've been thinking that too. I don't want to wear out my welcome, and I love our condo in the city." I took another sip. "Although, it will be very lonely with you not there."

Gabby's face turned ashen, and she fidgeted uncomfortably.

"That's not it. He has no issues with you recovering here. I think he'd be heartbroken if you left, actually." She tried to reassure me, but the uncertainty and guilt behind her eyes was making me nervous.

"Please, just tell me. If you don't, I'll call Aaron and say you spilled half the beans and left me to drive myself crazy."

"He's going to kill me."

"With what he's done to you, let's just call it even. I'll make sure he doesn't hold you accountable."

"Aaron's going to Shenzhen."

"He's going to China? On a business trip?" I asked, not understanding what the big deal was.

It was silent for a few seconds and the tension between us rose. I glanced at the pond where a couple ducks landed and then back to Gabby.

"To live," she whispered, her lips twisting into a frown.

"Wait. What?"

"His transfer was planned months ago. I think." Gabby continued talking, but I heard none of it. All that kept repeating in my head was that Aaron was going to live in China. China. My head started pounding, but that pain was quickly replaced with the ache in my chest. How long did he know that he was going to be leaving for China? Why had he been leading me on if he knew he wasn't going to be around? I knew there were long distance relationships that worked, but this was an entirely different scenario. Besides, was he even planning on continuing things? I shouldn't even presume that he had planned on us continuing.

"I don't understand." I shook my head as the ache spread from my chest to my entire body. "Why wouldn't he have mentioned this? I..."

"I'm so sorry. I just thought he had told you and—"

The tiny seed of hollowness began sprouting into full-fledged despair as I thought about

Aaron leaving Seattle, leaving me. Maybe I was just another conquest after all. I looked around the yard and back at the house. He undoubtedly had just felt bad, guilty, after the bike accident and took on a responsibility that wasn't his. Here I thought there was something more between us, but I was only his pity case.

I tried very hard not to sound devastated. I knocked the quiver in my voice out of range and looked at Gabby.

"You don't have to apologize," I swallowed the lump that threatened to give away my emotional state. "I'm glad I know. I can start planning to move back to the condo."

"Don't do that. He wants you to stay here."

I shook my head. "Don't think so. Wanna go inside? The temperature has finally gotten to me."

"Sure, hun." She stood up and turned off the overhead heaters as I half-waddled and walked to the house. The ache in my leg reappeared, and I somehow doubted it had anything to do with the break.

"Are you okay?" she asked, closing the door.

Sitting on the couch, I looked around the great room. There was no way I was staying here. Beside the fact that I didn't want to be someone's pity case, everything here exuded Aaron. I would be completely insane and masochistic if I wanted to be reminded of someone—something—I wouldn't be able to have any longer.

"I think I'm still in shock, but I'll be okay. I just never guessed this is how we would end it. Or how he would end it."

"Shit, Brandy. No, he's not trying to end it. Please-oh-please don't think that. Is that really what you think?"

Gabby grabbed the bottle of wine and poured some more.

"Moving across the globe without any consideration about your significant other is a bit of a red flag, Gabby. I'm not going to candy-coat this for myself. It is what it is. To be completely honest, I often wondered if this whole relationship went the way it did because he felt guilty."

I felt the tears begin to wet my eyes. Closing my lids tightly, I prayed the liquid would draw back in to where it came from.

"I'm getting Aaron on the phone." She reached for her phone and began dialing.

"Please don't. He'll be home soon and I'll talk to him then."

"I can't have you thinking that Aaron is trying to end it with you. That's the exact opposite of what his intentions are."

"I'm starting law school in January. It's not like I'm going anywhere or can move to China. Trust me. It's over."

The click of the front door signaled Aaron's arrival, and I quickly wiped my tears away as he came into the great room. His eyes connected with mine as he held a Gingerbread Latte out for me. His eyes stayed locked on mine and filled quickly with dread as he briefly glanced at his sister and then back at me.

"I got you this," he said, holding out the drink.

"I doubt that's going to cut it," Gabby said, standing up. "I'm so sorry, Aaron. I thought you'd told her."

"Shit," Aaron groaned, as his sister grabbed her purse and left out the front door.

"When were you going to tell me?" I asked, pushing away the tears again.

"Today," he said, coming to my side.

He sat next to me on the couch and I inched away.

"How long have you known?"

"Too long," he answered, placing the cup on the coffee table.

"How long is that?" I arched a brow, waiting for a response.

"I've known for about ten months that I'd be going there to oversee the opening of the plant."

"You've known for ten months?" I couldn't hide my anger. "And it never once occurred to you to mention it?"

My emotions were all over the place. I was sad, devastated, angry, guilty. I glanced around the room and felt completely out of place.

"Every time I was going to talk to you about it, something else got in the way. And then when the accident happened, it just didn't seem like the right time…"

"How long will you be there?"

He let out a deep sigh and rubbed his forehead. "Anywhere from one to three years."

I couldn't say anything. Instead I just looked at him as the world I had constructed slowly began to crumble away.

"I'm so sorry, babe. I love you so much and—"

"If you loved me, this would have been a more troublesome decision for you," I interrupted. "But I can tell you things are staring to fall into place for me. I was just your pity f—"

"Don't say that," Aaron yelled. "That's complete bullshit."

"Is it? When are you leaving?"

"Monday."

I started shaking my head, laughing. "You wanna know something completely pathetic? I've been daydreaming and planning about how to make your life better. How to make a life for us... I've even been planning an amazing Thanksgiving dinner for you that you won't be here for."

"Baby. Please, listen to me. I've been trying to find a replacement to send."

I crossed my arms in front of me. "You're trying to tell me that you couldn't find someone else to send in your place? Please. I wasn't born yesterday. You were always off-limits. I just chose to ignore it. You've got needs that I obviously can't meet," I muttered. "I wanted you to let me in your heart, but I'm not even sure you have one."

Aaron's jaw clenched as I scooted away from him.

"I'll get my things out of here by the end of the week."

"Please. Don't leave. You can stay here. Everything's set up here for you. Jackie'll be here and—"

"Jackie? Oh, that's great," I replied sarcastically.

"Listen. I don't know what you want me to do or say."

"That right there is what's so sad. You don't have a clue. I thought we had something, shared something special. But I was wrong, and I'm suddenly feeling sorry for Nina and everyone else who fell under your spell. But please. Don't worry about finding a replacement because there will be no one to come home to anyway."

I stood up quickly and felt lightheaded. My leg was aching, but I wasn't going to let that slow me down.

"I'll sleep downstairs tonight. And I'll pack while you're at work."

I glanced at Aaron and instead of seeing any regret or sorrow, I saw the same hardened gaze that scared me from day one. The look that told me I was never special. I was just one of many. I had been officially placed in his lineup.

I had the music pounding and was packing up the last of my boxes. I glanced up and scared the shit out of myself when I saw Aaron staring back at me. I saw a hint of a smile and pushed away the delight that tried to force itself into my psyche.

"You're usually done by this time of the day,"

he said, his voice distant. "I didn't expect you to be here."

I glanced at the clock in the kitchen.

Shit! It was a quarter past six o'clock. I was so in my zone I didn't even notice. Usually by now I was already at my place beginning to unpack.

"Sorry," I said. "Time slipped away from me."

I saw a shadow come from the powder room, and my jaw fell to the floor as a tall brunette walked into the room. Her hair was in a chignon, and she wore a pencil skirt with a tight-fitting, white sweater. She glanced at Aaron and followed his gaze to me.

"Hey. Sorry. I was just leaving," I said, reaching my hand out to Aaron's latest victim. "I'm Brandy."

"I'm Cheri," she said, shaking my hand. "Nice to meet you."

I couldn't help as a smile spread across my lips at the realization that I was damn lucky to get out of this with Aaron before anything worse happened to me, mentally or physically.

Aaron's voice interrupted my self-congratulatory mood, "Cheri is my translator for my trip."

I started laughing and locked my gaze on Aaron's. "I bet she is. I'll just leave these boxes for tomorrow and head out."

The collision of emotions that were piling up inside of me were threatening my sanity, and I knew I needed out...like now. I might be able to keep this smile plastered on my lips for another two to three minutes—tops.

Cheri, the translator, smiled as I limped out of the room, and all I wanted to do was punch something as the pair of eyes filled with sympathy watched me hobble to the door. This wasn't who I was. But this was exactly who he was.

The ache was spreading from muscle to muscle as I tried my damndest to keep my limp to a minimum. I, at least, had some shred of dignity left, even though he managed to crush most of it. The cold air blasted my face when I opened the door, and the moment I closed it, the tears unleashed. I walked as quickly as I could without tripping or feeling like my leg was on fire when I heard the door open behind me.

Damn him!

"Hey, Brandy. Wait up."

Yeah, right!

I opened my car door right when he pushed it closed.

"Excuse me?" I asked, staring at him.

He put his arms on each side of me locking himself in front of me.

"It's not what you think," he muttered.

"I don't even know what I think, Aaron. But to be honest we aren't together any longer so I'm pulling up my big girl panties and trying to ignore just how easy I was to forget."

"Brandy, she's just a translator, and I haven't forgotten about you. In fact, I can't think about anything but you," his words carved the pain deeper into my heart. I had to break free of him. "I'm lost without you."

A gutted laugh left my lips as I looked into his eyes.

"You promised me you'd never leave my side. I remember it. I remember a lot of things you said that day," my voice caught in my throat.

I never wanted to utter the words I heard him say. I never wanted to bring it up. I thought when the time was right he would. That he would ask me to spend the rest of our lives together. Instead, I was greeted with him moving halfway across the world to escape his demons, or maybe just embrace them.

Maybe, I was as delirious as everyone thought that day. Maybe, he never said anything to me. Maybe, I had imagined it all just as I'd imagined being able to talk, shout, scream, and move that day...

I wasn't going to bring it up. I had more pride than that. If he wanted to leave, he could leave. Who would I be to stand in his way, especially when he's already got the next hottie lined up?

"This was scheduled over a year ago... before I even met you. I've been trying to get out of it any way I can, but I told you I haven't been able to find a replacement. I've tried to get my father to—"

I interrupted him, "You know what's the saddest part of this whole thing?" I narrowed my eyes at him, hoping that would stop the tears from falling. "Is just how much your mother screwed up your life. You'll never trust any woman for the rest of your life because of what she did to your dad. And I just feel sorry for any woman who thinks she has a chance with you...A chance to change you because you're a lost cause. So runaway to China, Aaron. That's what you're best at."

I spun around and opened the door again and slid in my seat. He took a step back as I slammed my car door. Aaron was frozen in place, like someone had just dumped ice water on him.

I put my car in reverse just as Cheri opened the front door, sticking her big brunette head out the door, motioning for Aaron to come inside.

And that's when I heard him finally speak, looking directly at me.

"I'll be right in there, babe. Just seeing off my guest."

Exactly what I thought.

CHAPTER TWENTY-EIGHT

"I knew he was a jerk," Mason said, as he helped to unpack a box.

"He's confused. His family hasn't had the best track record of handling their personal business."

"That's no excuse," Mason said.

I sighed. "You're probably right."

"You deserve someone who wants to be all in with you. No matter what. I have to be honest...The way he stood up and took care of you after the accident, I thought it was a done deal. Mom and dad even thought that you guys..." he stopped.

"That we'd what?" I asked, narrowing my eyes on Mason.

"It probably doesn't matter at this point, but Aaron had asked dad if he could have your hand in marriage. He said it was something he promised you while you—"

"Say what?" I dropped the dress off of the hanger and stared at Mason.

He nodded and shrugged his shoulders.

"What did dad say?"

"Yes, of course. We really all got fooled."

"Tell me about it. I still don't want to believe it."

"What's Gabby say about everything?"

"She's been staying away, which makes me sad. I think she feels guilty that she spilled the news, but I wouldn't have known until I got a postcard from him, apparently. What little she did tell me was that she knew that the thing between her father, mother, and Bernie screwed him up, but she never guessed this was how it would end."

"It's amazing how parents do things that literally screw up the course of their children's lives..."

"He definitely has trust issues with women."

"Ayden and I wanted you and Lily to come out with us tonight...try to get you to forget about everything."

"You mean drink my sorrows away?" I asked. "No thanks. That never leads to good things for me."

Mason cut through the box for recycle and shook his head. "Just a plan."

"Thanks for being there for me." I smiled.

"I'll always be there for my knucklehead."

I narrowed my eyes at him and laughed.

"I'm gonna grab some chips or an apple,"

Mason said, walking out of my room. "When did you say Lily was getting here?"

"Any second."

I sat on my bed and stared around my room, feeling like a stranger in my own space. I let out a sigh and thought about what my brother said. There were no words to even describe what that news just did to me. Marriage? And then this? I laughed as I realized it was just another one of life's cruel jokes that I could toss into my pile of shattered dreams. At this rate the pile would turn into a mountain and crush me in the next few years.

I grabbed my new phone and scrolled until I hit Gabby's number. I had taken a cue from her past relationships and had gotten rid of my phone and got a new number. And I was thankful I'd done that or I'd be texting Aaron right about now. I understood why she did it now. It really took away the desire to send a text or leave a message that would end up a drunk dialing souvenir.

But that still didn't stop me from texting Gabby.

Did you know your brother was going to propose?

I tossed the phone aside and looked around my room. Maybe, it just needed a new color to brighten things up a bit. My phone buzzed and I grabbed it. Worried what the message might reveal, I took a deep breath in and looked down at the screen.

I helped pick out the ring

My heart was pounding, and the tears came pouring down my cheeks just as Mason appeared with a plate.

"Want an apple?" he asked, shoving the plate in front of me.

My tears turned to laughter as I looked up at my brother.

"Call Ayden and tell him I'm coming to party tonight." I smiled, rubbing the tears off my cheeks.

"You look absolutely amazing," Lily said, fastening the strap on her heel.

"So do you."

Lily was dressed in a light green, tight dress that showed off all of her assets. Like always her outfit wasn't overly revealing, but her body certainly made it that way. Anyone who danced with her tonight would be loving the view. I looked down at my black dress and silver flats and was pleased.

"This is the first time I think in the history of going out to a club that I've worn flats," I laughed.

"Wise choice, my friend. I'm not sure any of us will be in a position to scoop you up if you fall on your ass tonight."

I laughed and dabbed on a bit of lip gloss as I caught Lily looking at me in the mirror. "You'll forget about him. You will. It will just take some time and plenty of good lays."

"Lily." I threw my gloss at her, but she ducked in time.

"I feel really horrible, like I was the one who told you to keep after him and all he was ever capable of was breaking your heart."

"Don't feel horrible. To be honest, feeling what I did with him reminded me of what it's like to be truly alive, enjoying the moment. All that stuff. Now I'll just try to find it with someone who might be on the same page as me."

"Or the same continent."

"That too. But seriously, I don't regret one second of being with him."

She nodded and smiled.

"I'm sure you don't regret being with that guy from high school," I said softly.

"You're right. Not at all. It's just a hard thing to recreate."

"But, at least, you know what you're looking for," I said.

She shrugged. "What a great idea Mason and Ayden had." Lily was always game for going out, and I was sure she was relieved that we'd be out in the city tonight rather than cooped up in my condo. "Is Gabby coming?"

I shook my head. "I didn't think to invite her."

Lily nodded. "Probably for the best. We've got four single people ready to party. She'd just hold us back."

"Right," I said, laughing. I glanced at myself in the mirror and was pleasantly pleased. Without the boot, I started feeling human again and was actually looking forward to going out.

A whistle came from the door, and I turned to see Ayden leaning against the frame. "A little short, don't ya think?"

I started laughing and tugged on my dress. "It's not like Lily's."

Ayden nodded. "I guess I should be grateful."

"Hey, now," Lily laughed.

"Ready?" Mason asked.

"Let's get out of here," Lily said.

"We have to stop in the kitchen first. We've got two shots each lined up for us all to get the night going," Ayden said.

I let out a groan and felt my body being pushed toward the kitchen.

"What are these?" I asked.

"Our specialty," Mason laughed.

"So anything you could find."

Ayden nodded. "Pretty much."

Lily did the first shot and puckered her mouth, squealing. "Whoa. That was hot. Your turn."

I grabbed the glass and swallowed the shot in one gulp, hoping the liquid would get me well on my way to forgetting about the love of my life.

"Next," Mason hollered, shoving the second shot glass in front of me.

I took a deep breath in and swallowed, hoping that would take away the bite but it didn't. It tasted as bad as the first time.

"Club Vertigo here we come," Lily shouted.

And we were off to a night full of forgotten memories and relived sorrows.

CHAPTER TWENTY-NINE

"So here we are enjoying a girls' night on a gorgeous fall evening. Next time, I'll come down to Portland. Maybe we'll even rip Gabby away from Jason." I stretched my arms along our balcony railing as I looked over the city landscape. "Remember when the girls' nights involved all three of us?"

Lily started laughing. "Our Gabby seems to be a bit infatuated."

"Can't say I blame her. Jason is beautiful and such a sweetheart. It was fun on my brothers' property though. All three of us..."

Lily picked up her empty glass off the table and began walking toward the French doors. "They seem like a really good fit."

"It seems impossible to find, and I have to admit that I kind of wonder how much fate and destiny play in all of our lives. I mean will I ever find that one perfect man who will show me what Jason has shown Gabby? How does someone get Mr. Right to show up? In fact, sometimes it feels like certain courses of events are already predetermined for my lifelong venture into singledom. I just want that one man to sweep me off my feet. Is that too much to ask?"

The door clicked, apparently giving me my answer, and I started chuckling to myself. Great. I was getting all philosophical and talking to myself once again. This was what my life had become.

I closed my eyes and drew in a slow breath as I felt the cool evening air kiss my skin.

And then I heard his voice from behind penetrating me to my core. "I hope you'll let me be that one man, Brandy. I never should have left. I'm so so sorry."

His smooth, deep voice wrapped around every cell in my body as his words sunk in. My heart flopped upside down as I let myself believe that there possibly could be a chance.

Aaron slipped his hand around my waist sending a charge up my spine, and I leaned on the railing for more support. Bringing his lips close to my ear, he whispered, "I think fate already has been working hard in both of our lives, don't you?"

His words sent a chill through me as I felt his mouth lingering next to my lobe, each breath skating across my neck. I didn't know what to say. My heart wanted to say yes. Scream from the top of my lungs, YES! But my mind was winning over my heart; the fear replacing desire with every passing second. I stood frozen until his hands slowly turned my body to face his. I stared at him with wide eyes, uncertain of what to say, uncertain of how to feel.

I stood, taking him in, letting myself believe that he was actually here. My hands ran up his black suit jacket, my fingers grazing his cheek. He looked down at me waiting for my response. I closed my eyes, trying not to be swayed by how good he looked in his suit and crimson tie. I didn't want to keep repeating the past.

"Do you agree?" his voice was low and strong.

Feeling the strength I needed, I opened my eyes. "Do you? You seem to be the one struggling."

His mouth collided with mine, and my world began spinning with every deepened kiss, every touch of his lips to mine. He hungrily ran his tongue along mine, leaving my mind and body completely at his mercy. I slowly nodded, leaning against the railing, feeling the burn of desire, excitement, and fear all bubble into one strong emotion of uncertainty.

My body became keenly aware of his powerful presence as his eyes penetrated deep into mine, searching for my forgiveness.

He knew what he wanted.

And it was me.

"It feels so right, doing the wrong thing," I whispered.

"That's because it's not the wrong thing," he murmured. "Just the complicated thing."

"You absolutely sure?" I asked.

"Beyond doubt, baby." His hands lowered to my hips, pulling me in closer to him as his eyes fell to my mouth, and I brought my hands to his chest imagining my life with him back in it even if only for tonight.

"Everything changes when I'm with you. I see the possibilities of a long, happy life. A future..." he whispered.

"Do you promise?"

"I gave up my position in China. I can't be away from you. I can't keep running. I made a promise to you that day that I'd never leave, and I never should have. I'm so sorry. But I want to spend the rest of my life with you. Forever and after."

A quiver ran through me as his eyes conveyed the same message. My hands wandered across his taut chest, and my heart began beating quicker as I thought about the possibilities of us, a future.

"Tell me you feel that way too," he said, cupping my chin softly.

"I do. I have. That's why—"

His mouth crashed onto mine as a low moan escaped my lips. I was his the moment I laid eyes on him. All of the worries drifted away as his kisses deepened, creating the safety I had craved. His mouth slowly parted from mine, and my muscles began to tense as he took a step back and smiled.

"I've got a little surprise planned for you," he said, grabbing my hand and pulling me through the door.

"I was quite happy right where we were," I teased, my body still on another planet.

"I think you'll like this even more."

"Are you planning on staying the night?" I asked.

We stepped inside and Lily was nowhere to be found. She was probably hiding out in Gabby's bedroom. Aaron proceeded to haul me through the family room, past the kitchen, right into my bedroom.

I heard the front door click and chuckled. Lily had escaped. I had the best friends in the world.

"So what's your plan?" I whispered.

"You'll see soon enough."

"Tell me something. Do I need to be worried about any translators whisking you away?"

His eyes drilled into me as his lip curled up slightly. "I deserve that."

"Damn right you do," I said, grabbing his crimson tie as I pulled him toward me.

"Nothing happened with her. I promise. I fired her that night." His gaze hardened on mine.

"I believe you."

And I did.

"I even got all dressed up for you," I teased, doing a half-twirl as I pointed down to my bootless leg. "Progress!" There was a slight squeal to my voice as the excitement pulsed through me. It had been a long journey, and I still had some light therapy to continue until the limp went away, but progress was progress. I had no idea how much I loathed that boot contraption.

"So is this what you wore to work?" he growled.

"I thought I was back on the market," I teased. "Besides, I figured the shorter the dress, the less they'd notice the limp."

"Baby, you always look amazing. But this...this is incredible." His fiery eyes canvased my body quickly and a rush of heat ran up me. I had on a red dress that showed all the right features, but the length more than made up for the looseness.

"You like?"

"I love," he growled, scooping me into his arms.

It felt so good to tease him this way. Watching his eyes hold the intense desire as I wriggled in his arms. He let out a small groan as he held me close to him. I felt his firmness against my belly and all I wanted to do was to take it in me. Make tonight last forever.

He pressed his forehead against mine as his fingers ran up my leg, skirting the edge of my dress. The hungry look in his eyes made my body warm with desire. His gaze stayed on me as he lowered me onto the bed, hovering over me. "I'll never hurt you again."

I let out a wobbly breath as my mind filled with all the hopes, desires, and dreams that I had forced myself to throw away.

"I promise I will never leave your side again. No matter how scared I get."

"Scared?" I asked, touching his chin.

"Scared...You were right. I didn't want to lose you the way my father lost my mother and—"

"You'll never lose me like that. Ever."

"When I was on the plane I realized I would be willing to feel that type of pain tenfold rather than be without you. To have you think I didn't love you..."

I kissed him softly as the tears began to fall.

"I love you, Brandy, more than I ever knew I could love anyone. I'll never be able to make you forget the hurt I caused you, but I beg for your forgiveness. I should have told you sooner. I should have worked harder on finding a replacement. All of it. You were right. But I think I was using it as an escape because I knew I was falling so deeply in love with you that—" he stopped himself.

"That what?" I whispered.

"That I could never live in this world without you. You're my soul mate."

Our faces were only inches apart as his words settled over me. He slowly began to remove my dress. His eyes sparkled as his gaze fell down my body. I looked down and began fidgeting as if it were the first time he had taken me in.

"Are you sure this time—"

"I've got everything under control. Believe it or not."

"Do you have to go back?" I murmured.

"No. I gave up my position."

"You what?"

"I quit."

"But why?"

"My dad was being a hard-ass and life's too short. I've got some other ideas that I want to develop."

"What about—"

"If you keep asking questions, I just might blindfold you and make you sit still until I'm done with you," he said, skating kisses across my belly.

"Is that necessarily a bad thing?" I asked innocently enough.

He smiled and turned my chin slightly. His lips brushed mine softly, sending a quiver of longing through me as he teased me with his mouth with the power he held over me. That same power that kept me coming back for more, no matter what life threw at me, at us.

"I'd be careful what you wish for," he said, his voice low.

"Is that so?" I asked, sliding down the bed. I wrapped my arm around his neck, but he pinned me to the bed. His lips parted slightly as his mouth traveled up my arm, to my shoulder.

"You're absolutely beautiful," he whispered, tracing his right hand along my thigh.

I shifted slightly, attempting to kiss him, but he restrained me gently by moving forward.

"You control so much in your life. Everything is so perfectly orchestrated," he murmured.

I let out a small moan of pleasure as his fingers continued gliding along my thigh.

"And I think it's time you allowed me to show you another way," he said. "No more games. Ever."

I slowly nodded as he brought his mouth back up to mine, his tongue diving deeper in search of quenching the need we both craved to find our forever.

CHAPTER THIRTY

I was arranging the bowls in the kitchen, trying to keep track of everything. I wanted Aaron to remember this Thanksgiving for the rest of our lives together. Gabby and Jason were on their way over and so were my parents and brothers. Aaron's parents were in Utah visiting Carla's elderly parents, which was kind of a relief considering the shows she put on for simple dinners. I already had enough stress wanting to make today perfect for Aaron and didn't want to think about trying to impress the almost in-laws. I wasn't quite ready for the Carla whirlwind.

I glanced at the clock and knew I was cutting it close. I had to get the turkey in the oven or we'd be eating at midnight. The turkey was brined and ready to go. I needed a little help shoving it into the oven. Ever since my accident, I still hadn't been allowed to carry things that were too heavy and bending was sometimes a problem, especially if I was holding something.

"Aaron," I hollered. "I need help getting Henry in the oven."

"Who the hell's Henry?" he asked, coming into the kitchen, wearing his red plaid pajama bottoms. I couldn't have made this moment more picture perfect if I tried. His hair was still stuck up in several different directions, and the dimple in his cheek was absolutely adorable.

"Henry is the wonderful bird who is allowing us to feast on him for our glorious Thanksgiving dinner." I adjusted my flannel nightshirt under my apron and grinned.

"Jesus! Naming the poultry doesn't really make it all that enticing," he laughed. "Besides, how do you know it's not Henrietta?"

I turned around and scowled at him. "Just stick it in the oven, big shot."

He grabbed the large roasting pan and shoved the bird in the already warm oven as I began slicing the sweet potatoes for my mom's famous sweet potato casserole. The corn pudding was already assembled in the fridge. All I had to do was pop it in the oven about an hour before the turkey was ready. I made the garlic mashers yesterday and only had to warm them up. So really, I just needed to focus on starting the appetizers.

The Macy's Thanksgiving Day parade was on in the background as I grabbed a cutting board and took in this moment of bliss.

"Your hair is so cute that way," I said, glancing

at Aaron.

"So is yours." His smile was gorgeous as he spoke but not as beautiful as the words he said.

I ran my fingers through my hair, which was still in its grow-out stage, and felt the bursts of hair that were sticking straight up. There were only a few places that were shaved and during the day I was able to strategically place my hair so that no one would even see the gaps. However, that definitely wasn't the case first thing in the morning.

"Thank you."

He grabbed the remote and switched the stereo on, blocking out the parade.

"Hey, what are you doing?" I teased. "We're going to miss something."

"Like a turkey float falling over? The occasion calls for some old school celebrations," he laughed. The next thing I knew Beastie Boys was blaring through the speakers.

"Finger Licking Good?" I started laughing.

"Ah-uh," he said, mimicking the song.

"Oh. My. God. What is the return policy on you?" I teased.

Aaron wrapped his arms around my waist just as I tugged on his pajama bottoms. "There. That's better," I laughed, admiring how low I teased the pajamas without him catching on. Or so I thought.

"Is that all you want from me?"

"Not all, but—"

He softly kissed me before letting go to turn off the Beastie Boys. "I'm gonna go shower."

"That's a shame."

He smiled and shook his head as he left the kitchen.

Curse these appetizers!

I grabbed the package of tortillas and began spreading the cream cheese mixture over the first tortilla to make the roast beef rollups.

"Forget this," I said tossing the half-done roll-up on the cutting board.

I heard the shower water come on upstairs and began making my way up the steps. Not every stair was my friend, but I knew the more I did it the better I'd be. Besides the payoff was worth it. As I made it to our bedroom, I saw the steam rolling out of the bathroom and tossed my nightshirt on the bed.

"Room for one more?" I asked, watching him stand under the shower.

"Always," he said, opening the glass door of the shower.

Stepping inside the shower, I watched his gaze follow along my body as I grabbed the soap and slowly began rubbing it along his chest.

"That feels nice," he murmured.

My hands continued moving lower and lower until I felt him in my palms. He let out a quiet moan as I gripped him more firmly. Looking into his eyes, he removed the soap from my hands and began to glide the bar along my breasts and stomach, lowering with each circular motion. His free arm cradled me next to him as he gently pressed me against the tile wall.

My heart was beating so quickly as he

continued the quick circular motions, and his lips followed along my collarbone. Slowing as he got to my breasts, my body trembled as his mouth traced over each curve.

I ran my hands along his back as he lifted me up the wall. The water pounded on us both as our bodies joined together and a cry of happiness escaped from my lips. This was definitely a holiday to remember.

Our house was filled with family and friends and the amazing aromas of Thanksgiving drifted through the air. *National Lampoon's Christmas Vacation* was on the television, and I was just happy to be in the moment.

I looked around the dining room table and felt so grateful to be surrounded by family and friends.

"I loved Onyx. Remember *Slammed*?" I asked Gabby.

She nodded her head and popped another cracker in her mouth.

Jason started cracking up and looked over at Aaron who was shaking his head.

"How old were you? Like two?" Aaron asked, his eyes narrowing. "How could you remember it?"

I shrugged. "I don't know. Maybe three. Blame my brothers."

Mason and Ayden started laughing. "Yeah. It is

our fault."

Aaron grabbed a dinner roll and passed the basket to Gabby. "How so?"

"We performed it in third grade for the talent show at our school."

Gabby burst into laughter. "Please tell me you're kidding."

"Yep. It's true. So my poor developing mind had it memorized before I even hit kindergarten. I think I even got written up for singing it."

My mom and dad started laughing, and I knew they remembered it too.

"That's not the only thing you got written up for," my dad chimed in.

"Really?" Aaron asked, grinning.

"I talked a lot back then."

"Back then?" Gabby teased.

"You know...I think we even have video of it. I think the moment one of you find that special someone, it's time to bring out the footage. You should have seen how they dressed," I said, not letting my brothers off the hook.

Mason threw a piece of dinner roll at me and it landed in my gravy. I plucked it out of the gravy and began aiming.

"Don't you dare," my mom said. "It's Thanksgiving for crying out loud."

I looked around the dining room table and felt overcome with emotion as I saw everyone enjoying this moment. It was hard to believe that I almost didn't make it to be here. I took a bite of the roll that was covered in gravy and glanced down at my plate.

"You okay, baby?" Aaron whispered as the rest of the family continued talking about grade school memories.

"Yeah. Just tears of joy," I said, giving him a quick kiss on his cheek. "I love you. I'm very grateful to be here."

Aaron's breath caught, and I watched him swallow hard. "You make the world a better place. I couldn't imagine living on this earth without you here by my side."

"I'm gonna hold you to that," I whispered.

"Okay, you love birds. Enough already," Ayden said, kicking me under the table.

And that was my perfect Thanksgiving with Aaron.

CHAPTER THIRTY-ONE

"Do you think we should do it? Like really hunt him down?" I asked, feeling a tinge of excitement at the thought.

"It only seems fair, doesn't it?" Gabby asked, laughing.

"All right. What are you two scheming in there?" Jason asked, bringing a cup of warm apple cider for Gabby.

It was a week after Thanksgiving, and I went on a Christmas shopping spree to get Aaron's house ready for the holidays. I think I managed to cover every surface with something holiday trinket.

"Mmm, delicious," she hummed.

"Hey, where's mine?" I teased Aaron.

"Coming right up." He opened the fridge and grabbed the whipped cream container and began squeezing the nozzle, topping the mug off.

Grabbing the chocolate sprinkles, he dusted them on top and looked over wearing a large grin.

"This is what I'm talking about," I said, taking the mug from him as he sat next to me. Slurping some of the white stuff off the top, I sat back and felt fully content and completely lost in the moment.

The Christmas tree was over eight feet tall and was decorated with everything I could throw at it. Silver tinsel streamed from the branches as the red and white lights blinked away. And there were so many ornaments on the limbs that there was a slight droop to most. The tree only had to last three weeks and then it could fall over if it wanted, but right now I wanted everything perfect. If Aaron had missed out on a decade of Christmases with loved ones, then I was certainly going to put an end to that this year. Jason had told me that last year he and Aaron bought a six-inch felt tree at the drug store and hung it on the fridge. So not happening in my world.

"So do you think we could pull it off?" Gabby questioned.

"I think so. We've got his name, age, approximate vicinity. It can't be that hard," I said, thinking aloud.

The idea of tracking down Lily's high school sweetheart was beyond exciting.

"This can't be good," Jason said, shaking his head.

"What do you mean?" Gabby said, pretending

to pout. "We are only up to good—only good. Speaking of which, I can't believe Carla is willing to relinquish the holiday to Brandy. This is completely unheard of. Do you think you can handle it? I mean hosting all of my family and your family is crazy." She glanced at me smiling, knowing full well I was up for the challenge.

"I've totally got it. All the menus are planned out, and you promised you'd bring over the desserts so I'm fine. Aaron needs to have the house smelling of gingerbread, ham, turkey..."

"What do you mean menus?" Gabby interrupted.

"It's an all day event. So I have to start with brunch then we'll do snacks all day and then dinner." Aaron gave me a big squeeze and I nestled in.

"Do you want me to come over on Christmas Eve to help prepare?" Gabby took a sip of her cider.

"No, because you need to make sure all the desserts are ready."

Jason's phone rang, and we watched him dig it out of his pocket and glance at the screen.

"Is it her?" Gabby asked.

Jason nodded. "It'll just be a second."

"Is it who?" I asked as he answered the phone.

Gabby motioned for me to be quiet and then whispered, "We think we found his sister."

I didn't know much about Jason's family other than he didn't really seem to have much, if any. He'd been in the foster care system for most of his childhood and only recently began researching his past.

Jason walked toward the French doors and went out onto the patio. It was freezing outside with a chance of snow, and Jason only had a sweater on so I grabbed my throw blanket and threw it at Gabby to give to him outside.

"Are you serious? Did he have any idea that he had a sister?" I asked, completely bewildered.

"Not a clue," Gabby said, grimacing. She grabbed the blanket and started walking toward the door. "He's been able to slowly start piecing together his family. They are all over the place. He tracked down an aunt, and it started spiraling."

"Tell him he can invite her."

"I don't know if he'd be ready for that," Aaron said.

"Exactly," Gabby agreed. "It's all kind of new."

"True and I guess he can always call her back if he wants," I said, taking a gulp of the whipped cream as Gabby opened the door slowly and handed the blanket to Jason.

She gently shut the door and scurried back to the warmth of the fire. "I think it really is her."

"That's crazy," I muttered, shaking my head.

A slight ache in my hip began radiating down my leg, and I shifted to change positions. I really was looking forward to when everything would be healed completely. If it would be healed completely.

The ache in my leg was getting worse so I stood up slowly to stretch it and noticed Jason pacing back and forth on the patio.

"Do you maybe want to go check on him?" I asked Aaron who craned his neck to see Jason rubbing his temples.

"Sure."

I shook out my leg and slowly started making my way to the kitchen as Aaron went outside, flipping the patio heating on and pulling out a chair for Jason to sit on.

"You doing okay?" Gabby asked.

"Yeah. It just knots up sometimes." And felt like my leg was on fire, I wanted to add. "I think the artichoke dip is ready."

"Awesome. Let me help." Gabby hopped up and got to the kitchen before I could even turn her down. She knew very well that I didn't want people going out of their way for me or thinking I couldn't handle things. But I had to admit the ache wasn't making things very easy. She grabbed the set of potholders off the counter and took the dip out of the oven. The top was a beautiful golden brown and it smelled delicious.

"You can set it right here," I said, pointing to the trivet.

I walked to the pantry and grabbed the crackers while Gabby began slicing the French bread.

"This smells phenomenal."

"It does," I agreed.

"Looks like Jason's not on the phone anymore," Gabby said, glancing through the window.

"Hope everything's okay."

"Me too."

Gabby carried the steaming hot dip to the coffee table, and I followed with the slices of bread and crackers just as the guys were coming back inside.

"Everything okay?" Gabby asked.

Jason nodded and Aaron's eyes connected with mine. Something was definitely bothering Jason and if I could pick up on it so could Gabby.

"Doesn't seem like it," she said softly, putting the tray down on the table.

"Meh. Doesn't matter. I don't know what I was expecting anyway. I don't want to ruin what we've got going on here," he said, plastering a smile on his face.

Aaron nodded and came by my side, whispering softly, "I saw you limping a little tonight. Don't overdo it."

I nodded and smiled at him, placing a soft kiss on the crook of his neck.

"Now, let's dig in and hear your bright idea," Jason said, scooping the dip on top of the cracker.

"We are going to track down Lily's first love," Gabby said, curling into Jason.

"Do you really think that's a great idea?" Jason teased. "She hasn't had the best track record."

"That's exactly why we need to do this. He was her first love, and in her eyes, he was perfection. If we can get them to meet and fireworks go off, it will be absolutely amazing," I gushed.

"And if they meet and she can't stand the toad he turned into then she can start living her life without always thinking about the what-ifs," Gabby continued.

Aaron and Jason started laughing in between bites.

"Seriously. She was in love with him and it has colored everything," I said, nibbling on a piece of the bread.

"I guess we're lucky we weren't toads," Jason said.

"So where is this poor soul? Do you even know if he's single?" Aaron asked.

"He's in Utah and I have no idea if he's single, but we devised a plan that should work flawlessly as long as you guys follow our rules," I said.

"Really?" Aaron raised a brow. "And what are those?"

"The first one is to be ready to go to Utah after the holidays. We're making it a ski trip so Lily shouldn't catch on."

"And the other rules?" Jason asked.

"There's only one," Gabby replied.

"And?" Jason said, the sparkle appearing in his eyes once more.

"Never ask questions," she said.

"It will never be boring with you two, will it?" Aaron said, holding me tightly.

"Not as long as I can help it," I said.

"Life's too short not to make it interesting," Gabby said. "Besides, we haven't been on a vacation yet. We should make sure we're compatible."

"And if we're not?" Jason asked, a smirk appearing on his lips.

Gabby just shrugged, smiling. "Beats me."

"A toast to Utah and a life never dull," Aaron said, grinning as he grabbed his mug full of eggnog.

"Utah it is," I said, snuggling in to Aaron. "And to a life full of love."

If only Lily would agree.

To read more about
Brandy, Gabby, and Lily
be on the lookout
for
Beyond Reason(Book 3)

Thank you for reading about Brandy and Aaron!

I hope you enjoyed the second book in the
Beyond Love Series.

Continue reading for recipes and excerpts
from other Karice Bolton books.

THANKSGIVING MENU

Sweet Potato Casserole

3/4 cup firmly packed brown sugar
2 tbl orange juice
2 tsp vanilla extract
1 1/2 tsp ground cinnamon
1/2 tsp salt
1/2 cup flour
1 cup pecans
3 lbs sweet potatoes, cubed
6 tablespoons butter

Preparations

Preheat oven to 400°F.

Mix 1/4 cup of the brown sugar, orange juice, vanilla, 1/2 teaspoon each of the cinnamon, and salt in large bowl. Add sweet potatoes; toss to coat well. Pour into 9x13-inch baking dish and place 2 tablespoons chopped butter on top. Cover with foil and bake for thirty minutes. Remove from oven.

Mix flour, 1/2 cup brown sugar, and remaining spices in bowl. Cut in remaining butter until course crumbs form. Stir in pecans and crumble on top of sweet potato dish and bake uncovered for 20-30 minutes more, until sweet potatoes are tender

Corn Pudding

1-15.25 ounce can whole kernel corn or fiesta corn
1 (15 ounce) can cream style corn
1 8.5 ounce package dry cornbread mix
1/2 cup butter, softened
1 cup sour cream
1/2 cup cheddar, shredded

Preparations
Preheat oven to 350°
Grease a casserole dish. Mix together all ingredients and pour into casserole dish. Top with shredded cheddar and bake for 45 minutes or until knife comes out clean.

Herb and Garlic Mashed Potatoes

3 lbs white potatoes (red potatoes work well too)
½ stick of butter
1 Garlic and Herb Rondele Spreadable Cheese
Splash of milk for desired consistency

Boil potatoes until just tender. Drain and lightly mash potatoes. Add the butter, garlic and herb cheese, and splash of milk. Continue to mix until desired consistency is reached.

Pecan Pumpkin Pie

Prepare one shell piecrust and bake according to recipe.

Preheat Oven to 350°

Pumpkin Filling:
1 egg
1 cup pumpkin puree (canned or fresh)
1/3 cup Sugar
3/4 tsp cinnamon
1/8 tsp cloves
1/8 tsp nutmeg
pinch of salt

Pecan Pie filling:
2 eggs
2/3 cup dark corn syrup
2 tbl butter (melted)
1 tbl vanilla
1 1/4 cup chopped pecans

Preparation:

In a bowl, combine egg, pumpkin, sugar, cinnamon, cloves, nutmeg, and salt. Spread in already baked pie crust.
Next, prepare the pecan pie filling by lightly beating the two eggs. Stir in remaining ingredients and mix lightly.

Carefully spoon the pecan pie mixture on top of

the pumpkin pie mixture. Bake 55 minutes; once filling is set on edge.

Cool before serving.

LONELY SOULS
WITCH AVENUE SERIES

CHAPTER ONE

"Mom!" I hollered more for my benefit than hers.

I wasn't in earshot yet, but I loved the way my voice carried into the wind off the sea. The constant sloshing of the waves guided me to the rocky beach where my mom was collecting her thoughts and anything else that might catch her fancy. It was a pleasant night with only the moon's warm glow lighting my way on the very uneven path that weaved through the overgrown blackberries and tall beach grass. Doing my best to dodge the prick of the thorns, I carefully managed to stay on the trail. I didn't need to be all scarred up for my upcoming celebrations.

This little stretch of beach was hard to get to and rarely frequented by anyone, which was why we loved it. The beach wasn't what most people pictured when they thought of a beach. The beaches along Washington's coast, more often than not, had tiny rocks and pebbles in place of sand and many boulders and downed logs that made for awfully fine seating, not places to spread out on a beach towel and soak up the rays.

The makeshift trail finally ended, allowing me to spot my mom's pile of things. I hoped she was ready to leave. It was getting a little chilly, and I hadn't prepared to be here long. We had a crockpot full of chili waiting for us both, but she wanted me to meet her here at our special spot, so she could tell me something. I had no idea what it was that she wanted to tell me, but since so much was going on in my life right now it could be about anything. I just graduated from high school. My eighteenth birthday was almost here. Our huge summer solstice celebration, Litha was fast approaching, along with the big event, my acceptance into the Witch Avenue Coven on the same day.

"Mom?" I yelled, as I trudged my way over to her bag, looking around the empty beach.

Only the crashing of waves answered.

I didn't see her anywhere.

"Mom?" I tried again, batting down the worry that wanted to make its way into my consciousness.

Realizing my voice was no match for the roar of the waves, I started walking toward one of the larger boulders, in case she was sitting where I just couldn't see her. The pebbles were loose, creating an extra treacherous journey since I was only in flip-flops. Poor planning on my part, but I didn't think that I'd have to hunt her down. She could be sidetracked so easily.

Finally making it to the mammoth piece of black rock, I became annoyed when I saw she wasn't there. I wasn't in any way prepared to be marching up and down the beach looking for her. I grabbed my cellphone out of my pocket and dialed her number as I went back toward her pile of things to sit. Maybe I should stay put, and she'd return soon enough. As the phone rang on my end, I got closer to my mom's pile and heard her bag ringing. Darn! She didn't take it with her—odd. That was always a rule of hers when hiking or at the beach. We carried our phones with us at all times.

I squatted down to see what she brought with her, hoping an item might lead me in the right direction to find her. If she were gathering plants, then I'd know better where to go. I opened up her bag and panic set in immediately. The shirt she was wearing when she left our house was stuffed in her bag, wrapped around the shoes she was wearing. This made no sense. Her wallet and jewelry were in this bag. She wouldn't just leave all this stuff for a stranger to steal. Something was wrong. Jumping up, the insides of the bag dispersed onto the beach, but I didn't care.

"Mom!" I screamed, kicking off my flip-flops so that I could run up the hill closest to me.

Reaching the top of the hill, I scanned the

grassy area quickly seeing nothing. Spinning around, I looked back toward the rocky beach. From this vantage point, I was able to see everything and nothing. My heart started pounding as I began dialing 9-1-1.

"911, what is your emergency?" The operator answered.

"My mom. She's missing," I cried into the phone, dread spreading everywhere.

"Calm down, ma'am. Where are you located?"

Calm down? I'm not hyper, just scared!

"I'm at the beach just off of Snoqualmie Avenue, down the trail," I replied

"Is your mother in the water? How long has she been missing?"

"I don't know!" I screamed into the phone. "Please just send help."

Okay, now I'm panicking! I can't calm down. My mom isn't where she's supposed to be.

"Ma'am, help is on the way. What is your name?"

"Triss," I replied, as I ran back down the hill to search the beach or the water, or anywhere but where I was.

Could my mom be in the water? I didn't even think of that. She wouldn't be in the water, would she?

"And what is your mother's name?" the operator asked blandly.

"Veronica Spires," my voice panted with the exertion.

"Where are they? When will they get here? She needs help!"

I reached the edge of the water. The waves were lapping against my bare feet. Looking out toward the sea, I saw nothing but water and rocks illuminated by the moon's light. There was no way she would be out there. She never went into the water without someone with her. Oh, my God, where could she be?

The police sirens, off in the distance, were becoming louder by the second. Help was on the way but not nearly soon enough.

"Veronica! Mom! Veronica!" I kept hollering. "Where are you?"

"Ma'am, help has arrived. They're making their way down the trail. I'm going to stay on the phone until they reach you."

My body crumpled. Falling on my knees, the tears began pouring down my face. This couldn't be happening. I turned off my phone. The police were almost to the beach, and I didn't need the operator to hear my cries. The police chatter of CB radios began rolling through the air mixed with the barks of the K-9 units.

This was a nightmare. There was no way this could be happening. My eyes darted back to the hilltop that I had just left. A man was standing on the hill, watching me, with the darkness working in his favor.

"Hey," I yelled, looking at him, trying to see any sort of distinguishing features. He froze in place.

I jumped back to my feet, with my jeans soaked from where I had been sitting. I started running up to the hill, and the stranger took off.

"Miss!" a policeman yelled.

"Someone was watching me!" I cried, not stopping my run. "They might have my mom!"

I reached the top of the hill in a flash, and there was no one to be seen.

A policeman came up right behind me.

"Are you, Triss?" His voice was gentle, probably used to dealing with lunatics, not sure which way they were headed in any given situation. "I'm Officer White."

"Yes, my mom. She's not here." The tears started again. "I was supposed to meet her and all that's here are her things. I can't find her. Clothes, wallet, jewelry are all that's here." I took a deep breath. "Then there was a guy, I think staring at me."

"Where at?" he asked immediately.

"Right here," I replied. "He was standing right here. I think it was a guy. That's why I came this way. It's so dark it's hard to tell. I was sitting on the beach right before you got here and noticed the person."

"Where are your mother's things, Triss?" he asked, scanning the area and coming up with the same thing as me, nothing. There was no one here.

I pointed over to the beach, completely defeated.

He nodded and looked briefly at the ground for any sign of tracks besides mine; he then turned to the officers at the base of the hill and signaled for them to wait.

We walked back down the hill, and Officer

White explained to the others the situation. I had no idea how he got so much from my few sentences. He pointed at the two officers who were in control of the German shepherds, and he motioned for me to come with them to where my mom's belongings had been dumped by my carelessness.

"Triss, we are going to allow our K-9 members, Sunny and Brandy, to smell some of your mother's items, okay?" Officer White asked, looking intensely into my eyes. He had to be well over six feet tall and commanded the attention of anyone who looked in his direction.

All I could do was nod. It felt like if I even opened my mouth to breathe, I would break down again.

One of the female officers, who had her hair pulled back in a severe ponytail, came over to me and touched my shoulder softly. She quieted her chattering CB on her belt.

"Is there someone we can call for you?" she asked.

"My aunt," I muttered, staring off over the darkened sound again, my eyes filling with tears.

One of the other female officers gave commands to Sunny and Brandy and off they went in the direction of the hill. The very same hill I had just come from with Officer White. They were racing off into the distance with the humans following right behind. My mom had been in that area. The dogs caught her scent.

It seemed like hours, but Aunt Vieta finally arrived. Her eyes wide with horror from the scene she witnessed in the parking lot. I couldn't even begin to count how many police and search and rescue arrived. There were divers already out in the ocean, and everywhere I turned, there was activity.

I had shutdown. I was merely operating on autopilot. Aunt Vieta started running toward me and scooped me into her arms.

"We'll find her, Triss. We'll find her," she kept mumbling into my ear, but it did little to comfort me.

"I know we will," I nodded in agreement.

She released me and stood back looking at me.

"Here, I thought you might be freezing." She shoved a coat into my arms that she had tied around her waist.

"Officer White's over there," I said, pointing toward his direction. He was busy getting updates from the teams that had spread in various directions. "He'd be the best person to fill you in. I don't think I could."

I appreciated my aunt's presence, but I would rather just sit on the beach listening to everyone's updates, hoping I would find something out that would bring my mom back immediately. Instead, I was bombarded with statistics about the longer the victim was missing how exponentially the odds of finding them decreased. I doubt that was for me to hear, but I did. And those words would forever haunt me.

"The waters are getting a little rough. We'll start again in the morning," were the first of many sentences that etched a place in my mind, creating a level of despair I didn't think possible.

AWAKENING
THE WATCHERS TRILOGY

CHAPTER ONE

The screams shattered my sleep. My heart was pounding seventy miles an hour. I felt for my fleece blanket to throw off, since I seemed to be stuck to my sheets with gallons of sweat. I looked around my blackened room, with only the red glow of the alarm clock displaying 2:00 am to comfort me. My heart sank as I lost the battle for another night's sleep. I heard the gentle snore of my bulldog, Matilda, rattling through the air. She was used to my screams by now. I promised myself with a little whisper that I was safe. It was only a nightmare — another nightmare. That was all it was. It couldn't possibly be real, that kind of terror. The dreams were coming closer together now, and worse yet they seemed to lead to nowhere but sleep deprivation.

I commanded myself to take deep, steady breaths to stay calm. Still shaky from the last images that had blasted into my brain, I tried to rid myself of the awful scene replaying over and over in my mind — my death. The mere thought of the attacks made me want to hide from the world in my closet. The black, swirling creatures were coming at me and through me from every direction. Their mouths open, displaying several sets of teeth with blood dripping from their lips, waiting for me to make a mistake. This was not a world I recognized. How could my mind even create such deadly monsters? The elements of realism spooked me beyond belief. I grabbed a tissue from my nightstand and wiped the dampness from my forehead, unsure of how much longer I could keep this up. Every night and every dream seemed different. They all had similar storylines, to a degree. Sometimes the unfamiliar characters reappeared to haunt me over and over again. It just depended on the night. Part of me felt as if I should know these people or at least the events that kept taking place. Why else would they keep reappearing? However, the events were so fantastical, the thought that I should recognize them made me feel even crazier for thinking it.

Fully awake now and completely disappointed in the prospect of another long and drawn out day without sleep, I trudged to the window and opened my heavy, red velvet curtains to expose the serenity of a dark outside world. The snow was slowly floating down leaving a beautiful pattern on the sidewalk, illuminated only by the streetlight. The sight brought a shiver to my bones. Even though a minute ago I'd had to wipe the wet heat of fear from my body. I couldn't keep chasing and being chased like this. I couldn't go on thinking my life was in danger every time I closed my eyes. I needed rest. I needed sleep. Lack of sleep was making things worse. I was sure of it.

"What is all of this telling me? I don't even know the people in my dreams!" I whined to Matilda.

She responded with her usual snorts and snores, sprawling out even more on my mattress now that I had left a larger area for her enjoyment. I flipped on my nightstand light, which cast its familiar glow, as I attempted to move back into bed without displacing Matilda. A sigh escaped as I grabbed my latest book, which was ready and waiting for another night like all the others.

I opened the book to the third chapter as my mind attempted to identify the people in my dream. Seeing crumpled remnants of humans discarded all over was never something that I could get used to regardless of whether it was a nightmare or not. I was getting used to seeing the swirls appear to attack me, but I was also intrigued by the thought of trying to figure out the identity of the random strangers who appeared time and time again. Sometimes they were the same people. Other times, a completely new set would make an entrance. I always avoided looking into their eyes because, during one of my very first nightmares, all I saw was the dull glow of death staring right back at me. I couldn't stomach it twice, and somehow my subconscious self knew to never look them in the eyes, whoever they were.

Thankfully, the latest batch of characters had seemed kind — as if I knew them from somewhere although that wasn't possible. I'm sure they must have made an appearance in other dreams. I just don't remember them. One stood out in particular. He was trying to save me, but it was too late. The black, soulless swirls got me. My nightmares had never gotten to that point before. Never did I know the conclusion to these nightmarish adventures before tonight.

This time, I saw how it ended. I didn't make it. It wasn't a painful process. I didn't feel tortured. It seemed like I should have felt the attack. I didn't. What I was left with were horrible feelings of despair and loneliness wrapping their way through every aspect of my life. My soul felt like an empty cavern as I saw myself being blown away into the wind. I remembered looking back at the strangers on the ground. They were looking up towards the sky at me as I left to wherever bodiless souls go. The one guy who was so memorable was staring back at me, tears streaming down his face. He was the one who tried to save me. He'd risked his own life against the monsters for me. He was only a minute too late. My heart now longed for him, this figment of my imagination. I didn't know why.

I couldn't shake the images this time. They were too haunting, too real. And now I was going crazy believing that these things had some sort of significance. Lack of sleep was finally catching up with my fragile state of mind.

RecruitZ

CHAPTER ONE

I sat in the passenger seat horrified, but I didn't dare drag my gaze away. The world had been told zombies no longer threatened human existence. Yet I was staring at an onslaught of them taking slow, deliberate steps toward our vehicle. We had barely pulled into our driveway when the horde descended out of nowhere.

I managed to slide my fingers along the door to the electric lock. I didn't know why I thought that would save us. The undead had never let a lock deter them before. I looked around our house and it looked untouched. These creatures were only in our yard, coming for us at a most vulnerable time.

Gavin attempted to take the car out of auto-drive, pressing the buttons frantically and commanding it with voice controls. The car only responded with words. We didn't control it. The car controlled us.

"Pedestrians within minimum safe distance," the car said, acknowledging Gavin's attempts to drive us out of danger.

No shit! We want to run the pedestrians over.

Tiny beads of sweat began forming at my hairline as I watched Gavin repeatedly engage and disengage various controls. Nothing would let us override the car's safety features.

Gavin's foot pressed on the accelerator trying to override the computer system, but the car still refused to budge. His foot slid off the pedal, and he quickly replaced it.

Damn these self-driving cars!

The engine red-lined with each attempt from Gavin's override, but the brain of the car overruled Gavin's actions with every rev of the motor. Gavin kept shaking his head as his finger slid up and down the dashboard. He glanced at me, his green eyes connecting with mine. I didn't want to believe what I saw behind them so I turned to look out the window.

I gripped the console as I watched the twitches and spasms of the zombies' movements closing in on us. They were everywhere...the grass, the sidewalk, the driveway. There was no mistaking the rotting, grey flesh that exposed the muscle and bone of the undead. They were something I'd run from countless times, but this time we had nowhere to run. The undead had us trapped. They would rip us to shreds in an instant.

"I think some of 'em are new," I said, turning my attention back to Gavin.

There were some clean-looking zombies staggering toward us, their flesh mostly intact. That made no sense. The outbreak had been contained for months. There should be no freshly infected roaming around. Everyone had been vaccinated. The only stragglers evading capture had been around awhile, so their bodies were beat up badly by the time they were caught. Not these.

"Let's hope not," he murmured, not bothering to look out the window to confirm nor deny my suspicions.

"We can't run. They'd totally get us before we got away," I said, hoping he'd correct me, tell me that we had a chance.

He didn't.

He slammed his fist into the steering wheel and looked over at me. When the outbreak happened, we never looked back. We were always on the move, running from the disease that took our families and friends. That was the key to survival. Never stay in one place. Always stay on the move. Now we had nowhere to move. I glanced over at Gavin and saw the fear in his eyes. Even with everything we'd encountered, his eyes had never held this amount of terror.

"Babe, whatever happens..."

"Knock it off," I said.

"We have nothing to fight them with, and a horde this size needs a distraction."

"Don't you dare," I hissed, shaking my head. The fear was pulsing through me at an unstoppable rate. "We didn't live through the outbreak to die now."

I gritted my teeth, grabbed the civilian anti-zombie kit from under my seat, unzipped it, and looked for anything inside that might help. We were instructed to drop these kits off at government collection stations. I was grateful we never got around to it.

Gavin held down the ignition and reverse buttons at the same time in a vain attempt to override the safety sensors.

"Damn it," he muttered.

"Try rebooting the car. Turn it off and take the key out. Give it a few seconds and slip the key back in. Maybe if you pop it in reverse before the car can sense the zombies, it'll let us reverse," I directed.

He nodded, biting his lip, and turned off the engine allowing the moans of the horde outside to be heard. I took a deep breath and looked out my window that was now completely blocked by tattered shirts and non-oozing wounds pressed against the glass. It would only be a matter of time before they began to break through the glass. The moans turned into a chorus of humming.

"One-Mississippi-two..." Gavin's words wrapped around me.

I prayed silently to the same God I'd prayed to many nights before. He listened then and I hoped he'd listen now.

I grabbed two knives that were in the kit and flipped the blades open, locking them in place. The anodized orange handles were larger than the actual blades. Not comforting. I handed one to Gavin.

"There's still a Louisville Slugger on the floor behind us," Gavin said. His brown hair was cut short. That was one of the first things he did after we were vaccinated. A haircut and a shave to celebrate our survival. He still looked young but not as young as we both did before the outbreak.

I slid toward the center console, crawling as far from the passenger window as I could get. Gavin's breathing was heavy, and I felt the heat rolling off him as he continued to struggle with what we were facing.

I dug around in the bottom of the bag for the zombie deterrent. My hand clasped around the ADD, also known as the Audible Distraction Device, and I dropped the kit to the floor.

The car rocked back and forth as the number of beasts grew on both sides, creating a trance-like rhythm that was terrifying.

"Grab the bat," Gavin instructed, his voice low.

I slid my hand to his knee, squeezing it hard before I reached behind us and grabbed the wooden weapon.

The challenges we faced living off the land paled in comparison to what we faced confined in this car.

Gavin turned the engine on and sunk it into reverse, only to be stalled right where we were.

"Pedestrians in minimum safe distance," the car warned again.

"Shut up!" I shouted at the car's inhuman voice.

An oily residue smeared against the glass all around us from their bodies touching and gliding along the surfaces. They were crawling on the hood, metal pops sounded with every dent created. Their bodies slowly snaked up the windshield as they climbed toward the roof. Their mouths opening, jaws clicking as they tasted our scent. That was all we had separating us from zombies—glass. It would be only a matter of time before they mangled the metal above us and shattered the glass around us.

"If I get out of the car, I can distract them and you can run. I need you to run," he said slowly, his eyes locking on mine.

"No way. I'm not—"

The glass shattered, interrupting my objection. The shards of glass crumbled down the door and into Gavin's lap. Several mismatched arms shoved their hands through the nonexistent barrier, reaching for Gavin as I let out a scream and lunged with the knife in hand.

"Don't watch what happens, babe. Promise me you'll look away," his voice pleading, as he struggled against the fleshy fingers that twisted and pulled at his shirt.

I reached across Gavin and began breaking off fingers and slicing hands and anything I could connect with that was attempting to gouge at Gavin. Pieces of flesh tumbled into the car.

We'd been vaccinated.

We'd be okay.

The stench of the decaying flesh filled our small car with every crack of a bone and tear of the skin. Gavin and I were shoving the arms, bodies, and heads back the other direction, but they kept pushing through the small driver's window. Gavin grabbed the bat, shoving and poking the zombies through the window. The space was so small it was hard for him to hit with any force.

It wouldn't be long before they broke the other windows. The first thump on the roof made me jump and then the second. The metal was crunching with every step above, and I looked up to see the roof dipping in places.

The moans grew louder as more arms pushed through the opening, scraping and digging at our flesh. Fingers with calloused skin grazed my face, poking at my eyes and scraping my cheeks, but they would fall from my face almost instantly in search of Gavin. Why Gavin?

Gavin propelled the bat into the crowd with such velocity that he managed to run it through the stomach of one of the beasts, spreading the group out momentarily. The zombie collapsed, but the swarm returned, descending on us again.

I jabbed the knife directly into the neck of the most insistent intruder and pulled it out, severing the head from the neck. The head toppled into the car as the body slumped outside against the door. There was a brief hesitation as they stepped back, and I grabbed the ADD, removing the pin and flipping the lever. I threw the ADD out the window, but it bounced against an undead girl in the back of the crowd. It dropped to the ground with a thud. My heart sank with the realization the zombies wouldn't be running anywhere.

Broop-Broop-Broop

Maybe I was wrong.

Once the ADD sounded, the zombies peeled away from our car and turned toward the device, but there wasn't enough distance to open the door or escape through the window. They'd get us in a heartbeat. The deafening sound made it hard to think. I watched as each zombie turned back toward the car and shoved their arms back at us. A set of hands latched onto Gavin's neck, and I slashed clear through the zombie's wrists—bone and all—, stopping only because the blade encountered the softness of Gavin's throat.

"They're not going to stop until they get what they want," he whispered, punching back at the beasts.

The windshield began cracking from the weight of the bodies. The ADD siren stopped blaring, and I was almost completely positioned in Gavin's lap, stabbing at anything and everything in the opening. Hands had broken through all of the windows. The passenger side window had arms flailing as bodies attempted to squeeze into the narrow opening.

"I don't know what to do." My yell could only be heard as a whisper of desperation above the noise of the horde.

"Becca, there's some research in my folders from the campus..." his voice trailed off. His eyes began to cloud over, and I dropped my gaze. Dodging rotten, fleshy fingers and elbows, my hands ran protectively over his chest as I fought the undead. There was nowhere for us to hide.

"Don't start saying goodbyes," I commanded, noticing blood on my fingertips, lots of blood. Where was this blood coming from? There was no pain beyond the scratches on my arms. I felt no pain. Elbowing the beasts, I looked at Gavin. His eyes on mine—locked on mine—as his lips curled up slightly.

"What are the odds?" he whispered weakly.

A cry wanted to escape my lips as I watched Gavin blink slowly. His breathing became shallower with each passing second. I searched feverishly, gliding my hands along his chest and stomach. My fingers fell into his wound.

The zombies had torn through his shirt, through his abdomen. Blood was pooled on the seat, blood was everywhere, and I watched the hands of the undead still stirring and grabbing pieces of him. I swallowed my horror. A gasp wanted to escape my lips, but I was stronger than that. We were stronger than that.

I continued slapping the hands away but none were after me. They only wanted Gavin.

"I've loved you since your sixteenth birthday," he murmured, closing his eyes.

"No!" I screamed, grabbing him, attempting to move him from the window.

But it was too late. Several arms had wrapped around Gavin's neck and chest, hauling him through the window. I grabbed his body but he told me to let go. I couldn't let go. I wouldn't let go.

My hands slid from his waist...to his thighs...to his knees...to his ankles. I was holding on so tightly, but it wasn't enough. Only his feet were left inside the car, and I held on with a strength I didn't recognize as my own. As they pulled the last of him out the window, I followed right through the opening, collapsing on the concrete driveway. None of them attempted to attack me beyond the accidental push or scrape. They weren't after me.

I watched in horror as the love of my life was torn to pieces and thrown about. Why didn't they take me too? Why were they leaving me alone? My screams did nothing. I wasn't sure I was even screaming. The zombies huddled together, and I forced my eyes away from what was left of my husband.

"Please, kill me too," I whimpered.

Two unmarked, black vans came barreling down the street, stopping right at our driveway. The back doors flung open and the killers vanished inside. That wasn't possible. I couldn't trust my own eyes.

I was hallucinating.

The last of the undead stepped inside the vans, and the doors closed before the van peeled off.

"Is there anyone out here? Can't anyone help us? Please? Can't someone help us?" I sobbed, crawling toward what was left of Gavin.

I heard the screams of the neighbors as they ran toward us, stopping just short of our driveway. Their mouths dropped open, speechless. There was nothing anyone could do. The sobs and cries for help continued, and I didn't know if they were coming from me or from everyone else. I was numb. I heard apologies about not coming out when they heard the ADD, but it wasn't their fault. The ADDs were the equivalent of fireworks nowadays. Everything was in slow motion or people were moving slowly. I slumped over Gavin, holding the remains of his torso, listening to the ambulance siren make its way down our street. I wrapped my arms around him tightly for the last time.

That's what I remember from that day—and that I never told him I loved him.

.

The Camp Excerpt

CHAPTER ONE

The Cessna 180 engine rumbled through the small six-seat aircraft cabin, but unfortunately it did little to block out the words of the other passengers. I glared at the back of the Captain who was lucky enough to be wearing a headset.

"I'd love to see what's under her jacket." I heard the guy behind me say to no one in particular.

"I'll second that, and I bet we'll get the chance," another one said.

The gnawing in my stomach only grew with every passing minute, but there was nothing I could do. I was stuck in a plane where I could literally touch the pilot. I didn't need to start something that I couldn't finish and have the plane crash because I couldn't handle a little heckling.

I looked out the small, oval window pressing my head against the cold glass covered in water droplets. I couldn't really see anything out the window because the weather was so bad. It was like we were trapped in one continuous rain cloud that was sent from the Gods to mess with me.

Getting tired of seeing nothing but ominous grey,

I looked down at the pamphlet hoping the description would magically change, but I wasn't that lucky. My fingers trembled as I silently read the overview once more.

The ReBoot program is a juvenile camp for mid-range offenders who have yet to become established criminals. Youth in their mid to late teen years are often responsive to this type of program which includes occupational training and behavior rehabilitation. We've found that the potential criminals at our work camp for forestry and conservation in Southeast Alaska never become repeat offenders. We generally only accept less dangerous delinquents but all cases are subject for review.

I loved the 'yet to become established criminals' part, as if the first time around didn't really count for these misfits. I so didn't belong here. It wasn't like I needed to be reminded that my newfound campmates weren't savory characters. All I had to do was turn around in my tiny airplane seat to see their predator eyes taking me in.

I couldn't believe my mom let this happen to me. There's no way she could have been fooled into thinking this was a conservation-slash-forestry camp... although I was fooled. I actually thought my stepdad was trying to do something nice for me, for once.

God! I hated my stepfather, and he obviously hated me. This was his last sendoff before I went to college, and it was a doozey. As if living with him since my father's death wasn't horrible enough, he just wanted one more way to stick it to me.

The tin can I was riding in suddenly took a plunge, and all of the instruments went berserk. Gasps and whines filled the air as the high-pitched warning beeps sounded through our tiny capsule. My hands immediately became clammy as my heart raced. There was no calming down in a situation like this, especially when a person was born as jumpy as I was. My fingers gripped the armrest so hard that my nails hurt, and I took a deep breath in and exhaled slowly.

"It's okay, everyone. Just a little turbulence," the pilot told us as the beeps silenced, but the heavy breathing from everyone continued long after his announcement.

I was tempted to turn around in my seat and gloat at all of the guys who were big and tough only a few minutes ago and suddenly turned to pansies, but the Cessna took another huge dip, sounding the bells and whistles again. Man! I hated small planes. Actually, I don't even think this would qualify as a small plane, more like a car that could fly.

As the beads of water continued rolling down the tiny window, I noticed we had begun our descent. *Finally!*

"We'll be landing in approximately fifteen minutes," the pilot said as he continued adjusting controls.

Things were looking up. The dampness on my palms began to evaporate, and I looked back out the window as our plane flew barely above the treetops. The conifers looked like a brightly massed green quilt underneath us. Turning my head in any direction gave way to a completely different landscape. Alongside the deep green woodlands, there were rocky peaks, and monstrous cliffs that trees avoided calling home. If I wasn't so scared to death, I might be able to appreciate the beauty of everything.

I maneuvered my head so that I could see out the pilot's window. Directly in front of us there was a grassy field with small ponds surrounding it, or at least I think they were small ponds. I craned my neck as far as possible searching for the airport. Not only did I not see any buildings, I didn't see any sort of landing strip.

But I did catch a huge bear. I'm sure it was a bear. There was nothing else that big that walked on all fours.

"Whoa, check it out," one of the guys behind me said.

"That thing's huge," the guy next to him said. "I could totally take it down."

I couldn't handle it any longer.

"Why don't you? I'd love to see it," I taunted without looking behind me. There was no way I'd undo my seatbelt in transportation like this even if it meant I couldn't give him my best scowl.

"She does speak," he replied sarcastically.

Gritting my teeth, I watched as we passed by the brown bear with the plane descending at what felt like record speed.

"Please make sure your seatbelts are fastened. I'll make the landing as pleasant as possible," the pilot told us.

What? Landing? There's no runway!

This can't be possible. I've got a bear as an official greeter and our plane was landing on gravel or dirt or something. The only saving grace of this observation was that it kept the other passengers on the plane as silent as me.

I continued to watch the pilot pulling and pushing on things, and realized I really didn't want to see how little control he had over the situation. I'm sure he felt he had it handled, but from this viewpoint it was utterly terrifying. I clamped my eyes shut just in time to feel the plane shudder as the wheels began to touch down.

There was nothing smooth about it as our plane briefly greeted the gravel before pushing back up, only to quickly meet again with the surface below. It felt like a rollercoaster that had no tracks and no intention of stopping. Our plane continued to jump and skip its way down the non-existent runway. I slowly peeled open one eye and watched as we whipped by the tall grass and water finally coming to a slow stop.

The guys' celebratory hollers were deafening. They began throwing off their seatbelts, but I refused to budge. The pilot turned around and I wanted to hug him, but I restrained myself. Instead I looked out the window at the wilderness wondering if I'd survive.

"I'll be around to open the door, and the CLs should be here to greet you any minute. It's best if you don't wander off," the pilot instructed.

"CLs?" I asked, turning my attention back to him.

"Camp Leaders," he responded, his eyes connecting with mine. He opened his door and got out of the plane.

"Newbie. We've got a newbie on our hands," the guy sitting directly behind me shouted, kicking my seat. *What was he, twelve?*

"I wonder if that makes her a newbie in all areas? I can't wait to find out," he continued.

That was it! My seatbelt came flying off, and I leaned over the back of my seat, grabbing the guy's shirt, surprising him and myself. I was gripping the fabric so tightly I raised him slightly off his seat. He looked to be a year or so younger than me with blond hair that was greased back. His clothing was ten times too big for him, but he was still bigger than me.

"If you even look in my direction while we're at this camp—" I began, but the pilot opened the side door interrupting me. I pushed him back on the seat and turned back around in mine.

"Jeez, chill out," he mumbled under his breath.

"Still gonna get some, Luke?" I heard someone whisper.

Everyone on this plane was so sleazy, except for the poor pilot. I didn't even want to imagine what everyone else at the camp would be like.

I was the last to jump out of the plane, as I looked around the land void of civilization. I couldn't believe my mom fell for allowing my stepdad to send me here.

"Emma Walton?" A girl asked.

I turned around and relief spread through me

instantly. The girl looked to be a couple years older than me, so probably twentyish. And she looked normal. Her dark brown hair was bundled into a loose ponytail, and she was dressed in green cargo pants, a black T-shirt and rubber boots. Her smile was friendly, and I knew I'd be sticking around her as much as possible.

"I'm Steph," she said, smiling as she stuck her hand out for a handshake, "one of the CLs here."

Wow! That's formal. I shook her hand quickly.

"Nice to meet you." I grabbed my duffle bag and backpack

"Got everything?" she asked.

I nodded, and she waved at the pilot who was already preparing the plane for takeoff. "See ya in a week," she yelled at him.

A week! I'll be eighteen in a week, and then I can get out of here.

"We're in bear country out here," she began as our group followed her and the other CLs through the tall grass.

"I saw one on the way in." I adjusted the large strap on my shoulder, hoping we wouldn't be hiking all that far.

"It's all part of being in the backcountry," she replied. "We'll go over everything when we get to camp, but it's nothing to mess with. A ranger went missing a week ago on Baranof Island, and they just found his remains."

A shiver ran down my spine.

"And Baranof Island doesn't have nearly as many brown bears as we have," another CL replied from behind.

Not what I wanted to hear!

CONTACT THE AUTHOR

To contact the author, please visit her online at
http://www.karicebolton.com or via

Twitter/Facebook @KariceBolton.

If you'd like to be included on her mailing list to find
out about new releases, go to Karice Bolton's
website.

ABOUT THE AUTHOR

Karice Bolton lives in the Pacific Northwest with her awesome husband and two wonderfully cute English Bulldogs. She enjoys the fact that it rains quite a bit in Washington and has an excuse to stay indoors and type away. She loves anything to do with the snow and seeks out the stuff whenever she can.

Made in the USA
Charleston, SC
07 March 2014